Time After Time

5/29/09

To: Vale

Enjoy!

Margaret Michaels

Time After Time

Margaret E. Michaels

Copyright © 2007 by Margaret E. Michaels.

Library of Congress Control Number: 2007907783
ISBN: Hardcover   978-1-4257-9593-1
             Softcover   978-1-4257-9587-0

All rights reserved. No part of this book may be reproduced or transmitted in any form or by any means, electronic or mechanical, including photocopying, recording, or by any information storage and retrieval system, without permission in writing from the copyright owner.

This is a work of fiction. Names, characters, places and incidents either are the product of the author's imagination or are used fictitiously, and any resemblance to any actual persons, living or dead, events, or locales is entirely coincidental.

This book was printed in the United States of America.

To order additional copies of this book, contact:
Xlibris Corporation
1-888-795-4274
www.Xlibris.com
Orders@Xlibris.com

DEDICATION

To Debbie who always praised my stories
To Gail who took the time to read and edit
To Judy for the cover illustration
And to Claudia's dog, Bowser, who made this all possible

Prologue

A fog rolled in off the ocean water and climbed lazily up toward the house that sat high on the cliff. It was a forlorn-looking place. Years of neglect had turned the once majestic mansion into a place where only rodents and creatures of the forest would inhabit. The fog lay heavy on the ground, circling the house in a cloud of mystery. The sky was dark. Every once in a while the moon would peek out from behind a cloud and cast an eerie light upon the house. A sadness radiated through its halls. It sat there alone, waiting. It waited for that person who would come and make it into the place that it once had been. It waited for that person who would unlock all its secrets. To look into its windows was to look into the past, for only the past lived here. It roamed its rooms and cried out for deliverance from the things that tortured it.

Behind the great house lay a cluster of trees. If one were to look closely into this woods they would see the path that wind through the trees until it came to the little cottage that lay hidden there. It was a cottage that lay forgotten and neglected, except by the two that lived there.

The old lady sat rocking slowly in her rocking chair. Her face was deeply wrinkled and her eyes held all the secrets that now only the dead knew. Her gray hair framed her face in disarray. Her arms were wrapped around her holding her shawl tightly to her shoulders. She stared out the window into the darkness. But she was somewhere in the past, a place she visited often. She was tiny and frail and held no importance in this world except to those that were long gone. A whisper came from her lips. It was so low that the woman standing at the mirror arranging her hair had to turn around to inquire what she had said.

Nell was a robust woman of sixty. She lived in this cottage with her aunt Cora. She had no purpose in her life but to care for the big house. For thirty-five years she had taken the path through the woods to look after it. She was not capable of maintaining a place of that size. But she tried. It was all she had, and she had dedicated her life to it. Today all that was about to change. Today she had dressed in her maid's uniform and arranged her salt-and-pepper hair in a neat bun at the nap of her neck. "What's that, Cora?" She looked down at the old woman sitting in her rocking chair. "You're mumbling again. I've told you before I can't hear when you mumble." She walked to the stove and poured coffee into a cup and held it out to the woman. Cora ignored her and continued to rock and to stare out the window with unseeing eyes. Nell set the cup down on the stand beside the chair and turned again to the mirror to finish her hair.

Cora forced her mind back to the present and to concentrate on her niece. She wanted to warn her, to let her know that things were soon going to change for all of them. She spoke in her cracking voice. "She's coming. I tell you, she is coming."

Nell turned from the mirror. "Who? You mean the family is coming? I told you weeks ago. Today is the day the family comes to take over Brier Cliff. I for one am glad to see it. That place has sat too long without a family to care for it."

Cora shook her gray head. She could not make her understand. It was more than just a family. It was the one that the house waited for. "The girl" she said. "She's coming and there will be no good come of it."

Nell was puzzled over her aunt's words. "The Mitchells have a daughter. Is that what you mean?" She turned back to the mirror.

Cora shook her head. "Mark my words. Things are going to happen that even I can't stop. Take a look at her. Look into her eyes. She's the one. She is like the other one. The dead will not rest with her there. The house had waited a long time. Those that still live there have waited. They will have their way, and she will suffer for it." She grabbed her niece's arm. "You heed my words, Nell. No good can come of it."

Nell felt a chill run down her spine. She would not let her aunt's ravings ruin things for her now. She had looked forward to having a family to take care of again. She pulled away from her aunt's grip and pulled on her sweater. "I have to hurry. They are to be here by noon and I want to have a good meal prepared."

She hurried from the house and into the darkness. She made her way through the path in the woods until she came to a clearing. In the distance sat the house shrouded in fog. A strange feeling came over her, but she shook it off. She attributed it to the strange words her aunt had said. She walked through the yard and up the steps to the veranda. With a shaking hand she placed the key in the lock and opened the door.

Chapter 1

The door is opened. We walk in
unaware that time will not
let time remain in the past.

March 1942

Black clouds rolled over the landscape darkening the sun and casting a shadow over the car as it traveled at a leisurely speed down the road. The white-capped waves of the ocean beat relentlessly against the shore. Sea gulls circled in the sky then dove to its surface for food. The wind began to pickup force and the smell of salt water permeated the air. Palm trees bent under the force of the wind then rose back to salute the sky. The distant sound of thunder rolled over the land and grew louder with each minute. The sky opened up and a downpour of rain fell to the ground. The windshield wipers of the car beat a rapid report as the rain blinded the two occupants of the car.

Soft music filled the air in the car and caused an atmosphere of calm over it two passengers. Joan's mind began to travel back to that place that she and her daughter had just come from. She smiled as she remembered that it was there that she had met her husband, Charles. She was in her first year of college. She was a perky blonde, free from the restrictions of home and eager to try her wings. Baltimore seemed like such a big place after her eighteen years in a small rural community in the northwestern part of the state of Maryland. She was eager for a good time and college was where to find it. She didn't worry about studies. Learning came easy for her and she didn't care if she passed with an A or a C. She would graduate but she was determined to have a good time doing it.

Charles was standing in front of the library doors staring into a book that he had just checked out when she came flying around the corner and ran right into him knocking the book from his hand. She had apologized and stooped to pickup the book. Then she stopped. She took a good hard look at the man standing in front of her and she knew. Right from the first meeting. From that day on all her efforts went into landing him. He really didn't stand a chance. She smiled as she remembered. Poor Charles didn't know what hit him.

He had come to college to earn a degree. He was very studious. He was tall and handsome. He had dark hair and blue eyes and an irresistible smile. He took a second look at the pretty blonde, but he was not at all sure she was his type. He didn't care for girls that were into the party scene and that was exactly what she was. She made him forget what he was at college for and that made him nervous. He tried to stay clear of her but that was impossible. She had swept him off his feet, he liked to joke with her. Within the first year they were married and she was pregnant. Times were hard for the newlyweds. Charles had another year of college and had no way to support his new family. They had moved in with his parents. Joan continued to attend classes and graduated her first year of college. Two weeks later, Beth was born.

Beth had always been a beautiful girl. Charles remarked often that she was special. She could warm her father's heart with her smile. She cared about everything and everyone. She hurt for people she had never met. She could read an article in the paper and cry for days about some poor soul who had lost everything in some tragedy. Joan often thought she carried the world on her shoulders.

After graduating from college Charles had landed a good job with an agency that handled the buying and selling of commercial property all over the country. This meant a lot of traveling but the money was good and they were able to move into their first apartment. Later they moved into a bigger apartment in the city of Baltimore. Things were good for the little family. When Beth started school Joan got a job as a substitute teacher. She enjoyed working with the children and enjoyed the extra money the job brought in.

Things drastically changed for the family when war broke out. Charles enlisted and, within six weeks, was shipped overseas. Joan and Beth were alone in their apartment in a big city. Joan hated coming home to an empty apartment. She had always been a good cook and enjoyed cooking for her family. Now Mother and daughter often ate soup and sandwiches while listening to the radio. She had taken on a fulltime job at the elementary school just so she didn't have to spend long hours alone in their apartment. She wrote often to her husband and he could detect the despair in the tone of her letters. She missed him terribly and she was very lonely.

Beth tried to help with the work in the apartment. It seemed such a forlorn place with her father gone. She too missed him and she was concerned about her mother. She was like a mother hen seeing to it that her mother was entertained and not left alone for long periods of time. They began to spend an evening out every week to go to a movie and then to dinner. These were good times for mother and daughter. They began to know each other as they never did before. Out of all this they became friends. They had something in common they never had before. They both waited for a husband and a father to come home from a war.

Joan felt guilty over taking up so much of her daughter's time. But Beth did not heed her mother's suggestions to go out with her friends. She had forgone her own life to be with her mother. Joan could not help but be grateful to her daughter. She didn't know what she would do without her constant companionship.

Charles worried about his wife and his daughter. He had been raised in a rural community in South Carolina and thought of it as home. He wanted to protect his family from city life. He had purchased a house, sight unseen, from a realtor and wrote home to his wife of his plans to move them there. He had written glowing reports of the house and property. He said that it was a large house that sat on a cliff facing the ocean. He had gotten it for a good price because it was in need of work. But he was sure that his efficient wife could whip it into shape. It was a place, he said, where they would be safe. Beth could attend college and not have to leave home. He was full of enthusiasm about the place and assured his wife it would be the perfect home for them. So here they were, Joan and her twenty-year-old daughter, Beth, driving through a rainstorm heading for their new home.

Joan had not regretted leaving behind the city and the harsh winters of Baltimore. But that was not the case with Beth. Baltimore was home for her. She had friends she would have to leave behind and a college she had planned to attend. Joan's heart ached for her daughter.

Soon after Charles had left for overseas, Beth had found a job near home. She said she wanted to delay college until her father returned. She didn't want to go away and leave her mother. She said it was her place to stay close to home until things were back to normal. Joan was glad to have her daughter near. She realized it was selfish of her to accept Beth's decision and so unselfish of Beth to forgo something she wanted so much.

When the time came to leave Baltimore, Joan could see the sadness in her daughter's eyes. She wanted to reassure her but she did not know the words. It was an important step to leave everything one knew and to begin again in a strange place. Joan too had felt apprehension but she agreed with her husband that the city was no place for two women alone.

She looked over at her daughter. She was now a beautiful woman. She stood five foot four inches tall and had a delicate small frame. Her hair was light blond and hung to her shoulders in soft waves. Her eyes were as blue as the ocean and her smile was perfect. But besides being beautiful on the outside, that beauty reached to her very soul. She had an enormous heart. Mother and daughter had the same look but Joan did not possess the giving and loving nature of her daughter. Joan did not let others take advantage of her. She had an ability to see people for what they truly were. Beth did not have that ability. She took people at face value and was easily hurt.

A clap of thunder brought Joan back from her thoughts. She reached over and turned down the radio. She needed to concentrate on her driving and not be daydreaming about the past. A bad storm was erupting all around them. She glanced over at her daughter and saw that she was beginning to have a worried look upon her face.

Beth had never been a strong person. She had serious bouts of asthma as a child and of late had begun to suffer from headaches. The doctor had attributed this to her stress from moving. Beth never complained. She never wanted her parents to worry. She thought her mother had enough to worry about with her father away at war. She kept all her emotions locked inside. She had, over time, learned to deal with her problems.

She dated off and on all through high school. But there had never been anyone that she was serious about. Her best friend was Tim Alexander. He was a boy she had gone to school with and the two shared a special bond of friendship. He was someone she could tell anything to and he would understand. Saying goodbye to him had been the hardest thing Beth had to do. She knew that once she moved they would slowly lose contact with one another. Time would take away the bond she shared with him.

Beth knew her mother and her father shared a genuine love for one another and Joan strived to make her husband happy. What made him happy made her happy as well. Even before she and her mother had discussed the move, Beth knew what the outcome would be. A month after receiving the letter from her father they were packed and on the way to Hampton South Carolina. The drive had been pleasant. The weather was warm and the scenery breathtaking. They had taken their time and often stopped to rest. Joan was always a cautious driver and believed in obeying the posted speed limit. She was not used to driving on narrow rural roads. She joked, if she could drive in city traffic she could drive anywhere.

The storm had come up suddenly. What had first been a pleasant drive on a narrow country road had turned into a nightmare. The sky opened up and sheets of rain poured down on the couple as Joan slowed the car to a crawl. She leaned forward in the driver's seat to see through the windshield. Joan turned up the speed on the windshield wipers and took out her handkerchief to clear the window.

Beth rolled up her window and turned on the heater fan to try and clear the windshield. Visibility was practically zero. She felt her heart race with fear. She grabbed the door handle and held on as the puddles forming on the road threw the car from side to side. Lightning danced over the ocean and thunder cracked loudly. The sky had turned to a dark gray. Threatening black clouds rolled in from the ocean.

Beth tried to relax. She took her hand and wiped at the passengerside window. The ocean lay as far as she could see. But what at first had been a beautiful blue was now black and menacing. She thought, South Carolina was not as welcoming as her father said it would be. She tried to get her mind off the storm. She remembered what her father had said about the house. He had called it Brier Cliff. It was an old Southern mansion. Her father had bragged that there were over a hundred acres and that there would be plenty of room to plant flowers and even a vegetable garden. It had all sounded so wonderful that at first, Beth had been looking forward to their new home. But as time drew near to leave she began to have second thoughts. The warm winters and an ocean at her doorstep held no appeal to her. She would rather be back in her safe apartment than on these narrow roads in this terrible storm.

A loud clap of thunder rocked the car and its occupants. Beth jumped in fear. She looked at her mother who was intent driving. She tried to think, to pray, but no words would come to her mind. She knew she was being foolish. This was just a rainstorm and they were safe but even that logic could not ease her tension.

Beth saw the car first. It was coming on the opposite lane at a very high rate of speed. She looked to her mother and grabbed at her elbow to warn her. But Joan was already alert to the approaching car and the danger it posed. She applied the brake and slowed even more. The car was across the centerline and coming right at them. Its driver tried to pull the car back into its lane but the high rate of speed and the wet road made it run onto the gravel brume. The driver pulled the car back onto the road, and it again crossed the centerline and headed straight for Beth and her mother.

Joan whipped her car off the side of the road and slammed on the brakes. They came to a jarring halt. She leaned her head forward onto the steering wheel and took a deep breath. The other car narrowly missed hitting them and continued on down the road, not bothering to stop.

She looked toward her daughter and took in her pale shaken condition. "Are you all right?" She asked.

Beth could only nod her head. She straightened herself from where she had fallen and tried to stop from shaking inside.

The two women sat there alongside the road and gained control of themselves. Finally, Joan pulled the car into gear and pulled back onto the road.

As fast as the storm started, it ended. The sun peeked from behind a cloud, and the rain stopped. They continued on down the road, each realizing how close they had come to being injured in an accident.

Beth again rolled down her window and let the warm air into the car. She had gained control of herself and a lighter mood began to come over her. She had to let the past go. This was a chance for a new start for the entire family. She would not be the selfish one and cast a cloud on their moving into a new home and to a different state. South Carolina was a beautiful place.

She looked to her left and saw the high cliff that ran along the road. She turned to her mother. "Is this the cliff that Brier Cliff sets on?"

"It must be." Joan turned to her daughter and cast her a quick smile. "We're very close. Only a mile or so. I'm getting excited. How about you?" she added in an attempt to lighten the mood.

Beth returned the smile. "Yes, I'm anxious to see our new home. Do you think it is everything Father said it was in his letters?"

"I'm sure your father exaggerated a little." Joan laughed. "But it's got to be better than that tiny apartment."

Beth turned her attention back to the road. She could only imagine what life held for her in this new place.

Ten minutes later they came to what appeared to be a driveway cut out of the rock of the cliff.

Joan pulled the car to a stop so they could look up at their new home. As her husband had said, it sat high on a cliff facing the ocean. Two white pillars reached to the second floor and supported a balcony. French doors opened onto the balcony. Two dormers protruded from the roof. A whitewashed porch stretched around all sides of the house. The porch had white railings and beautifully carved posts.

Joan pulled the car up the drive and stopped in front of the house. A plump, elderly lady with salt-and-pepper hair stood on the porch. She was dressed in a maid's uniform with a white apron. Her hair was pulled back in a tight bun, and on her head she wore a white lace cap. She came running down to the car and opened the driver's-side door.

Joan stepped out and offered her hand to the lady. "Nell?" she asked.

"Yes, ma'am." Nell beamed her brightest smile. "I'm so glad you had a safe trip."

"It was, except for that rainstorm. Does it always storm so hard?"

"Rainstorm?" Nell looked surprised. "We had no rain here."

Beth came around the car and stood beside her mother. "This is my daughter, Beth," Joan said.

A strange look came upon Nell's face when she looked at the daughter, but she quickly masked it. "Good to have you here, miss. I hope you will love this house as much as I do."

Beth took her offered hand and Nell shook it. "I am sure I will."

Beth looked up at the old house. It was much in need of a paint job, but it still showed the signs of once being a grand place. The grounds around it were well manicured, and trees circled it in all directions except the front. With a resigned heart, she followed her mother and Nell into the house.

They walked into the foyer, and both women gasped. The floors were of wood and ran halfway up the walls. The remaining wall was plaster. The ceilings were cathedral and were of the same wood. A tarnished and dusty chandelier hung in the middle of the ceiling. The sitting room, as Nell called it, was the same as the foyer, except that against one wall there was a huge stone fireplace. The dining room was the same, filled with beautiful antique furniture. Joan loved it. Everything was dusty and dirty, but they all held promise. The kitchen sat in the back of the house and was more modern than all the rooms. New cabinets and appliances lined the walls. Nell explained that the owner had remodeled the kitchen and had added three new bathrooms, making a total of four, in hopes that it would help sell the house. The upstairs was in worse shape than the downstairs, but all the rooms were clean. Nell said she and three other maids had cleaned the upstairs when they heard the new owners were arriving.

Joan turned to her daughter. "This house will be a showplace when your father sees it." Joan could not contain her enthusiasm. She would work tirelessly to make this house a home for her husband when he returned.

Beth agreed. She had no doubts with her mother's determination that Brier Cliff would once again be a grand Southern mansion.

Beth tossed her luggage upon the bed and stared down at the neatly folded clothes. Jeans, sweaters, and blouses met her eyes. First order of business was to change out of the traveling suit her mother had insisted she wore and change into a pair of jeans and a tee shirt. Her mother would frown at her choice of wardrobe. She often said Beth wore jeans far too often. She stepped out of her skirt then pulled off her jacket and blouse. Next came her full slip and hose. She sat down on the edge of the bed and pulled on her jeans and tee shirt. Now she felt comfortable. She removed a stack of hangers from one of her suitcases then picked up her suit from where she had discarded it and walked to the closet to hang it up. She opened the door and stopped short when she saw the dress hanging there. She removed it from the closet and held it up to the light. It was white with tiny pink rosebuds. The neckline was scooped and the sleeves puffed. It was of an odd design, more like a dress from the 1800s than a modern dress. But she thought it beautiful. She walked to the mirror and held it against her. It looked like it was made for her. She twirled around in the room and laughed aloud at the rustle the material made at her movement. She thought, *I must show Mother.*

She held it to the light once again then hung it up in the closet. Now began the tedious job of hanging up her clothing.

An hour later, she hung up her last piece of clothing. The closet was full, along with the drawers of the dresser. She sat down on the bed and looked around at her bedroom. It was a spacious room with high ceilings. The floors and half of the walls were a dark mahogany wood. She thought to herself that it was much too dark for a woman, but she could brighten it up with new curtains and maybe an area rug. The bed looked like an antique with its high headboard and tall posters. She loved the bed and planned to get a new spread that would match the curtains and brighten up the room. All in all, she thought it was a nice room. Better than the tiny one she had back home. She stopped. Already she was comparing this huge place to their tiny apartment back in Baltimore. And the apartment was falling short in the comparison. She felt guilty. Baltimore was her home, and she owed it her loyalty, for at least a few days. She laughed to herself. She rose and hurried down to join her mother for lunch.

Downstairs her mother sat at the kitchen table and motioned for her to take a seat. "I hope you're hungry. Nell has prepared us a wonderful meal."

Beth turned to the cook standing with her back to her at the stove. "Something smells good."

"Thank you, miss." Nell turned around with a large platter of turkey. "I cooked a large bird so we can make sandwiches while we're working on the house this week."

"Excellent idea," Joan said. "Please take a seat and join us. You have worked so hard on this meal. It wouldn't be right not to enjoy it with us."

"Oh no, ma'am. It wouldn't be proper." Nell blushed with embarrassment.

"Please do. We'd love to have you join us," Beth joined in her mother's invitation.

Nell reluctantly took a seat at the table with her new employers. She was overwhelmed at their kindness.

The table was full of delicious food—turkey, stuffing, gravy, mashed potatoes, corn on the cob, and a loaf of homemade bread.

"Tell us of Brier Cliff. How long have you worked here?" Joan said as she filled her plate with food.

"I grew up here. I've been caretaker for the last thirty-six years. Of late, I was beginning to think the house would fall into ruin before someone came. But she is built on solid rock and will stand a hundred more years now that you are here to care for her."

Beth marveled that someone could love a place so much that they would dedicate their life to it.

After the meal Joan and Beth retired to the sitting room to enjoy a second cup of coffee while Nell cleaned up the dishes.

Joan turned to her daughter. "This old house has a lot of promise. I can't wait until we get started restoring it. Your father is going to be pleasantly surprised when he gets home. I mean to make this place something he will be proud of."

"It's going to take a lot of work. But I can see what it can be," Beth said as she sipped at her coffee. "Nell is a wonderful cook. Where did Father get her?"

"She came with the house. She cooked for the owners of Brier Cliff many years ago."

Joan leaned back in her chair and began to look around the room. "Nell calls this the sitting room. That's quaint, but I like it."

Beth laughed. "Everything about this house is quaint. But it does have a charm to it."

Joan smiled. "This is our home. Doesn't that have a nice sound to it?"

Beth agreed with her mother. "Home" did have a nice sound about it.

Beth set down her coffee cup and leaned back in her chair. She closed her eyes and tried to relax. But something would not allow her to get comfortable. She sat up and looked toward her mother. "I almost forgot. Upstairs, in my closet, I found a beautiful dress. It is made in an old-fashioned design, but it is lovely. It is white with tiny rosebuds. I held it against me, and it looked like it would fit. But I wonder were it came from? Did some woman live here before us? The dress looks like it is new."

"Your father said in his letters that no one has lived here for the last thirty-six years," Joan answered, looking toward her daughter, instantly interested in the dress.

They went up the flight of stairs to Beth's bedroom. She hurried to the closet and pulled open the door. She gasped when she saw the dress was no longer there. "I don't understand," she said as she moved the hangers aside in the closet. "It was here. Someone must have moved it. Nell!" Beth turned to her mother.

Joan came up to the closet and looked inside. "Nonsense. Nell wouldn't remove the dress. What reason would she have? Besides, she's been working in the kitchen since you came downstairs."

"But it was here! Mother, it was here!" Beth's voice rose in alarm.

"Dear, we've had a long trip, and we are both tired." She led her daughter to the bed and sat down with her. "Perhaps you fell asleep and dreamed the dress. Things like that can happen, and they seem so real we get them confused with reality."

Beth rubbed her temples as they began to throb. She shook her head. "No. It was here. I saw it. It was just as I described."

"Well, it's not that important." Joan laid her daughter's head down on her shoulder. "We've had a long day. I know I am tired, and I imagine that you are too. Why don't you lie down and rest? I'll get you something from my purse for that headache." She had seen these headaches come on Beth before when she was upset.

Beth stretched out on the bed and closed her eyes. Joan returned a moment later with two aspirins and a glass of water.

Beth took the pills and lay back down. Her mother covered her with a blanket and left the room, turning out the light behind her.

Beth was tired, but she couldn't sleep. She had not imagined the dress, of that she was sure. But she had no explanation for why it had disappeared. The room was very dark. There was no moon tonight. She lay there in the darkness and felt a chill run over her body. Someone was in the room! She pulled the blanket up to her chin. She could hear them breathing and the slight shuffle of feet on the hardwood floor. She wanted to scream, but she could not. She opened her mouth and tried to call out. All she could say was, "Mother?"

A gentle hand touched hers. A voice, so soft it was almost a whisper. "Rest, dear. It will be all right."

Beth smiled. How foolish. It was her mother. She had remained in the room until she fell asleep. How like her to be so kind and loving. She closed her eyes and, with the reassurance that her mother was near, fell asleep.

She slept so soundly she did not hear the whispers that took place in her bedroom. They were soft and low. A person would have to strain to hear and understand them. "She's come! Thank God! She's come at last."

Chapter 2

Can we stop the ravages of time?
We fight against time, but it is
of little consequence.

Beth opened her eyes to a dark room. She had taken the aspirin her mother had given her and fallen into a deep sleep. She was surprised to see she was wearing a long white nightgown. Her mother must have dressed her, but she had no memory of it. She sat up in bed and turned on the night-light. It was past midnight. She stood and retrieved her robe from her closet and opened the door to her bedroom. The hall was dark and the house silent. Obviously, her mother was asleep. Silently, she crept down the hall on tiptoes. Placing her hand on the railing, she started down the flight of stairs. Halfway down the stairs, she stopped. She saw a flickering light coming from the sitting room. Someone was awake and had lit a candle. She couldn't imagine her mother doing such a thing. Why would she light a candle when she could turn on a lamp? She stopped at the landing and listened. She could hear faint voices and the crackling of a fire. Soft music was coming from a piano. She listened again more intently this time. There were people in the sitting room. How strange! Who could it be? She stood in the darkness a long moment, listening to the sounds coming from the other room.

    She heard female laughter and the soft tinkle of glass touching glass. Her heart picked up its pace, and she suddenly was frightened. She tried to reason away her fear. Was her mother entertaining? But whom? There was no one that she knew in South Carolina. Mustering all her courage, she cautiously made her way on bare feet up to the doorway of the sitting room. Taking a deep breath, she peeked into the room. Her eyes met only darkness. There was no candle flickering, no fire in the fireplace, and no one talking in the room. She felt along the wall until she found the light switch and flipped it on. Nothing was out of place. It was just as she and her mother had left it earlier. She walked into the room and stopped. The sweet smell of jasmine assaulted her senses. She turned around as the hair on the back of her neck stood up. She expected to see someone standing behind her. She could have sworn she had felt their breath on her neck. There was nothing behind her. Instead, she heard a soft whisper. It was a voice, and it was calling her name. She slowly turned her head back around, afraid of what she would see. A mist was rising from under the windows and through the draft in the fireplace. A mist that was more like fog than anything else. It crept toward her. It came slowly and deliberately. At times it seemed to take the form of a woman. Then the figure within the mist would disappear, and it would return to what it had been before. She screamed as it began to envelop her body and swirl around her. But it did not harm her. She felt warmth coming from the mist that seemed to go throughout her body. She stood there, letting this apparition envelop her. She somehow gained control of herself and pulled away from the hold it had on her. She began to run. She ran back up the stairs and into her bedroom. She fell into bed and drew the covers up over her head. She lay there for a long time. She heard sounds in the room. Of floorboards creaking as though someone was walking in the room. She listened, and then she heard something that made her heart race. She heard a voice. A soft female voice, and it was calling out to her. She pulled the cover down an inch and looked into the darkness, but she could see nothing. Whatever had been in the sitting room had followed her up the stairs to her bedroom. Then a most peculiar thing happened. A cool breeze blew over her, and with it came that sweet smell of jasmine she had smelled in the sitting room. It seemed to calm her, and she knew instinctively that everything was all right. She pulled down the blanket and sat up in bed and turned on the lamp on the nightstand. She looked around the room. Everything was in order. Then she saw something on the floor. She threw back the blanket and rose from the bed. There on the floor was a gold bracelet. It was very wide and had a man's name engraved on it. Justin MacCarthy. She looked closer. There were two names engraved inside the band. One was Elizabeth, the other was Dillon, with the date 1866. She laid the bracelet on her nightstand and returned to bed. She would investigate this further in the morning. She turned out the lamp and tried to go to sleep. Sometime in the night, sleep overtook her.

Sunlight streaming through her bedroom window woke her. She lay there for a minute and remembered the dream from the night before. It seemed so real, but she realized it could not have been. She tried to laugh it off, but the laughter didn't reach her face. She felt frightened. She knew it was because she was in a strange house. She prayed she would get used to her new surroundings. She walked over to her dresser. She had laid the bracelet here last night. She thought. There was no bracelet. She began to relax. It had been a dream. No matter how real it seemed, it had been a dream. She began to dress. She knew her mother would be waiting to eat breakfast with her. Their first day here, and she had overslept. She hurried down the stairs. It was already past eight o'clock, and she knew her mother had planned to rise early. The servants were to arrive at seven, and Joan would have been there to greet them.

She descended the stairs and found two maids on their hands and knees, scrubbing the foyer floor. She tiptoed around them, greeting them as well as she could. She found her mother in the kitchen talking with Nell. Instantly, a frown came to her face. "Dear, are you all right? You look so pale." Her mother felt her forehead to see if she had a fever. Beth laughed it off. "Mother, I am not a child. Of course, I am all right." She took the offered coffee Nell held out to her and took a seat at the table. "I had a crazy dream. I didn't get much sleep after that. It frightened me."

Joan looked concerned. "This big old house, it's enough to give you frightening dreams. But not for long. I have plans for this place. It's going to be a grand house once again."

Nell handed a cup of coffee to Joan. "How is your headache?" she asked.

"All gone." Beth sipped at her coffee. "The aspirin helped."

"Good. Do you feel like working today?"

Beth nodded her head. "I'm game if you are."

She sipped her coffee and smiled at her mother as she took a chair to join her at the table.

"Mother, it wasn't necessary for you to dress me in my nightgown and to stay in my room until I fell asleep. But I do love you for it." She reached across the table and took her mother's hand.

Joan looked astonished. "But, dear, I didn't dress you in your gown and stay in your room. I came back downstairs and helped Nell clean up before I went to bed."

Beth felt the same chill she felt the night before run down her spine. She tried to hide her reaction to her mother's words. She shook her head and laughed. "I must have been dreaming again."

Beth finished her coffee and followed her mother into the foyer to help with the work. First order of business was to wash everything down. Nell set a bucket of water at Beth's feet and handed her a rag. Beth did not know if a thank-you was in order. For the next three hours, the team of servants and mother and daughter worked. At noon Joan called a break for lunch. Beth wiped the sweat from her eyes and thought, *Thank God.*

Beth washed up for lunch in the upstairs bathroom. When she entered the kitchen, she took a chair beside her mother. Everyone was eating and talking around the table. Her mother added to the conversation. "I heard the strangest sound last night after I went to bed. I thought I heard voices in Beth's room. It was so real that I got out of bed and went to look in on her. Of course, there was nothing to it."

Beth laughed. "I was probably talking in my sleep. I told you I was having a crazy dream."

Nell looked intently to her employer. "I've heard strange things in this house too. My aunt says there is nothing to hurt anyone here. She says the house is waiting for the right person to come. Whatever that is supposed to mean. She rambles a lot."

Beth picked up her turkey sandwich and took a bite. She turned to Nell. "Does your aunt know Brier Cliff as well as you?"

"Better, miss," was all Nell would answer.

Patty, the youngest of the maids, spoke up. "When we were cleaning for your arrival, I was upstairs alone one day, and I heard whispering too.

It near frightened me to death. It sounded like they were saying something about someone coming. I ran downstairs and got Nell, but by that time, it was gone. She swears I was imagining it. But I know better."

Joan laughed off the comment. "Well, if this place is haunted, I hope they are friendly because I'm not moving."

"Brier Cliff has a soul of its own. It wanted and needed a family to come and love it as the rest of us do. She won't frighten you off. She welcomes you," Nell said.

Nell's words affected Beth more than anyone knew. She never thought a house could have a soul. But, she thought, if one could have a soul, this one surely would be the one.

After lunch they resumed their work and worked for the next four hours. When her mother called it quits for the day, she was more than glad. She had never been so tired in her life. Joan laughed when Beth rubbed her lower back. "You'll get used to it, dear. And the rewards for our hard work will be well worth it."

After bathing and changing into a white sundress, Beth lay down on the bed to rest before dinner. She had only closed her eyes, and she was asleep. She began to dream.

It was dark. She was standing on the cliff in front of Brier Cliff. She was wearing a long white nightgown. The wind was blowing, and her hair was flowing out behind her. The nightgown caught the wind and clung to the contours of her body. She stretched out her arms to the night and looked up at the star-studded sky. Below her the ocean pounded against the shore, and she could feel the spray from it on her face. She felt free. The wind and the night were taking away all her inhibitions, and she was set free. Suddenly, she felt two hands in the middle of her back, hands that pushed her forward over the cliff. She began to fall through the air. Falling into the night and heading toward the rocks below.

She awoke with a jerk. Beth sat up and shook her head. "What a dream," she spoke aloud. She climbed out of bed and hurried down the stairs to where her mother waited for her.

After dinner Beth walked outside for some air. Her mother stayed behind to read her book. The night was still, and a full moon shone from above. She walked, enjoying the night and the pleasant surroundings. "This is a beautiful place," she said into the night. She stopped beneath a tree and leaned against it to look up at the sky. A shooting star blazed across the sky and made Beth smile. The smell of jasmine came to her on the wind. It was such a pleasant smell she turned toward it. She stopped short as she saw a figure in the night. A figure of a woman standing only a few feet from her. The fragrance of jasmine was coming from her. Beth did not move. Fear grabbed her. As suddenly as it appeared, it was gone.

Beth forced herself to walk to where she had seen the figure. She laughed when she saw a bush swaying in the night breeze. Her imagination was surely running away with her, she thought.

Beth turned around and started back toward the house. She looked up at it and smiled. *So,* she thought, *this is what a house with a soul looks like.* She had to agree with Nell that Brier Cliff was unusual, but could a house have a soul? She stepped onto the veranda and stopped. She could hear the pounding of the surf below the cliff. Tomorrow, she thought, she would walk down the path that led to the water and take a look around. Even with all her misgivings about coming here, she had to admit that it was a beautiful place.

The work continued day after day. The only time Beth had to herself was in the evening when she left the house to take a walk. Her mother seldom accompanied her, wanting instead to relax with her book. But for Beth, the quiet of the night and the beautiful surroundings were relaxing. She began to feel something special for this old house. She could not put it in words, but her heart began to warm toward it. She saw in its peaceful beauty a place that held promise of better things to come. She had not forsaken her love for her birthplace, but she had to admit that Brier Cliff was a place where a person could find peace and contentment. She didn't have any more dreams. For that she was grateful. She had dismissed them by blaming it on a vivid imagination.

Beth stood at her vanity mirror braiding her hair. She was dressed in an old pair of jeans and a baggy sweatshirt. She finished the braid and wrapped a bandana around her head. She laughed aloud at her appearance. Today was Sunday and she and her mother were alone in the big house. They were going into the attic to explore and hunt for antiques for downstairs. The attic was the one place that neither had gone, but Nell said it was loaded with old things from the past.

Joan could hardly wait to explore the attic. She had a genuine love for anything old and had a history to it. She had made these plans days in advance even though it was to be a day of rest for her and her daughter.

They had been at Brier Cliff for a month now, and for the entire month, they had worked. Joan was a stern taskmaster. She had worked along with the servants and her daughter from early morning till late each evening. They had stripped all the wood of layers of wax and replaced it with new. Hours of buffing had brought the wood back to its original shine. The walls were scrubbed down and given a fresh coat of paint. All the fixtures were taken down and polished until they shone like new. The furniture was scrubbed and polished. The downstairs windows were cleaned. All the curtains and rugs were removed and replaced with new ones because they were too old and worn to salvage. A month later, the downstairs was the showplace Joan had desired. She planned at a later date to have the ceilings done by a professional. It was just too difficult for the women to accomplish. Brier Cliff was now a home, and Joan worked tirelessly out of love for the place. Each night Beth and her mother fell into bed too exhausted to even dream.

In the hall, she met her mother and had to smile. They both looked like miners going into a mine. Joan handed her a flashlight then pulled down the trapdoor and the folding steps. One by one, they climbed into the attic.

The attic was dark and had a musty odor. Over everything lay a thick dark layer of dust.

Joan turned to her daughter. "Let's try and open these windows."

They pulled and tugged at the windows that had not been opened for more then eighty years. With both women pushing up on one window at a time, they were able to open them.

The attic was bathed in sunlight. They laid down their flashlights and began to look around. Every corner was filled with precious objects that Joan relished. She knelt before an old trunk and opened the lid. It was filled with dresses—dresses that had once been expensive and beautiful. At the bottom of the trunk lay a Bible and a journal. She handed them to Beth and continued her rummaging. In one corner of the trunk, Joan found a box. She opened it and gasped at what she saw. It was a complete set of silver. It was tarnished with age, but once it was polished, it would adorn the china cabinet in the dining room. Joan was full of energy as she began to pull objects out of the trunk. These were things that to the average person would have no value but to Joan were priceless.

Beth took a hand and wiped over the cover of the Bible to remove the dust. Carefully, for it was very old, she opened the Bible. On the inside page, someone had written in bold scroll, "The Preston family Bible." On the opposite page was written the names of the Preston family. "Look at this, Mother. The names of the family that lived here in the 1800s."

Joan stood and came to her daughter's side. She read aloud the names written on the page. "Charles Lee Preston, born 1820. Joanna Wilson Preston, born 1822. Married 1839. Daughter Elizabeth Ann, born 1840. Daughter Willowmenia, born 1842." Joan stared a moment. "That's strange."

Beth raised her eyes from the page. "What is?"

"The names, dear. Don't you see? Father, Charles. Your father is named Charles. Mother Joanna. My name is Joan. Daughter Elizabeth. Your name is Elizabeth." She returned to the trunk and began to dig through it. "Very strange." In a moment, she had forgotten about the Bible in her quest for treasure.

Beth again felt a chill run down her spine. She felt like she had just stepped on a grave. She quickly shook off the feeling and laid down the books so she could continue to explore. She came upon something leaning against the wall covered in a blanket. She pulled away the blanket, and dust flew all around. She fanned the dust away from her face before she knelt to look at the paintings leaning there. A dust-covered landscape met her eye. It was of the view of the ocean that was in front of Brier Cliff. In the distance could be seen sailboats clustered together as though they were about to begin a race. She called out to her mother. Joan again was at her side. She knelt before the first painting and exclaimed over it. She carefully set aside the first painting to reveal the second. It was Brier Cliff in its glory days. Joan was ecstatic. "This will go over the fireplace in the sitting room." She had adopted the name for the room that Nell called it.

The third painting was of a young girl. She was blonde; her hair was braided and circled her head like a crown. She was not smiling, but that could not subtract from the beauty of her face. Her eyes were a light blue, and her skin as white as alabaster. She sat on a high-backed chair, her hands resting n her lap. She wore a white dress that was dotted with tiny pink rosebuds. The dress was cut modestly but still revealed her white shoulders and long slender neck. In one hand, she held a single rose. On her wrist was a wide gold bracelet. Beth thought, *Just like the one in my dream. It couldn't be the same bracelet. That had been a dream, nothing more.* Even with all her reasoning, Beth was not as sure as she wanted to be.

She stared at the portrait for a long time. Something was so familiar about the dress the girl was wearing in the painting. Then it came to her like a powerful blow! She began to sway. Joan was quickly on her feet, grabbing at her arm to hold her up before she fell. "What is wrong?" Her voice rose in alarm when she looked into her daughter's pale face.

"The dress!" Beth found it hard to speak. "It's the dress that was in my closet the first night we were at Brier Cliff!" Her head was spinning, and her knees were weak. For a moment, she felt like she would faint.

Joan led her to a cot set along the wall and sat her down. "That's nonsense. That dress would be more than eighty years old. The dress you described was new."

Beth placed her head in her hands and tried to think. Her mother was right. It couldn't be the same dress. It just resembled that dress. She shook her head and tried to clear her mind. She looked up at her mother and tried to laugh. "You're right. I am so silly to let a thing like that disturb me." She spoke more to reassure her mother than anything else. She was confused and uncertain. How could the dress in the portrait be identical to the one that was in her closet?

Joan was not convinced her daughter was all right. "Does your head hurt? It's too hot in the attic for this. Let's go down to the kitchen and get us a cold drink. It will make you feel better."

"No." Beth rose to her feet. "I am fine. My head doesn't hurt. Let's finish with the pictures before we go downstairs. I am as anxious as you are to see them." She forced herself to continue. She was still shaky, but she would not let her mother know that doubts still plagued her mind.

"Are you sure? This can wait until another day." Joan still held on to her daughter's arm. "I've been working you too hard. I should have been more considerate of your feeling. I am so sorry, dear."

"Mother, I told you I'm fine. I don't want to wait to see the pictures." Beth took her mother's hand and led her back to the pictures.

"Look at that bracelet she is wearing." Beth leaned close to examine the picture. She recognized the bracelet as the one from her dream. She held her breath and let it out slowly. She would not frighten her mother further, but she didn't know how much longer she could contain her apprehension. Beth moved back and let her mother take a closer look. She could not imagine what was happening. But these things could not be a coincidence. She tried to still her racing heart. She would not let her silly imagination spoil this day that she and her mother had planned for days. She would take deep breaths, and soon she would feel better. But nothing seemed to help.

Joan began to relax and accept that Beth was fine. She leaned forward to look at the bracelet. "It's almost as wide as a man's. Why would a young lady wear a man's bracelet to be painted in her portrait? It must have a significance to her. Perhaps it belonged to her father."

She brushed at the right-hand corner, and a name was revealed. It read, "Randolph 1862."

Joan set aside the portrait to reveal another. The painting was of a girl, younger than the first and the complete opposite. Her dark hair was worn long and flowed behind her as though she was standing in a wind. There was a bright smile on her face, and she appeared to have a wild and adventurous spirit. Her dress was a dark green cut daringly low, revealing ample breasts. Her skin was not the white alabaster of the first girl, and her eyes were as dark as night.

Again, Joan brushed away the dust to reveal the name of the painter and the date. It was the same as the first. She stood. "Well, that answers that. The first painting is Elizabeth, and the second is Willowmenia. How could two sisters be so different?" Joan brushed her hands together to remove the dust "All these paintings will go downstairs. They will have to be cleaned, but they will look good in our new home." Joan looked around the tiny room. "This room is far too dirty to continue. We'll have to do some cleaning before we can get a good look at what is here. I think I'll get right to it tomorrow. Let's go to the kitchen for that cold drink."

Beth was glad to finally leave the attic. She had gained control of herself, but she was not sure how long she could keep up this facade.

Beth and Joan carried the paintings down the steps along with the other treasures Joan had discovered. It was then that Beth remembered the Bible and the journal. She climbed back up the steps and found the books just where she left them. As she turned to leave, she ran into something hanging from a nail on a wooden beam. She turned it toward her and was surprised to see a Confederate uniform. She looked at it closely. It seemed to be a captain's uniform, but she could not truly tell. She dismissed it and started down the steps. Beth stopped only two steps down. She saw movement in the corner of her eye. She looked around her and spotted the mirror sitting in the corner. She laughed. She had seen her own reflection. She knew the attic was a spooky place, and her mind was running away with her, as always. She hurried down the remaining steps to join her mother in the hall.

Joan folded back the steps and raised the trapdoor. She brushed at her clothes. They both were covered with dust. "Let's leave these things here until tomorrow. They're just too dirty to fool with today."

Beth agreed. "I am going to shower." She wanted to go to her room and think about what had happened. She knew she was not going crazy, but no one else would believe that. She thought it better to keep it all to herself.

"Me too." Joan started toward her bedroom. "I'll meet you downstairs. We'll have lunch. Today is our day. We are going to relax and enjoy ourselves." She disappeared into her room.

Beth entered into her bedroom and pulled the bandana from her head. Dust flew from it. She coughed and brushed away the air in front of her face. She entered the bathroom and began to remove her clothes. The knocking at her bedroom door made her pull on her robe and walk to the door. She opened it and was surprised that her mother was nowhere in sight. She crossed the hall and rapped on her mother's door. There was no answer. She opened the door and was met with only silence. She called again and entered the room. Her mother's clothes were laid out on the bed. Beth walked up to the bathroom door and pushed it open. Water was running in the tub, and the shower curtain was pulled closed. She called out again. Again she was met with silence. She didn't know what to do. Should she pull back the curtain to check on her mother? "Mother," she called in a loud voice that she was sure her mother could hear over the running water. There was no response. She pulled the curtain slowly open. She gasped when she saw a bloody handprint on the tub wall. Tiny streams of blood ran from the print, down the wall, and into the tub where the blood mixed with the water and ran toward the drain. She stepped back and ran into a solid object. She turned and screamed as her mother grabbed her by the shoulders.

"What is it?" Joan didn't release her hold on her daughter.

"Mother." Beth was close to tears. She looked back at the tub and found the print was gone and the water was running clear, draining in a whirl into the bathtub drain. She tried to get hold of herself. She didn't want to frighten her mother. "I . . . I called out to you, and you didn't answer. It frightened me when you were not in the shower," she managed to say with a shaking voice. She buried her hands in her robe pocket so her mother would not see them tremble.

"I'm sorry, dear. I went downstairs to get a bottle of shampoo. Nell picked it up for me yesterday, and I forgot it in the kitchen." Joan leaned over and turned off the water. "Was there something you wanted?"

"I thought you knocked on my door." She wanted to get back to her bedroom where she could completely break down if she needed to. She started for the door. "The noise must have been you shutting your door and going down the stairs."

Beth reached her door and stopped to turn back to her mother. "I'll hurry so I can help you with lunch." She closed the door behind her.

Beth sat down on her bed and leaned back and closed her eyes. She took several deep breaths to try to stop her racing heart. She could not explain what had happened in the bathroom, but she knew that it was not real. How could it be? Her mother had seen nothing. "No," she said aloud. It was something going on with her. She had to get control of herself. She reasoned that the atmosphere of the attic, seeing the dress in the portrait, the bracelet, the names in the Bible being so similar to her own family members' names—all contributed to her mind playing tricks on her. She lay there for a few minutes more until she could rationally explain away what she had seen. She rose and headed to the bathroom to take her shower.

Chapter 3

Voices call out in torment and pain. Are they only echoes from the past?

Beth stood under the shower and let the warm water wash over her, relaxing her. She scrubbed her body and hair, rubbing away the decay from the past. She tried to stop her mind from returning to what had happened today. But it was of little use. She could not stop herself from remembering. First there was the dress in the portrait. She knew it was the same as the one that was hanging in her closet. But her mother's reasoning made sense. The dress she saw was new. It couldn't be the same dress. But the bracelet had been the same as the one in her dream. And then there was the bloody handprint on the bathroom wall. She knew that couldn't be real. Was someone trying to play a cruel joke on her? If so, who could possibly be doing it? Her mother trusted Nell and insisted it was not her. But who else was in the house? No one but herself, her mother, and Nell. Who else could it be?

But what reason would she have for doing such a thing? She could only let things go until she knew what was going on. She stepped out of the shower and took a towel and wiped the steam from the mirror, then she wrapped it around her body. She grabbed another towel and leaned over to wrap it around her hair. She stepped into a waiting pair of bedroom slippers and made it out of the bathroom. Dripping water, she hurried to her closet and pulled out her white terry robe. She had just sat down on the bed and begun to towel-dry her hair when her eye caught sight of the Bible and the journal lying on her nightstand. She wanted to open these books and find out more information about the Preston family and, especially, the two young women in the portraits. But the books were still covered with dust from the last eighty years, and she knew she had no time for that now. Her mother was waiting for her to have lunch.

She rose from the bed and returned to the bathroom. She braided her hair and dressed in a pair of jeans and tee shirt then hurried down the stairs to the kitchen. Her mother was standing at the stove when she entered. Joan had also showered and changed into a pair of jeans and a white tee shirt. She had pulled back her wet hair into a ponytail.

"Sit down, dear. It will be ready soon. I only made toasted cheese sandwiches and soup. I hope that is all right with you."

"That sounds great," Beth answered as she pulled out a chair and sat down. This is what she remembered most from her home in Baltimore. Her mother standing in the kitchen, having a meal on the table when she returned home. She smiled at the memory. It was a good memory. There had been no big house or servants. There had been only their little apartment and the three of them that shared it.

"What plans do we have for the rest of the day? It is Sunday, and I thought we would take it easy today," Joan said as she poured the soup into the bowls sitting on the table. She placed the sandwiches on two plates and set them beside the bowls.

"What to drink?" she asked.

"Coffee for me. Thank you," Beth answered.

Beth waited for her mother to pour the coffee into her cup. She added one sugar. "I've been thinking about those two women in the portraits. They have to be buried around nearby. Are there any cemeteries we could look through? I'd like to know when they died."

Joan pulled her chair up to the table. "Nell is the person to ask. She knows all there is to know about this place. She told me her grandmother worked for the Prestons and her mother after that. Of course, Willowmenia was the only one left alive at that time. Nell called her Willow. Isn't that lovely?"

Beth nodded her head. "What of Elizabeth? What happened to her?"

Joan laid down her sandwich and wiped her hands on her napkin. "She didn't say. But she did say Willow never married and lived closed up in this house till she died." Joan took a spoonful of soup. "In the old days, people buried their dead on their property. There could be a cemetery around here. Why don't we walk around the grounds and see what we can find? We've been so busy with the house we haven't taken the time to explore our property."

"That sounds like a good idea," Beth said before beginning to eat her food. "This is good, Mother."

Mother and daughter shared a good meal then cleaned up the dirty dishes before going outside.

The grounds around the house were all cleared for one hundred and fifty feet, but beyond that was all woods. Joan paused to look around. "This really is a beautiful place." The grass was green already in this early month. Flowers were beginning to bloom. The love she felt for Brier Cliff was reflected in her words. Beth wasn't surprised. She knew her mother had put too much work into the house not to love it. "You like it here—better than home, better than Baltimore."

"Yes, even better than Baltimore," Joan smiled. "You will too, dear. Just give it a chance. Look how beautiful the grounds are, and the house is coming along. You'll make friends once you start college in the fall. Think of the parties you can give with your new friends. This is a lovely place to entertain."

"I do like it here, Mother. But I still miss Baltimore. That will always be home to me."

Beth turned and looked out through the woods. She had spied a path leading back through the trees. "Mother, there is a path. Let's follow it."

Mother and daughter followed the trail deep into the woods. "This path has been well used," Joan commented as she walked behind Beth.

Beth stopped and stared to her left. Joan followed her gaze. Two old buildings sat hidden from the main house by the trees. "Let's see what those buildings were used for."

Joan and Beth left the path and made their way through the trees to the two old buildings. "This one was a barn," Beth said as she removed the wood beam from the door that was used as a lock. She opened the door, and a hoard of bats flew from the interior. Joan screamed and knelt to the ground. Beth was soon to follow. The two women began to laugh as they rose to their feet. Beth walked over to the other building and began to remove the wooden beam from its door.

Joan did not follow. "I don't think you should open that door. I don't want more bats flying at my head."

Beth did not answer as she opened the door. She could only stare at the sight that greeted her. A black stallion stood alone in the middle of the room. It pawed at the ground and raised its head to snort at her. It wore a saddle with the letter *C* on the side.

Joan came to her side and looked into the building. It was obvious she did not see what Beth saw. "These buildings will have to be torn down. They are not safe. I will have to hire men from the town to do that, and as soon as possible."

Joan led the way back to the path. Beth walked silently behind her, her mind in a whirl. She was losing her mind. She had no other explanation for what was happening to her. She felt tears gather in her eyes. But she was determined not to cry. She knew she could not tell her mother. She would not understand. How could she when Beth herself couldn't understand what was happening?

They followed the path until it opened into a clearing. In the clearing sat a little house. The house was not well kept. One side of the porch roof was falling down. The porch had broken boards sticking up. And it was long past a good paint job. On the porch sat a rocking chair and a lounge. It was obvious someone lived in the house.

The two stopped at the gate that opened into the front yard. "Should we call out?" Beth asked her mother in a lowered voice.

At that moment, an old woman appeared at the door to the house. She stepped out on the porch when she spied the two women. She was stooped over, leaning on a cane. Her hair was snow white, pulled back into a disheveled bun. She was dressed in a black dress with a white shawl over her shoulders. "You there!" she yelled, waving her cane into the air. "Get off my property!" She slowly made her way down the three steps off the porch to the walkway.

Joan and Beth stood their ground as the old woman approached. "We're sorry to disturb you. I'm Joan Mitchell, and this is my daughter, Beth." Joan held out her hand.

The old lady ignored Joan's outstretched hand. She stopped a few feet from the gate. Her dark eyes moved slowly over the two women. "You're from the big house," she said. Her eyes fixed on Beth and held for a long moment. "Beth, you say? How old are you, girl?"

"Twenty," Beth answered, not liking the intent stare the old lady gave her. Something about the woman frightened Beth. She knew she was being foolish. This was just an old woman. But when she looked into her eyes, she saw something there that caused her heart to race.

She raised her cane again and pointed through the woods in the direction of the big house. "You heed my words girl, get out of that house. You'll find no happiness there. Only pain and sorrow just like the Prestons."

Beth was visibly frightened. "Mother, let's go." She wanted to get as far away from this place and this woman as possible. Too many things had happened today, and she didn't need to be frightened by this old woman.

Joan tried to control her anger. "I don't appreciate you frightening my daughter."

"My name's Cora. I've been living here all my life, and I know these things. I know that house and the people that lived there. They all came to a bad end, and so will you, if you stay." She looked directly into Beth's eyes. She saw the fear her words caused. "That girl." She pointed a crooked finger in Beth's face. "She's the right age and the same look as the other one. Even the same name. Don't you see? It's not safe for her there."

Joan tried to laugh. "Surely you don't believe that?"

"I do. And soon, so will you. If you stay long enough," Cora returned.

Joan turned away and took Beth's arm. "Let's go, dear."

"Wait," Cora called after them. "The old cemetery is that way." She raised her cane to point down the path.

Beth and her mother stopped in their tracks. Joan turned back to the old woman. "How did you know we were looking for the cemetery?"

Cora chuckled. "I told you. I know these things." She turned and slowly made her way back into her house.

Beth tried to shake the fear the old lady's words evoked in her, but there was no way she could. Cora had threatened her. Cora knew what was happening in the main house. Beth could sense that. She couldn't reason or explain the feelings that washed over her. It was more than fear. She was experiencing that, but it was mixed with doubt. These things could not be real, but she had seen things that she could not explain. How could she justify everything by saying it was her imagination? If that was true, than she was losing her mind. She tried to overcome the emotions that were causing her heart and mind to race. She wanted to relax and enjoy the day with her mother. Her mother had worked so hard on the house that she deserved a day that was not filled with worry for her daughter. Beth stuffed her shaking hands into the pockets of her jeans and willed herself to calm down. She was not some child to let things like this disturb her.

As though Joan sensed her distress, she turned to her daughter. "Dear, don't let that foolish old lady disturb you. There is nothing to harm you here. And if there were, I won't allow it." She smiled at Beth, trying to reassure her. "We are having such a good day together. Let's not let anything destroy it."

Beth forced a smile to her face. "Nothing can, Mother." Beth would endure her troubled mind to protect her mother.

They continued on through the woods until they came to a clearing. A broken-down wooden fence surrounded a small area in the clearing. Rows of stones filled the space.

Beth turned to her mother with excitement in her eyes. She tried to pull open the gate to the fence, but it was buried in years of soil and could not be moved. She walked around the fence until she came to an opening and climbed over the fallen rails.

Joan stepped in behind her and silently surveyed the cemetery. It was unkempt and overgrown with weeds. Many of the markers had fallen over, and the lettering on many was hard to read. After much searching, they were able to locate Charles Preston's grave and his wife Joanna's hidden behind a growth of brush. Their headstones were over six feet tall and dwarfed all the others in the cemetery. Below their names was Willowmenia's. Charles s had died during the Civil War in 1863. His wife died the following year of 1864. Willowmenia had died in 1906.

There was no marker for Elizabeth.

"Well." Joan took Beth's arm to lead her out of the cemetery and toward home. "I presume she died away from here and was buried there."

Beth turned once to look back at the tiny cemetery. "I don't think so, Mother. She would have wanted to be buried here beside her parents." Mother and daughter walked slowly back to the house. When they came to the clearing, they walked around it so they would not have to go near Cora's cottage. Each was in deep thought. Joan knew her daughter was still upset by the old lady's words. She didn't want anything to mire her happiness in this new place. She would have a talk with Nell and see if anything could be done about Cora's threats to her daughter. Nell surely would know the old woman since she lived so close to Brier Cliff. Maybe the old woman would listen to Nell.

Beth's mind was a jumble. Too many things had happened today. And the old lady's threats had been more than she could stand. She wanted only to find a quiet place and think this out. She knew she could make sense of all this if given the time.

They returned to the house, and Joan made them a glass of iced tea and carried it out to the yard where Beth sat waiting for her.

"Thank you, Mother," she said as she took the tall frosted glass and took a sip. She set the glass down on the table beside her chair.

"Do you have a number for Nell? I'd like to talk with her. I bet she knows where Elizabeth is buried."

"She may," Joan answered. "But do you think you should bother her on her day off?"

"She won't mind." Beth rose from her chair. "Where is the number?"

"Written on the front page of the phone book." Joan was not at all sure this was the right thing to do. "Don't keep her on the phone too long. She may be busy," she called after her daughter's retreating figure.

"It will only take a minute. I'll be right back." Beth hurried to the house and leafed through the phone book until she found the number. She dialed it and waited impatiently for Nell to answer.

"Nell?" Beth said into the phone. "This is Beth. Mother and I found the old cemetery today. But there was no grave for Elizabeth. Do you know where she is buried?" Beth was filled with anticipation. She knew Nell would know where to find Elizabeth's grave.

There was a long silence on the other end of the line. Finally she spoke. "She's buried in the family cemetery, beside her father and mother."

"But there is no headstone. We couldn't find the grave." Beth could not hide her annoyance.

"One minute," Nell said.

Beth knew she had covered the mouthpiece with her hand and was talking with someone. After a few minutes, she came back on the line.

"There is no headstone. There never was. I guess Willow did not purchase one."

"But why not just add her name to her parents' stone? There was no need to buy a headstone." Beth was trying to understand why a sister would not add another sister's name to the family headstone.

"I have no idea," Nell answered. "Is that all you need?" Nell was dismissing her. She did not like where this conversation was going, and she wanted to get off the phone.

"Yes. I am sorry to bother you," Beth returned. She knew that Nell knew more than she was telling. But she seemed not to want to talk about it. There was nothing Beth could do but let her go.

"Miss, leave it alone. I mean no disrespect, but the past is the past. Besides, my mother always said a soul did not rest in an unmarked grave." Nell hung up the phone.

Beth returned to the yard. She sat down and picked up her drink.

"Did she tell you anything?" her mother asked.

"She told me Elizabeth is buried in the family cemetery, but her name was not added to the family stone. Don't you find that strange? Evidently, Elizabeth died before Willow, and she didn't see fit to give her sister any recognition in death." Beth was troubled about the idea of Elizabeth being buried without a marker. "Nell said the strangest thing—that a soul could not rest in an unmarked grave."

Joan sipped on her tea. "People believe all kinds of strange things. But I do find it odd that her sister did not see fit that she had a proper stone to mark her grave."

Beth tried to shake the morbid mood she was in. "Did she not care about or love her own sister? It sounds like that was the case."

Joan nodded. "It's good that you are interested in the history of Brier Cliff. You realize the Prestons built this house. It seems only proper that Elizabeth Preston should have a stone to mark her grave. Perhaps we could take care of that if it bothers you, dear."

"That's an idea." Beth was thoughtful. "But I don't think it is our place. It should be family, someone who cared about her. It's a shame none of the family is left."

"How about you and I go into town for supper tonight? I don't feel like cooking, and it would be good for you to get your mind off this subject. We'll go somewhere nice, then ride around town and see if we can locate the college. You know, it won't be long before you will have to enroll."

Beth smiled. "All right. That's a great idea. We need to change. Meet you in the foyer in an hour." She stood and raced toward the house.

After eating a good meal in an expensive restaurant, the two women walked across the street to a museum. The building was full of artifacts from the 1800s. And to their surprise, one section was dedicated to the Prestons, the lumber mill, and Brier Cliff. There was a large portrait of Charles Preston standing outside his mill. He was a big man, tall and muscular. But there was no mention of his two daughters. In one corner, they found a picture of Brier Cliff and some furnishings that were donated by the family. Brier Cliff stood proud and majestic facing the ocean. Joan stood in awe of the picture. She wanted the place to look like that again. Her heart filled with pride that a whole section of a museum would be dedicated to her home.

They left the museum and drove through town until they found the college. It was a small college, but Beth liked the idea of attending a small school. She would not fall through the cracks with a small population of students. They parked the car and walked around the grounds. The lawn was well manicured, and palm trees lined the walkways. It was a beautiful campus. Beth was excited about attending class here.

As it grew dark, they turned the car toward home. Joan pulled the car up to the door, and the two got out. She turned to her daughter. "I thought we left a light on?"

"Perhaps the bulb burned out," Beth offered.

"Perhaps." Joan put the key in the lock and opened the door. She felt along the wall and turned on the light. The foyer was bathed in light. They stepped into the house and removed their jackets and hung them in the closet by the door. "I'm going to go upstairs and change into something comfortable."

Beth followed her mother up the stairs to change her clothes as well.

In her room, she turned on the lamp and pulled off her shoes. She was tired. It had been a long and interesting day. She had felt better getting away from the house. She pulled off her clothes and hung them back in her closet. She pulled on a worn pair of jeans and a tee shirt. Walking up to the nightstand, she ran her hand over the two books from the attic she had laid there. She sat down on the bed and picked up the Bible and flipped through the pages. Her eyes caught something and turned back to it. There in the pages of the Bible was the marriage certificate of Joanna and Charles, along with a rose pressed between the pages. She fingered the rose carefully because it was so delicate. She smiled at the fact that they had kept this important document in the pages of a Bible. She assumed that it was probably the safest place in those times. A few pages beyond, she found the birth certificates of Elizabeth and Willow. She lifted them carefully from the Bible. The paper was yellowed with age and very fragile. She marveled that these papers were so old. She read them then placed them back where they had been for many years. She closed the Bible and returned to the bathroom to wash her hands.

Downstairs she found her mother in the sitting room enjoying a cup of hot tea. "There's a pot of tea in the kitchen. Help yourself."

Beth walked into the kitchen and poured herself a cup of tea and added two sugars. She went back into the sitting room to sit with her mother. "Did you check that bulb, Mother?"

"Yes, and it was fine. I guess I didn't turn it on," she said before sipping on her tea.

Beth did not reply. She remembered her mother turning on the veranda light before leaving the house.

"Do you think you're going to enjoy that little college, dear?"

"Yes. It is what I have been looking for in the way of a school. There won't be that many students, and it will be easier to fit in," Beth answered.

At that moment, a loud sound came from upstairs. Joan looked at her daughter. "What could that be?"

Beth rose to her feet. "It sounded like it came from my room. I'll go up and check."

Beth hurried from the sitting room and up the stairs. In her room, she flipped on the light and was surprised to see the Bible and the journal lying on the floor. She walked over and picked them up. From the pages of the Bible, something fell to the floor. Beth leaned down and picked it up. It was a piece of brown paper with something wrapped in it. She opened it and looked down at a single blond curl. On the inside of the paper was written the date *1865*. Beth carefully wrapped the paper around the curl and placed it back in the Bible. This time she opened the drawer to the nightstand and placed the books in it. There would be no chance of them falling to the floor again. She turned out the light before closing the door and hurrying down the stairs to her mother.

"What was it?" her mother asked.

"I must have placed the Bible and the journal too close to the edge of the nightstand. They fell to the floor," she answered as she seated herself and picked up her cup of tea.

Later that evening, Joan and Beth sat on the veranda and enjoyed the cool air and the peaceful night. In the distance, they could hear the pounding of the ocean. No longer was it a foreign sound, but one that reminded them of home. The sky was full of stars, and a quarter moon shone down on them.

Beth felt content, something she had not felt since coming to Brier Cliff. She was trying very hard to fit in and learn to love this place as much as she knew her mother did. She turned to her now and asked, "Mother, do you think this house has a soul as Nell says?"

Joan remained thoughtful for a moment before she could answer Beth's question. "I think a place that has seen as much history as this one has a certain atmosphere about it. But I don't think any house has a soul. It would have to be alive for that."

Beth listened intently to her mother. "Don't think I am silly if I tell you this. But I think this house is trying to tell me something. I have felt it since I first arrived. I feel that those who lived here before left part of themselves behind. It's as though we are living someone else's life."

Joan reached over and took her hand. "I'll admit I have felt something in this house that I have never felt in a place before. Brier Cliff is special. And you have always been sensitive to the feelings of others. Maybe there is a secret hiding in the walls of Brier Cliff. But you must remember, those that lived here are long gone and with them their secrets. There is no way to know what has happened here. The incident with the dress was unusual. You described the dress Elizabeth was wearing in every respect. I have no explanation for it. But I wouldn't jump to conclusions and say it was supernatural. There has to be another explanation."

Beth thought over what her mother had said. "Maybe it is just me. You always say I am sensitive to other's feelings. I think at one time there was a lot of pain in this house. Didn't Cora say all the Prestons came to a bad end? I believe the pain is still here, and I am in some way picking up on it. That sounds strange, but I don't have any explanation for what is happening to me. It's not happening to you. You don't have strange dreams or hear and see things that are not there. It only happens to me. I'd like to know why."

Joan looked intently at her daughter. Were all these things happening to her? A deep concern filled her heart for her daughter. "Dear, I know that you have seen many strange things since we came to Brier Cliff, but you have to realize that these things cannot be real. You and I are alone in a big house that has not had a family live in it for many years. There are bound to be strange things happening that do have an explanation. I want you to promise me, the next time something happens that disturbs you, you will come to me with it and we'll talk it over. We'll come up with a how and a why. Don't let it fester in your mind. That's what I am here for. I love you, and your happiness and well-being are most important to me."

Beth knew she had revealed too much. She didn't want her mother to worry. She smiled and reached out to take her mother's hand. "Thank you, Mother. I will come to you. But there are things that I have to work out for myself. I'm going to start reading the journal tonight. Maybe it will tell me what I want to know." She stood and leaned over to kiss her mother's cheek. "I love you too. I'm going to go up to bed. Don't fall asleep out here."

Joan smiled. "Don't worry about that. I'm almost ready for bed myself. I'm only going to spend a few more minutes out here enjoying the night. You know we'd never be able to do this in Baltimore. It is so peaceful here. There is no traffic, no horns or sirens blowing, and no smog. How did we ever live in the city for so long?"

Beth did not answer. She missed all those sounds of the city. But she had to admit that Brier Cliff was a special place. She started toward the front door. "Good night, Mother."

"Good night, dear," Joan said as she leaned back her head and stared up at the stars.

Beth ran up the stairs to her room. She took off her clothes and pulled her nightgown over her head, then pulled back the blanket and climbed into bed. She picked up the journal and opened to the first page. She stopped and thought about her conversation with her mother. Had she hit upon what was happening in this house? Was she just sensitive to the pain that had taken place here? It was a thought. She had always known when those close to her were in pain. She could sense things others could not. She had always thought of it as a gift. But now she was not so sure. This gift was now bringing her nightmare and strange happenings that she did not like. She wanted to be rid of whatever it was that had taken hold of her mind and would not give her rest.

There had been times in the past when she had sensed her mother's pain. When her father went off to war, it was as though she knew just what her mother was thinking. She knew her worries and fears, but could that be considered the same thing? She was very close to her mother. These people that lived in this house before were long gone.

Could such terrible pain and heartache remain in a house after the people were gone from it? She didn't have the answers. She opened the book again and began to read.

Chapter 4

Love does not know the bonds of time.

Beth placed the pillow behind her head and lay back in her bed. Carefully she opened the journal.

June 5, 1859

Today is my birthday, and Mother has given me this journal to keep. She says she had one at my age and found it great fun to read it now that she is married and has children. Father took the entire family out to dinner to celebrate my nineteenth birthday, then to the theater. It was such great fun. Everyone had a wonderful time. After the play, all the young men came to our box to greet us since it is rare they see us out all together. Of course, Willow was the center of attention, and she basked in the attention. Mother swears Willow will be married and carrying her first child before I. But that is no matter to me. I do not intend to marry the first man that asks me. John Drake paid me court a few months ago, but once I made it clear to him that I would not marry him, he moved on to the next. I hear he and Julia Thomas are to wed this fall. I swear he was only after Poppa's money and never gave a fig about me. In fact, I thought him more interested in Willow. He paid her more attention. But isn't that always the case?

Beth flipped through the journal and stopped at a page marked with a news clipping. She looked at the yellowed piece of paper and read the heading on the column Elizabeth had underlined: "SOUTH FIRES ON FORT SUMTNER." She laid the clipping down on the nightstand and read the entry in the journal.

January 12, 1860

Tonight at the dinner table Poppa said there is going to be a war. Mother cried, and Willow squealed and clapped her hands. I only sat there, trying to make sense of it all. To not be part of the Union. What nonsense is that? Of course, I take Poppa's views seriously and understand how he feels. This man Abraham Lincoln will destroy our economy if he frees the slaves. We have every right to withdraw from the Union if we choose. But what a terrible thought to fight our neighbors in the North. Poppa says the war will not last long, six months at the most. He says the Northern soldier has not been born that can win over a soldier of the South. I only hope he is right.

Beth closed her eyes and fell asleep with the journal lying across her chest.

The knocking at the door woke her. "Yes?"

The door flew wide, and a young girl ran into the room. "Elizabeth! Wake up! I have wonderful news! Poppa has returned from town, and he says there is to be a grand ball next week to celebrate our independence from the North! I need you to help decide what I should wear. Oh, there is so little time! No time for a new gown." She flopped down on the bed and began to pull the covers from Beth. "Get up! I swear! Aren't you excited!"

Beth could only stare. This was Willow! How could that be! And Willow thought her to be her sister, Elizabeth! Then the realization came to Beth that she was dreaming. That was it! How foolish of her to be so frightened! This was only a dream, and this girl on her bed a figment of her imagination! Beth decided to play along with her dream. Why not have fun with it? "If you will move, I will get out of bed and try to understand what is going on."

Willow jumped up and began to clap her hands with joy. "Everyone is going to be there! And our boys are going to be dressed in uniform. Just think: this could be the last time we will see some of them alive. They will be fighting for our country!"

"What a terrible thought," Beth answered as she pulled on her robe. "Now tell me everything. When and where is this going to be?"

"I told you, silly. Next week. Next Friday. In the town Community Center. The women are going to decorate with our new flag. Poppa says he is going to wear his uniform. And it is important that I look my best."

"You can always wear the dress you got for the Fourth of July ball. It was lovely," Beth answered then gasped in wonder. How did she know of the Fourth of July ball and that Willow's dress was lovely? This was her dream, and she could say or do anything she liked.

"Don't be foolish! Who would wear the same dress twice? That may be fine for Mother or you, but not for me."

"So what choice do you have? You said yourself there is little time for a new dress." Beth was exasperated with this woman-child.

"Well . . ." She hesitated only a moment. Then her eyes began to sparkle with her plan. "You remember that new dress you bought last month when you and Mother went to visit poor sick Aunt May? I thought with a little work, it would do nicely. Just a few tucks and a slight hem, and it would fit perfectly."

"You could have gone with us, but you said you were no good in a sick room. Mother bought me that dress because I was so helpful with Aunt May. You envied me that dress from the beginning, and now you have plans to take it from me and make it over to fit you. It would never be mine again." Beth didn't spare the girl's feelings. But the insult went right over her head.

"But that was so unfair. Mother bought you a dress and not me!" She pouted. "She knows how I love a new dress. You have always been her favorite. While you and Mother were off shopping, I was sitting at home entertaining Poppa."

"I won't fight with you over this, Willow." Beth turned her back on the girl. "The dress is mine, and that is the way it will stay. You can wear any number of dresses, all of them beautiful. Choose one of your own. Not mine."

Willow stomped her foot and folded her arms over her chest. "We'll just see about that! I'm going to have a talk with Poppa. I'm going to tell him about you and John Drake."

"What about John Drake and me?" Beth asked, surprised at Willow's determination.

"Last Fourth of July dance, you and John Drake left the dance and were gone for a very long time. Gossip has it you two were in his carriage. Doing what, only you and he know." The smile on Willow's face made Beth ill.

"You know that isn't true. And if you go to Poppa with that lie, I'll deny it," Beth returned.

"We'll see whom Poppa believes." She moved toward the door. With her hand on the doorknob, she turned back to Beth. "You know that I am Poppa's favorite."

She wanted to say, "Do your damned best." But that was hardly the way a lady spoke in the 1860s South. Instead she said. "Do what you will. You still will not get my dress."

Willow left the room, slamming the door behind her.

Beth woke with a start. For a long moment, she didn't know where she was. Was she still in her dream or back where she belonged? She looked over to her nightstand and saw her electric clock sitting there. With a sigh of relief, she pushed back the covers and crawled out of bed. What a dream! It was so real! She knew she needed to distance herself from this obsession she had with the two Preston girls. When a person started having dreams that were more real than not, it was time to stop. She dressed and ran down the stairs to find her mother. Seeing her mother dressed in her old work clothes, with a bandana tied around her head, made her smile. She had never seen anything more welcome.

"You slept late this morning." Joan smiled.

"Yes. Why did you let me sleep so long?" Beth asked as she poured herself a cup of coffee.

"After yesterday, I thought you needed to rest." Her mother came up to her side and retrieved a cup from the top cabinet. She poured herself a cup of coffee as she spoke. "Did you sleep well?"

Beth pulled out a chair at the kitchen table and sat down. "Mother, I had a crazy dream. I was back in the 1800s, and Willow was there. We were arguing over a dress." She laughed. "It sounds funny when I tell you, but it frightened me. It seemed so real. She thought I was Elizabeth."

Joan joined her at the table. "It doesn't sound funny. All day yesterday we talked of those two women. Of course, you'd dream about them. I couldn't go to sleep last night for thinking of them." She took a sip of her hot coffee and set the cup down before she continued. "We need to get on with our lives and let the past go." She smiled at her daughter. "Today I want you to rest. There'll be no housework for you."

"But, Mother—," Beth began but was interrupted by her mother.

"No. You will rest today. We are working on the staircase, and there will be little room for the three servants and myself. I want you to take a book outside to the lounge chair and just relax. You have been a great help to me, but today, I don't need you. Besides, your health is more important than this house. Some fresh air and warm sun will do you good." Joan reached across the table to take her daughter's hand. "Do this for me."

Beth nodded her head in agreement. "Thank you, Mother."

Beth stretched out on the lounge and opened a new book by her favorite author. The sun was warm, and a cool breeze rustled the leaves of the trees. She put on her sunglasses and began to read. A shadow fell over her face. Beth removed her glasses and sat up to look in the face of Cora. The old lady was leaning forward on her cane, staring intently at Beth.

"Didn't mean to frighten you, miss," Cora said. "Not now or yesterday. I came here to tell you that."

Beth smiled. She knew the old lady was apologizing in her own way. "Please sit down." Beth pointed to one of the lawn chairs. "You have walked such a long way. Do you care for a glass of lemonade?"

Cora lowered her stiff body into the chair. "That is kind of you, but I haven't the time. Besides, I don't think your mother would like that I am here."

"What do you know of Brier Cliff, Cora?" Beth asked. "I know there is more to this than anyone knows. Except, maybe, for you."

Cora leaned forward in the chair with both hands on the top of her cane. "There is, girl, but I'm not the one to tell you. I'm just an old woman who saw more in her lifetime than she should. This house holds a secret that no one knows. Maybe it will choose you to reveal it to. I tried to warn you yesterday. Now I know that it has to be revealed. Maybe then the dead can rest in peace. Then maybe we all can find peace." She stood up to leave.

"Please don't go." Beth rose from her lounge to take the old lady by the arm. "Elizabeth and Willow came to me in a dream last night. The dream was so real! In the dream, I was Elizabeth."

Cora shook her head. "You're the very picture of her. Look again at the portrait. Look into Elizabeth's eyes. Yours and Elizabeth's eyes hold the same light. The same kind and gentle soul radiates in those eyes. Don't be afraid of what you will find. She is not the one to fear. She'd never harm you." Cora shook her head. "But the other one, Willow, she's the one to watch. Maybe things will be different this time." She turned to walk away.

Beth called out to her. "Please! Talk to me! Tell me what is happening!"

Cora disappeared into the woods.

Beth sat back down on the lounge and leaned back. She closed her eyes and tried to will away her fear. The sun was warm on her face, and she had had little sleep the night before. She took several deep breaths and slowly began to relax. Within minutes, she was asleep.

Elizabeth stood alone in a crowded ballroom. She fanned herself to bring some relief from the heat. She was dressed in her new dress that her mother had bought her on their trip to visit her Aunt May. Willow had not managed to take it from her and had not gone to their father with the lie she concocted. Instead she had worn her dress from the Fourth of July ball, removing bows and ribbons, cutting off the puffy sleeves and plunging the neckline lower. Beth had to admit, Willow's dress was beautiful, and she was beautiful in it. In her gloved hand she held a dance card with only one name on it. The young soldier, dressed in a captain's uniform, had approached her only moments before with a request for the next dance. His smile was so friendly she had accepted readily.

Willow was lost somewhere in the crowd of dancers, dancing every dance and being the belle of the ball. The music stopped, and everyone moved to their corners to wait for it to begin again.

She saw the young man approaching from across the room. He stopped inches from her and knelt at the waist. "I believe this is our dance." She smiled and took his arm. The music began, and he led her out onto the floor. He was head and shoulders taller than she. Beth had to lean back her head to look into his face. His dark green eyes stared back at her, and he smiled. "I know I didn't introduce myself to you. I'm Dillon MacCarthy."

Beth returned his smile. "MacCarthy? Then you're not from here? I don't recall the name."

"No. They sent me from Atlanta to bring in the new recruits. You'd be surprised at how many of them are at a loss to this sort of thing." His hand about her waist was firm as he swirled her around the dance floor.

"I'm Elizabeth Preston. My father owns Brier Cliff. I've been here all my life," she said as she looked over his handsome face. His hair was dark with a slight wave. His chin was square and strong. His dark green eyes were enclosed with thick black eyelashes. His smile was as perfect as the rest of him, his teeth white and straight. He was by far the most handsome man at the ball, and for the life of her, she couldn't understand why he chose her to dance with.

His eyes traveled over the crowd of people then back to her. "There's a young lady standing in a crowd of men who is staring at us. Someone you know?"

She looked in the direction of his gaze. "My sister, Willow."

"Willow? Odd, but nice." The music stopped, and he led her back to her place against the wall. He knelt again at the waist. "May I talk with you awhile, or are all your dances taken?"

"Please do stay and talk with me. You see, I'm not the most popular girl here. My sister has that title taken. Men don't ask me to dance in fear of making her upset," Beth answered with her head down.

"She must be a powerful woman to put that much fear in the hearts of these young men." Dillon laughed.

She couldn't tell him that her sister told any number of lies about her to keep the young men from her. Lies such as she was promised to someone else and didn't care for the attention of other men, or that she wasn't feeling well and would rather be left alone. A stranger would not believe that of beautiful, carefree Willow. But Elizabeth knew it to be true. Willow had all but bragged to her of the many things she had told the young men. It had never bothered Elizabeth until now. Anyone who knew the two sisters knew the truth. Friends and family knew that Willow had to be the center of attention. That she wanted everything that her sister desired. To forgo her pouting and anger, she usually got her way. Elizabeth too usually gave in to her sister's demands. Everyone knew but Poppa. To him Willow was an innocent child who adored him. He gave her anything and everything she wanted, even if meant taking it away from his oldest daughter.

She and Dillon danced several more dances before they found a place to sit down and talk. His attention overwhelmed her and made her smile more than she could remember. He held her delicate small hand in his larger one as they talked. He told her of his home in Maryland, of his brother who fought for the North. He told her of his three years at West Point that had guaranteed his appointment as an officer. His father was a professor at the University of Maryland, and his mother a wonderful woman who had raised her two sons to make up their own minds and go their own way.

"You would love my parents." He had a faraway look in his eyes as though he was trying to picture their faces. "My mother's name is Ruth, and my father's is Jason." He smiled as he began to remember his home and family. "Dad has a beard through the winter months. He says it keeps his face warm. Maryland is not as warm as South Carolina." He smiled. "But in the summer months, he shaves. Mother says he is more handsome in the summer than in the winter. They have had a good marriage. Almost thirty years. Mother teaches piano lessons to young children. Every Friday and Saturday, the living room is her domain. We are not allowed in there between the hours of noon to three. My brother is named Robert. He was studying at the same university where my father teaches. He left his studies soon after war was declared to join the Northern army. Father was not at all pleased. He said the war was not as important as Robert's education. Robert—Bob, as I call him—was angry with me when I chose to fight on the opposite side. We had a violent argument before he left. I hope he and I get home so we can mend our differences. My greatest fear in all this war is that we will meet somewhere on a battlefield and have to fire at one another. I realize there are many more brothers, fathers, and uncles that are in the same situation. This war is brother against brother."

"Why did you choose to fight for the South?" She was intently interested in everything he had to say.

"I believe in what they are fighting for. A state should be able to govern itself. The federal government has no place dictating to a state how they should live. I don't fight for slavery. I do have an opinion about slavery. One day it will have to end. There is no way one person can have complete control over another. I realize you probably disagree with me. You have been raised in the South where slavery is an institution. But in Maryland, it is not that way. There are slaveholders. But not in our home. We have servants, paid servants. My parents were very disturbed when I joined the Southern army. That was the first time I ever saw my mother cry." He stopped there and looked into her face. "It's strange, me telling you all this. I rarely speak of my family. I feel it is a personal thing."

She took his hand in both of hers. "Sometimes a person needs to talk to someone else. I don't disagree with you on the slavery issue. I too feel it is something that should have ended a long time ago. But it is a necessity here in the South. Entire plantations could not produce without slave labor. And for the most part, they are treated well by their owners. I realize that is not the case in some instances. And those few should be punished. Sometimes I feel these people could not get along without someone to guide them. Then I hear tales of Negroes that are educators. In the North, I have been told, they can manage well without us. It makes me wonder if the slavery issue is right. But I am just a female and have no voice in such things. I believe what my poppa tells me. He is a good man, and he has never lied to me. I believe what he believes."

They continued to talk for many hours. He made her smile and talked to her like she was a knowledgeable person, not just a woman. She liked the way his eyes lit up when he talked of things that interested him and the way he smiled often.

He stopped in the middle of their conversation and shook his head. "How impolite of me. I have been talking so much I forgot to ask if you would like some refreshment. You must think I have been raised with no manners."

She laughed. "Yes, I would like something to drink. If it's not too much trouble?"

He stood and bowed to her. "At your service, madam." He smiled before he disappeared into the crowd of dancers.

Willow appeared quickly at her sister's side. "Who is that man who has been monopolizing you all evening? He is very handsome." She sat down in the chair emptied by the young soldier.

Fear entered Elizabeth's heart. Men always found her sister more attractive than her. She didn't want Willow to ply her charms on Dillon. He was special, and she didn't want to lose him.

Elizabeth chose not to answer her sister. She saw him coming with a glass in each hand. He stopped when he saw Willow and smiled down at her. "I am sorry. If I knew you were here, I would have brought you a glass of punch."

Willow waved her gloved hand and smiled her brightest smile up at him. She could not help but envy her sister. He was an extremely handsome man. She was instantly interested in him. "Don't worry about me. I've had plenty. It seems every man in this room has brought me a glass of punch." She wanted him to know that she was very popular with the young men.

He handed Elizabeth her drink. "I am sorry it took so long. There was a line at the refreshment table." He did not look toward Willow.

Anger filled her and made her clinch her fists. Who did he think he was? She could have her pick of any man in the room. She did not have to sit here and be ignored by this stranger.

At that moment, a young man approached her and bowed at the waist. "I believe this is my dance."

She rose and took the man's offered arm. She did not bid good-bye to her sister or acknowledge the man who stood at her side. She disappeared into the crowd of dancers.

The evening flew by, and soon it was time for the last dance. Dillon led Elizabeth onto the floor and took her into his arms. Together they moved as one. Elizabeth's heart was light as he smiled down at her.

He helped her with her wrap and led her from the Community Center to her awaiting carriage. Her father stood holding the door for her. "Poppa, this is Captain MacCarthy. Dillon, this is my father, Charles."

Dillon held out his hand. "Good to meet you, sir."

Charles took the young man's hand in a hearty handshake. "Good to meet you, boy. Drop by Brier Cliff before you leave. I'm sure my family would be glad to meet you."

"Thank you, sir. I will." He turned to Elizabeth. "I look forward to seeing you again."

She climbed into the carriage, and her father closed the door behind her. She was so happy that she didn't let the dark looks from Willow bother her.

In her bedroom, she undressed and pulled down the covers to the bed. Without warning, Willow barged into the room.

"How dare you shame the family as you did tonight with that stranger." Her face was red with anger. "Everyone was talking about your behavior. You spent every minute with that man. You ignored everyone at the ball!"

Elizabeth removed her robe and laid it on the bottom of the bed. She made no comment to Willow's insinuations.

"Aren't you going to say anything! Aren't you going to try and justify your actions!" She approached Elizabeth with clinched fists. "We'll not be able to face people in this town after tonight. My sister! My innocent sister throwing herself at a complete stranger who, for all that you know, could have a wife in another state!"

As she came close to Elizabeth, Beth took control of the situation. "Get out of my room!"

Willow stopped short. "How dare you talk to me like that!" She took a step closer and raised a hand to strike her sister.

"You do that and I'll knock you on your ass." Beth's voice was firm.

Willow gasped. She had never heard her sister talk like this. With eyes wide and face pale, she ran from the room.

Elizabeth climbed into bed and blew out the lamp. In seconds, she was asleep.

Elizabeth rose early and began to dress for a trip into town with her father. She didn't normally go into town with her father. She wanted to buy material for a new dress, and she had hopes of meeting Dillon MacCarthy. This she did not tell her father. She wore a blue dress that matched her eyes. It had a modest neckline and elbow-length sleeves. It fit tight at the waist then fell into a full skirt. On her head, she wore a wide-brimmed hat with a matching blue ribbon.

She stared at her reflection for a long minute before she was sure she looked good. She hurried down the stairs and out the front door to the waiting buggy. Her father lifted her up into the buggy and joined her. He cracked the reins and slowly pulled away from Brier Cliff.

In town, Charles pulled the buggy to a stop in front of a row of stores. He lifted Elizabeth down to the street. "You realize I am going to be a good while. I always spend a few hours in town on Saturdays visiting with Judge Brown."

"That's fine. I'll be a good while. Mother gave me a list of things she needs, and I have to choose material for that dress I've planned." Elizabeth smiled up to her father.

"All right. I'll meet you back here at four." He knelt down and kissed her cheek. Within minutes, he had disappeared down the street and into the judge's office.

A half an hour later, Elizabeth's shopping was done. She placed her purchases in the back of the buggy and crossed the street to the cafe. She would have lunch while she waited for her father.

The cafe was crowded at this noon hour. She looked over the crowd of people to find an empty table. Then she saw him setting alone at a table. He looked up, and their eyes met. A smile came to his handsome face. He rose and made his way to her. "Elizabeth, what a pleasure to see you again. Will you join me, or are you waiting for someone?"

She returned his smile. "Thank you. I'd love to join you. I am in town with my father, and he will not be rejoining me for hours."

He took her hand and led her through the crowd to his table. After seating her, he returned to his chair and looked into her face. "Then you are free to show me around town?"

"I am afraid you would be bored with our town. It's not Atlanta," she answered.

"I'd never be bored with a lovely lady on my arm."

She blushed and looked down at the table. "I'd love to show you the town."

The waitress appeared at that moment, and their conversation stopped. After they had ordered and the waitress had moved on to the next table, he reached across the distance between them and took her hand.

"I was just thinking about you when I looked up and saw you standing there. Do you think that means something?"

She looked at him intently. "I enjoy your kind words, but, Captain MacCarthy, I know that you are a lonely soldier and far away from home. You need someone to cheer you. I am more than willing to spend time with you. You don't have to say all those flattering things to me."

He laughed. "I am a lonely soldier and far away from home, but I mean every word I say to you. I enjoy your company, and if you would permit me to say, you're not hard to look at."

She blushed again. Never had a man talked like this to her. She was enjoying his attention but found it hard to believe he would be interested in her. "All my life we have been known as the Preston girls. Willow is the beautiful one, and I have always been known as the sensible one."

"Are all men around here blind? Willow is beautiful, but not any more than you."

They had a good meal and a good conversation. Afterward he led her out onto the street. She took his arm, and they began their tour of the town. She pointed out the park and the community hall, the opera house and the school she attended as a child. She showed him the church her family attended every Sunday. She showed him the town hall where the mayor and the town council held their meetings. When there was nothing left to show him, she stopped and had to laugh. "I've talked for almost an hour."

He looked down at her. "I am having a wonderful time. What man wouldn't enjoy an hour with a beautiful lady on his arm and listening to her lovely voice?"

He again placed her hand in the crook of his arm and started to walk. "Why don't I hire a buggy and drive you home? It will give us more time to talk. And I am not ready to leave your good company."

She was flattered that he wanted to spend more time with her. "Father is with Judge Brown in his office. I will have to let him know. But I don't think he will mind. He and the judge have probably had a drink or two by now, and he will not be ready to leave for some time."

"Good." He turned to her. "I'll go speak with your father. Then we'll go to the stable to hire the buggy."

He led her to the judge's office, and she waited outside while he went inside. In only a few minutes, he returned, and they were on their way to the stables.

She sat close beside him on the buggy seat, but she didn't mind. She enjoyed the feel of him so close.

They had ridden a short distance from town when he pulled the buggy off the road into a grove of trees. He jumped down and came around to lift her down. He took her hand and led her to the river that ran through the trees. He took off his uniform jacket then seated himself in the grass beside her. It was cooler in the shade of the trees, so she removed her hat. Her hair cascaded around her shoulders in golden curls.

He took one strand and wound it around his finger. "You have such lovely hair. You should wear it down all the time." He was very close. She could feel his warm breath on her cheek. Her heart began to jump erratically. She turned to face him in hopes that he would take the initiative and kiss her. He looked deep into her eyes. Suddenly he pulled away and stood to offer her his hand. "We have to go. We don't want your father overtaking us on the road."

She rose reluctantly from the ground. He grabbed his jacket and pulled it on as he walked beside her. He was silent and thoughtful. He lifted her into the buggy seat and came around to climb in beside her.

He snapped the reins, and the horse pulled away from the grove of trees. Elizabeth turned and looked back. She knew that she would never forget this place.

At Brier Cliff, he lifted her from the buggy and stood her on the ground. He did not remove his arms from her waist as he looked down into her face. "May I call on you tonight? Or is it too soon?"

"No." She was overjoyed at his words. "Yes. Please do call. I am sure my family would be glad to have you." She didn't want to sound too anxious.

"Then tonight at seven. Is that all right?"

She nodded her head. She stood on the veranda to watch the buggy disappear down the driveway.

Chapter 5

A smile. A touch. And
time stands still.

Beth rose from the lounge and took a deep breath. A new resolve filled her. She needed to find out what was happening to her. Why was she having these dreams? Was it as her mother had said? It was normal to dream of what you had talked about or done that day. Or was something happening that had nothing to do with that? Was the past coming to her through her dreams to tell her something? But why? She needed to find out what was real and what was a product of her imagination. She rushed into the house and up the back flight of stairs so her mother wouldn't see her. She went quietly to her room and opened the door so it didn't make a sound. She went straight to her nightstand and grabbed the journal. Sitting down on the edge of the bed, she opened it and leafed through the pages. Something fell from the journal. She leaned down and picked up the small card. It was Elizabeth's dance card. On the card was one name. Dillon MacCarthy! He was real! This was proof that her dreams were real! She turned back to the journal and began to read of the night of the ball. Everything was just as she dreamed. Her heart was racing as she closed the book. What had happened? Why was it so important that she know? She needed answers. If Elizabeth and Dillon fell in love, did he return from the war and marry Elizabeth? Did he take her back to his home in Maryland? Is that why there is no grave in the cemetery? Beth laid the book back on her nightstand in exasperation. "What do you want to tell me?" she spoke aloud. There was only one way to find out. She stretched out on the bed and closed her eyes.

Elizabeth stood at the foyer window and watched as the rider and horse rode up to the house. She waited until he dismounted and the groom took his horse before she opened the door. The smile on her face was her welcome to this handsome man.

"Elizabeth, you grow lovelier each time I see you." Dillon took both of her hands in his.

"Come in." She pulled him through the door. "Everyone is waiting to meet you."

At that moment, Willow descended the stairs. Her beauty overshadowed Elizabeth's. Elizabeth's heart sank. She knew she could not compete with Willow. She had dressed with care this evening in an effort to impress their guest. Her gown was beige satin that flowed in layers of material. The neckline was cut daringly low. She moved as though she floated on air. Dillon's eyes fixed on the dark beauty, and a smile came to his face.

"Sister, you must introduce me to your new gentleman friend." Willow stepped in front of Elizabeth and held out her hand for Dillon to take. "It is so nice to have you in our home. I am afraid my sister was rude when she failed to make proper introductions the night of the ball."

"My sister, Willow," Elizabeth said. "And Dillon MacCarthy," was all she could manage. Tears came to her eyes as Willow took his arm and led him into the sitting room to meet her parents.

Charles Preston was a self-made man. He and his father had come to South Carolina when Charles was just five years old. His mother had died the year before, leaving the two on their own. His father, Carl, had owned and operated a sawmill in Ohio and had hopes of doing the same in South Carolina. After settling in town, the two went out and began to buy up property. The three hundred and fifty acres that would eventually become Brier Cliff was bought for a mere one hundred dollars. Father and son worked side by side to clear the land of its timber. But Carl did one thing that no other lumberman in the state did. With each tree he cut down, he planted a young one to take its place. He would say to his son that he was looking out for the future generations of Prestons that would one day own this land. The work was hard, but in a short time, his father had secured timber contracts all over the state. More men had to be hired to clear the land. In five years' time, Carl Preston had secured a small empire for his young son. He then turned his attention to the boy's education. Charles attended classes and graduated, but he had never been a good student. His heart was not in his studies. He wanted to be working side by side with his father.

It was at this time that Carl began to build Brier Cliff. All the lumber for the project was supplied by his mill, ensuring that it was of the finest grade. Carl hired the best carpenters in the state, and when it was finished two years later, it was the finest house in Hampton.

Preston and Son was now one of the largest employers in the state. This fact made father and son very proud.

When Charles was eighteen, his father was killed in a lumber accident, leaving the boy to manage on his own. Charles took over the company and, with his father's knack for doing business, began to see the company grow.

While on a trip to Atlanta, he met his future wife, Joanna Peters. She was the daughter of a Methodist minister. She was small and petite and the most beautiful woman he had ever seen. She had dark eyes and dark hair and had a life about her that inspired the best to come out in Charles. He thought himself no equal to her. He was too tall, he thought. He stood six feet two inches. His blond hair and blue eyes could not compare with hers. He was husky, weighing two hundred and fifty pounds. Why, he thought, he could crush her with his bare hands.

But for reasons he could not understand, she felt the same about him. He proposed the first week after their meeting, and she had accepted. They were married a short two months later in her father's church with her father officiating.

He had taken her back to Brier Cliff, and she had loved it as much as he had. The next year, their first daughter, Elizabeth, was born; and two years after, his second daughter, Willowmenia, was born.

Both of his girls were special to him, but Willow held a place closer to his heart. She had a way of manipulating him. He was no fool. He knew when she used her charms on him to obtain a new dress or a new piece of jewelry, but he could not refuse. Willow would climb onto his lap and lay her head upon his shoulder as he read. Sometimes he would read aloud to her. These times were special to him. But Elizabeth held back, preferring to read on her own. She was a quieter child and better behaved than the rambunctious Willow. Elizabeth seldom asked for anything. She was content with what he gave her. She was the sensible one, the one that would one day take over Brier Cliff.

Charles rose to his feet to greet the young man. "Good to have you, young man." He turned to his wife. "This is Dillon MacCarthy, dear. Captain Dillon MacCarthy. Captain, this is my wife, Joanna."

Dillon took the older lady's hand and leaned down to kiss her fingers. "My pleasure, ma'am."

Joanna noticeably blushed at the young man's actions. "Please take a seat. It is seldom that we have company anymore. What with everything that is taking place with the country and all."

Willow led Dillon to the settee and sat down beside him. Elizabeth took a chair.

Charles reseated himself. "Tell us the news. We have heard nothing for some time."

"There is very little to tell, sir. Men are enlisting from every state, and our resolve is growing stronger every day." Dillon slid forward on the settee to distance himself from Willow's attention. He now sat with his back to her. Every once in a while, he would look toward Elizabeth and smile. This made her heart warm even more to him.

"What of Jefferson Davis? Do you think him the right man for the job?" Charles asked.

"I only know what I've heard. And from that, he seems to know what he is doing. I think if he gets the right generals behind this, we will win."

At that moment, the maid entered the room to announce dinner. Dillon stood and walked up to Elizabeth and offered her his arm. Together they walked into the dining room. He held out a chair for her and seated himself beside her on the opposite side of the table from Willow. The conversation at the table consisted of talk of war. But Elizabeth didn't care. Every once in a while, he would reach under the table to squeeze her hand. The fact that Willow had noticed did not bother her. She was too happy to care what her little sister thought.

"I saw you in uniform at the ball, sir. Does this mean you have joined up?" Dillon asked before taking a sip of his wine.

"No. No. I would like to join, but my wife is opposed to it," Charles answered. "I fought in the war with Mexico. I was a major under Wayne. Damn good man."

After the meal, Joanna rose from the table. "Let us retire to the sitting room to continue our talk."

Charles and Dillon escorted the women back into the sitting room. Charles poured two glasses of brandy and handed one to Dillon. "We save this for only our most distinguished guests." He poured three more glasses and added three-quarters water to the mixture. He handed the glasses to the ladies.

"Thank you, sir. It has been a real pleasure meeting your wonderful family and sharing your meal." Dillon lifted his glass in a toast to the ladies. "I am sorry to have to go so soon after dinner, but I have to report to my commander. He left orders for me to do so only this afternoon. I hope that you will excuse me and invite me again into your lovely home. It has been a pleasure sharing a meal with you and your family."

Charles shook his hand vigorously. "We hate to see you go, but you know you are always welcome here."

"Thank you, sir." Dillon returned his handshake. "May I be permitted to have a few moments alone with Elizabeth to bid her good-bye?"

"Yes, of course," Charles returned.

He took her arm and led her from the house to the front porch. "I want to see you again." He leaned closer. But he only wrapped her hand in the crook of his arm. They walked away from the house toward the gardens that lay in the back. "You have a very nice family. I enjoyed my talk with your father. He would like to be in this war fighting, but I can understand why he stays, what with three beautiful women in the house to protect."

The moon was bright and full, making it easier to walk. Elizabeth enjoyed being this close to him. "Yes, I know he would like to be in this war. I am only glad that he is not. I don't think Mother and I could manage without him."

Beneath a tree, he stopped and turned to Elizabeth. "I know this is too soon, but I would like to kiss you. I feel like we've known each other a very long time."

She looked up at him in the moonlight. He smiled down at her and said, "When I look into your eyes, I feel like I can read your thoughts." He pulled her close and brushed his lips across hers.

He could see her blush, even in the dim light. She said, "Did you read in my eyes that I would allow your kiss?"

"Yes," he answered as he ran a finger down her lovely cheek. "I read in your blue eyes that you wanted my kiss and do so again." Again he pulled her into his arms. This time taking more liberties to explore the depths of her passion. The kiss lingered for a long moment as both were lost in the spell it created. He was the one to pull away. His breathing was heavy and unsteady. He looked down into her flushed face and tried to smile. "You surprise me, sweet Elizabeth. Who would think that such a tiny thing could hold such passion? But I should have known. I saw it in your face today. It frightened me." He laughed. "How could such a sweet thing like you frighten me?"

She didn't answer as she returned to his arms and laid her head on his shoulder. "Do I shock you?" she whispered so low that he could hardly hear.

He pulled away from her embrace and tilted up her chin to look into her face "I don't like the way you make me feel. This is not the right time for this. There is no future for anyone until after this war. You must understand that my intentions are honorable. But I cannot allow our feelings to interfere with my resolve to fight in this war." He laughed. He had not meant to make a speech. "After saying all that, I would very much like to see you again. I needed to let you know where we stand."

"Yes," she whispered up at him. "I would very much like to see you again."

He once again brushed his lips across hers before he turned and mounted his horse and rode into the night.

She stood for a long moment, staring after him before returning to the house. Her heart was light. Never had she met a man like this one. She knew that he was special and that she wanted more from him than a friendly relationship before he rode away to war.

The constant knocking on the door brought Beth suddenly awake. She raised her head off the pillow and looked toward the door. "Yes?"

Joan stuck her head around the door. "There you are. I was worried when I didn't find you in the yard."

Beth sat up in bed and swung her legs over the side. She was trying to shake the dream from her mind. "The sun was too hot. I came up here to read and fell asleep."

Joan entered the room. Concern was etched on her face. "Are you all right? Have you had another dream?"

"No." Beth turned to her mother. "I was sleeping so soundly, and you woke me."

Joan smiled, accepting the explanation. "Lunch is ready. Will you join us?"

"Yes, of course. Give me a minute to straighten myself, and I'll be right down." Beth rose from the side of the bed. She waited until her mother had left the room and closed the door behind her before she went into the bathroom to splash cold water into her face. She was not surprised to see her hands shake. She felt panic race through her, but still there was anticipation. She wanted to experience this new love that Elizabeth had found. How was it that she could have the same rush of excitement that Elizabeth felt each time she was near him? She changed out of her jeans and tee shirt and put on a bright sundress. She ran a comb through her long hair and applied a small amount of lipstick.

She left her room and descended the stairs to join her mother and the servants in the kitchen.

Joan motioned for her to take a chair. "We've been waiting for you." She allowed the servants helping with the restoration to take their meals with her and her daughter. They were all sitting around the table, their meal of homemade vegetable soup sitting untouched in front of them.

Nell ladled soup into a bowl and placed it in front of Beth. Beth turned and smiled up at her. "You're a wonderful cook."

Nell noticeably blushed. "Thank you, miss. I appreciate your kind words."

"Dear," Joan began, "I was in hopes you'd help me hang the paintings. They came while you were resting. I wouldn't ask, but I am anxious to see them hung. Everyone is busy, but I could get Patty to help. She's polishing the furniture in the sitting room."

Beth took a spoonful of her soup before she answered. "No. Don't do that. It will take only a moment for me to change back into my jeans and tee shirt. I just was tired of wearing the same old thing all the time."

Joan smiled. "I think it will take only a short while to hang them. I know I wanted you to rest today. But I swear, once this is done, you can do whatever you please."

"That's all right, Mother," Beth returned. "I'm looking forward to seeing the portraits hung. They are really going to add to the decor of the house."

Beth handed up the portrait of Elizabeth, then stood back as her mother hung it in place. The cleaning had brought out all of Elizabeth's beauty, and Beth stared for a long moment. Cora had been right. There was a similarity between her and this young girl. She could understand how the fact could have spooked Cora.

Willow's portrait now hung beside Elizabeth's portrait adorning the foyer. Visitors could see them when they first walked into the house. The painting of Brier Cliff was hung over the fireplace as her mother had wanted. Beth had to admit, her mother had been right. Brier Cliff had once been a grand place. Beth knew it would be again. Her mother had already hired painters to paint the outside.

Once the paintings were hung, Joan climbed down off the ladder and stood back to admire their work. "How could two sisters be so opposite?" Joan asked again. "Both were lovely in their own way. But Willow, her beauty was remarkable."

"Yes," Beth said as she turned away from the painting. "And she used that beauty to get whatever she wanted."

"And how could you know that?" Joan turned to her daughter.

Beth quickly answered, "From the journal."

"Well, I think I've done enough today. I'm going upstairs to bathe and rest before supper," Joan said as she pulled the bandana from her head.

Beth waited until her mother disappeared from the landing at the top of the stairs then turned to the kitchen. There she found Nell peeling potatoes. "Nell, I'd like to talk with you in the sitting room."

Nell wiped her hands on a towel before she followed Beth into the sitting room. "Please, sit down." Beth directed her to the chair. Once she had sat down, Beth sat in the chair opposite her. "I need to talk to you. But I don't know where to begin."

"I think I know, miss. It's about the house. You want to know about the house." Nell appeared nervous.

"Yes. The house and the two girls that lived here," Beth said. "There's no one else I can turn to. Cora refuses to tell me anything. You're the only one who knows anything about the past."

Nell wrung her apron in her hands. "Miss, your mother would not approve."

Beth smiled at the older woman, trying to put her at ease. "Mother will never know you told me anything. You can trust me. I'm at my wit's end, and there is no one else."

Nell sat with her head down, refusing to say a word. Beth stood and began to pace the floor. "All right. Then tell me about Cora. Where does she come from? How does she know so much?"

"My grandmother took Cora in as a baby. She raised her as her own. I've always thought of her as an aunt," Nell began, somewhat relieved that the subject had turned from the Preston sisters.

Beth took her seat again, interested in what Nell was telling her. "So Cora was at Brier Cliff with your grandmother?"

"Yes. Then later with my mother," Nell answered.

"Did she know Elizabeth and Willow?"

"Elizabeth was gone by then. But she knew Willow. Cora helped take care of Willow just before she died," Nell said.

"Tell me the story of this house, Nell. Tell me of what Willow was like and how she died."

"All I know comes from my grandmother and my mother. Mother said that after Elizabeth left, there was no one but Willow. Her father had died in the war, and her mother the year after from grief. Her mother locked herself in her bedroom and never came out again. Elizabeth and Willow took care of her, but they could not make her leave her room. In the end, she refused to eat. It wasn't long until she died.

"Elizabeth ran off with her soldier and was never seen again. Mother said that her mother, my grandmother, told her that after Elizabeth left, everything changed. Willow had always been the social one. She loved parties and loved being around people. But all at once, she started refusing invitations and was never home to callers. Soon the invitations stopped, and the callers stopped coming. She stayed secluded in this house with only her servants around her. Toward the end, Mother said she was quite mad."

"How did she support herself?" Beth asked.

"Her father had lost all his money with the war. But he had something that did not lose value. He had property. Willow began to sell the land through her lawyers and lived very comfortably."

"How is it that Cora lives on the property?"

"My grandmother was very devoted to the Preston family. Willow left that little house to her. In the old days, it was a very fine place. But since Willow's death, it has gone downhill. Willow always saw to it that it was taken care of," Nell answered. "In those days, it wasn't overgrown with trees and brush. It could be seen from the main house. My grandmother was very proud of that little house. When she died, she left it to my mother and Cora."

"How is it that Cora knows so much?" Beth stared intently at Nell. Trying to absorb every word.

"At the end of Willow's life, all the servants were gone but my mother and Cora. Cora was the only one that Willow would listen to. She had raving mad fits. Pulling out her hair and breaking things throughout the house. Mother said that Cora could talk to her in a soft voice, and she would drop whatever she was about to throw and follow Cora to the bedroom. Cora would sit with her for hours at a time, holding her hand and listening to her ravings. The day she died, Cora sat with her till the end. She made her confession to Cora and swore her to keep her secret. Cora has been true to her word and has never told anyone what the old woman told her. Not even to me, and we're as close as any two people could be."

Nell stood. "I should go before your mother comes down. I would never want her to know that I told you this."

Beth shook her head in agreement. "One more thing, Nell. Where do you live?"

"With Cora," she answered before turning and leaving Beth alone with her thoughts.

Joan had rested for two hours then showered and dressed for supper. She came downstairs, refreshed and ready to enjoy her meal with her daughter. She found Beth sitting in the kitchen, staring into a cup of coffee, deep in thought. No matter what she said, she could not bring Beth out of her thoughtful mood. Joan was beginning to worry. She reached across the table and waved her hand in Beth's face. "Do you hear me talking to you? I said we should go into town for a movie or shopping. Just to get out of the house for a while. We've been working hard all day. It wouldn't hurt to have a little fun."

Beth tried to concentrate on what her mother was saying. She had a lot on her mind. Everything Nell told her kept going around in her head. "That sounds like a good idea," she said at last.

At that moment, a roll of thunder sounded outside. It got suddenly dark, and lightning flashed in the sky. Sheets of rain pounded against the windows.

Joan laughed. "Well, that destroys that idea. After supper, I will curl up with my book and read until bedtime."

Nell announced supper, and the two left the kitchen for the dining room. They had just sat down to eat when a flash of lightning and a loud roll of thunder sounded outside. The lights flickered and then went out. Nell was quickly there with a candelabra. She set it on the table so mother and daughter could finish their meal.

Joan tried to make light of the storm. "This is nice. Don't you think? How often do we eat by candlelight?"

Beth stared into the flickering light of the candles. She knew that this storm was a result of the house not wanting her to leave. But that was ridiculous. How could a house do such a thing? She needed to get hold of herself. She couldn't go on like this. She shook her head and tried to concentrate. "Yes, this is very nice," she answered her mother.

Joan looked at her for a long moment. "Is there something wrong? You've not been paying attention all evening. Do you have something on your mind?"

"No. Nothing important. I'm just not that hungry." She tried to smile.

"Neither am I. Let us go into the sitting room and light a fire. A fire will be nice. We can just talk. I certainly can't read in this light." Joan rose from the table and followed her daughter into the sitting room.

Nell hurried into the sitting room to light the fire.

Joan said to Nell, "Sorry about not eating that wonderful meal. We just couldn't with this storm going on outside. We'll try to eat later."

Nell started to leave, but Joan called her back. "How are you going to get home this evening? With this storm, you can't walk. Do you want me to drive you?"

"No, thank you, ma'am. I've brought an umbrella for just such an occasion."

"An umbrella is not good enough to protect you. Listen to that wind. You'll just have to stay here for the night." Joan seated herself on the sofa and raised her legs to warm them by the fire.

A look came into Nell's eyes, and Beth knew that she was afraid to stay the night in the house. "No. I haven't that far to go. I'll be fine with my umbrella."

"Nonsense. You can make yourself up a bed in one of guestrooms. I don't want you out in this. Now that that is settled, bring us a cup of your good coffee. It might help shake off the chill of the evening."

Nell stood there a moment, twisting her apron in her hands. She wanted to protest but knew it was useless. She disappeared into the kitchen and returned a short time later with the coffee.

"Thank you," Joan said as she took the cup from her cook's hand. "Sit with us. There is nothing you can do in the kitchen in the dark. It will have to wait until the lights come on."

"I should get the food off the table and put it away," Nell said.

"Then go ahead and take care of that, then return and sit and talk with us," Joan said. She looked toward her daughter. "Why is everyone acting so strange this evening?"

Beth sipped on her coffee. "I guess it's just this storm."

Nell returned, carrying the candelabra. She set it on the mantel over the fireplace and seated herself beside Joan on the sofa.

"This is nice." Joan smiled at Nell. "It is so cozy with a fire."

"Yes, ma'am," Nell answered. She was visibly frightened. She kept glancing at her watch. She never stayed in the house past midnight. It was only eight o'clock. Maybe the storm would end before twelve, and she could go home.

Wind pelted rain against the window. Thunder rolled loudly, and lightning lit the room as day.

Beth looked toward the window and saw the tree branches scratching against the pane. She stared for a long moment before she saw it—a figure standing at the pane. Lightning flashed again. It was the figure of a woman. Her hair was long and wet and clinging to her face. Her eyes were wide, and her mouth was saying something that Beth could not hear. She could only stare. She could not say a word, nor did she want to. She would not frighten her mother. Nell was looking in the same direction as Beth and saw what Beth saw. A gasp sounded from her white lips.

Joan followed their gaze. "What? What is it?"

Nell stood from the sofa. "I really think I should go, ma'am. My aunt is all alone. She will be frightened in this storm."

Beth thought, Cora frightened? That was unlikely.

Joan looked concerned. She did not want her servant out in this storm; then again, she didn't want Nell's aunt all alone. "Call her. She'll understand. She'd want you here where you will be out of this weather."

Beth suddenly realized her mother did not want to be alone in this house, in a storm, with only her daughter. She wanted to ease her mother's mind. "Yes, Nell, call her. Mother is right. You shouldn't be out in this storm."

Nell reseated herself. She mumbled, "I'll call her later." She knew she was fighting a losing battle.

The wind picked up speed and began to howl. At times it sounded like the scream of a woman. Beth felt chills run up her spine. What was happening?

The three women jumped at the sound of a knock at the door. Joan looked around at the two women before she stood to answer it. "Who could be out in this weather?"

Nell came quickly to her feet. She stopped Joan before she reached the door. "No! Don't answer it! Don't let her in!"

Joan stood in the middle of the foyer and looked from the servant to the door. "This is nonsense. Someone is out in this terrible storm, and I am going to let them in." She started again toward the door.

Nell began to run toward the door. She reached it ahead of Joan. She hit the door with both hands. "Go away! You're not welcome here!" she screamed.

The knocking stopped, and the wind began to quiet. The rain began to slow, and the lights came on. As suddenly as it began, it ended.

Beth stood alone at the door to the sitting room. She knew, then, what had happened. Someone, or something, was trying to gain entrance to the house. Nell had stopped it when she had said it was not welcome. Beth knew that her mother was not aware of what had taken place right before her. It was better that way. She didn't know how her mother would handle the thought that an unfriendly spirit was trying to gain entrance to their home.

With the lights on, everyone calmed down.

Nell apologized, blaming the storm for her actions. She pulled on her coat, grabbed her umbrella, and soon was out the back door to walk home.

Joan opened the front door and laughed when she saw the branch lying on the veranda. The wind had caused it to rub across the door, making the sound of knocking.

Joan picked up her book, curled on the sofa, and began to read.

Beth ran up the stairs to her room. So much had happened tonight that she needed to think. She knew now that she was not losing her mind. Something was happening in this house.

Chapter 6

Time cannot erase the
spell that love weaves.

Beth lay in her bed and stared up at the ceiling. Something important had happened tonight. She knew that Nell had seen the figure at the window. Her mother had not. But that was not unusual. Her mother saw only what she wanted to see. Spirits and ghosts did not fit into her image of a normal life. This house was important to her and to her family. Therefore, she would not let anything interfere with that. Beth knew that something was in this house that was trying to communicate with her. It used her dreams to relay what it wanted to tell her. But where would this end? What good could come of letting the spirit, or spirits, take control of her while she slept? But how could she fight it? She had no control of her dreams. When she thought back on the events of this evening, she realized she had not been afraid. Whatever it was, it was not trying to hurt her. She knew that in her heart. But what it wanted she didn't know. She knew that something had happened to Elizabeth, and she was the one trying to communicate with her. The attempts to frighten her off were from a spirit that didn't want her to know the truth.

Beth rolled toward the window and looked up at the star-studded night sky. The rain had stopped, and everything was still. The moon had come out, and outside, it was almost as light as day. There was a sweet smell to the air, and she seemed to find peace in it. She was restless, so she rose from bed and walked to the window and looked down into the yard. She opened her window and breathed deep of the fresh air.

Her eyes moved across the yard as she heard a sound. A movement caught her attention. A figure stood in the shadow of a tree. It stepped out of the shadows and looked up at the window toward her. It was Dillon! But it couldn't be! She wasn't asleep! She groaned, "Oh my god!" It was Dillon! She began to shake. Were these images going to start to plague her even in her waking hours? Then she felt her heart pick up its pace.

She wanted to go to him. She heard his voice calling out to her. She leaned forward from the window and signaled to him that she had heard. Pulling on her robe, she quietly left her room and hurried down the stairs and out the front door. He pulled her into his arms, drawing her tightly against his chest.

"I'm sorry, sweetheart. But I had to see you one more time." He looked down into her moonlit face. "I don't know what has come over me. I have thought of you every minute since I last saw you." His lips brushed hers. "Is there somewhere we can talk in private? I wouldn't want your father to find us here like this."

"The stables." She grabbed his hand to lead him through the dark to the stables. He lifted the bar from the door and let her enter first.

Once inside, with the door securely closed behind them, he turned to her and drew her back into his arms. "Do you realize what seeing you like this does to me? Have you cast a spell on me? My mind is full of only one thing. You. I came here to say good-bye. I planned to never see you again. I received my orders tonight. We are to leave for Atlanta in three days. We have no future, and I do not want to hurt you by letting you think that we do. But when I hold you in my arms and kiss you, I can think of nothing but our future and what it could be. Send me away, dear Elizabeth. Send me away so that I will not say or do something that may hurt you." His eyes pleaded with her.

But she could not send him away. She loved him. The realization staggered her. She loved him, and she wanted him to know. "How could I send you away when you are my heart? Without you I am nothing. Maybe this war will not allow us to have a future, but I will not deny how I feel for you. I love you, Dillon. From the very first minute. You are so good, so kind. I feel you are my best friend and more. You are everything to me." She raised a shaking hand to his cheek. "I know how forward I am at this moment, but you said we have only three days until you leave. I could not let you ride away from me without telling you. Three days, and I may never see you again." She could not hold back the tears that came into her eyes.

"Elizabeth!" Her declaration of love was a shock to him. He had hoped and dreamed she would feel this way, but never had he imagined the depths of her feelings. The surprise was that he felt the same. He wanted her—not only in a physical way, but also in every way. He wanted to share his life with her. To father her children and to grow old with her. He had known her for only a few short days, but those days were the most important of his life. He saw her tears now, and it broke his heart. He lifted a hand to wipe them from her cheeks. She grabbed his hand and brought it to her lips. "Elizabeth." He spoke her name again, and she lifted her eyes to look into his face. "I love you too. No matter how foolish that may be at this time in our lives, I can't help the way I feel. Nor do I want to." He drew her into his arms and held her to him, never wanting to release her.

"How could loving one another be foolish? It doesn't matter what is happening in the world. This is our time to love. The foolish thing would be to let it get away from us," she said with her head resting against his chest.

He pulled away from her and looked down into her face. "We will do this right between us. I do not intend to cause any shame to fall upon your head. I have only three days left until I have to leave. That means I have three days to convince your father that I'd be a suitable husband for you."

Elizabeth laid her head against his chest and closed her eyes. "Do you mean it? Do you really want to marry me?"

He tilted up her chin. "Elizabeth, I know it is too soon to be talking like this. A lady such as you should be courted for a long time. I should get to know your family. But there is little time for us. I have to go. There is a war.

Some say it won't last long, but no one knows for sure. I only know that from the first time I saw you standing alone at the dance, I was drawn to you. I knew that you were someone special, that you were someone worth getting to know better. That evening we sat and talked, you touched a place in my heart. Never had I talked so freely to anyone, especially a woman. But you were interested even in the trivial things I had to say." He looked deep into her eyes. "I tried to fight it. I didn't want to care for you or any woman. But how do I fight your loveliness or your beautiful eyes or your gentle spirit? Tell me, sweetheart, how do I fight that?"

"I would never tell you to fight how you feel about me. Why should I want you to? I could never deny my love for you. We came together because that is the way it was supposed to be. Can anyone fight fate?"

He laughed, and he pulled her back into his arms. "Now if only your father can see it that way. Let me talk with him. I'll tell him we love one another. I'll tell him I can't ride away without first having you belonging to me. He'll see how much you mean to me. He wants what is best for you, and when he sees I can take care of you, that I can give you a good life, that we have a good future together, he'll agree." Dillon smiled down into her tear-streaked face.

He pulled her back into his arms and lowered his lips to hers. Her arms came around his neck and held him to her. She pressed her body to his and felt him respond to her nearness. He placed his hands on her back and moved his hands up and down, feeling the soft contours of her body. He knew they were going too far, and he tried to pull away. Already he was hard with need of her. But a soft moan escaped her lips, and she held him to her, making it impossible to pull away. The feel of her warm body so close to his and the taste of her sweet kisses were driving him beyond reason. He wanted her and needed her as he never wanted a woman before. He lowered her to the soft hay on the stable floor. He kissed her lips, her cheeks, and down her neck to the top of her breasts. She entwined her fingers in his hair and held him to her. He pulled down the fabric of her nightgown and exposed the pink-tipped nipples of her breasts. He gently took one in his mouth and sucked. Another groan escaped her, and she raised her hips to push herself closer to him. She was his to do with as he pleased, and the realization was driving him over the edge. She wanted this as much as he did. Why shouldn't he take what he wanted?

Then sanity came crushing down on him, and he knew that this was wrong. He couldn't do this to the woman he loved and ride away the next day. It wouldn't be fair to her.

He pulled away and rose to his feet. He held out his hand to her to help her to her feet. She stared up at him, not believing that he would leave her when she needed him so.

He looked down at her and shook his head. "I am sorry, Elizabeth. I shouldn't have let this go so far. I know it is hard for you to understand. But someday you will. Please forgive me."

She rose to her feet and straightened her clothing. She found it hard to look into his face. She had all but begged him to make love to her, and he had refused her.

He tilted up her chin so she could look into his eyes. "I love you, Elizabeth. If I didn't, I would have taken you tonight. I'll not harm you in any way, because you mean so much to me. And if I allow this to happen between us, it will only hurt you. Believe that I love you and want you, more than I've wanted anything in my life."

She felt tears come to her eyes. She knew that he loved her. She wiped at her eyes and smiled up at him. He was a good man, one that put her above his own wants and needs. She should be grateful, but at that moment, she felt the hurt of his denial running through her body and making her weak with her need for him.

"You go back into the house. We wouldn't want to get caught and ruin everything for us. Tomorrow I'll call again, and we'll spend more time together. I'll speak with your father tomorrow evening."

He leaned down and pulled her lips to his. He tried to control his passion, but again he got carried away. The kiss left Elizabeth shaking anew. "There will be plenty of time for this once we're married," he tried to reassure her. "Now go."

She started to leave then turned back to him. "I have to ask." She hesitated a moment before continuing. "Why would you choose me over Willow? Men find her more attractive."

He laughed aloud. "I told you I find you special. There is nothing special about Willow. Pardon me for saying this, but you asked. You can find her type in any town. She's just a little girl playacting like a woman." He stepped up to her and kissed her lightly one more time. "I said to go before I don't want you to go."

Elizabeth ran from the stables and back to the safety of her room. Her heart was as light. She loved him. And she wanted to shout it so the whole world could hear. She opened the front door and ran up the stairs as quietly as she could. She paused in the hallway to listen for her father's snoring. She smiled when she heard it. He was fast asleep.

Beth entered her bedroom and closed the door quietly behind her. "Dear God," she spoke aloud. "This is really happening." This was no dream. She had been awake this time. She wasn't merely dreaming about Elizabeth's life, she was Elizabeth! She went to the window and pulled it closed. For a moment, she stood there. She could still feel his kiss on her lips. She could still feel the warmth of his body next to hers. Her heart was still racing from the excitement he caused her. Beth knew she was falling in love with Dillon MacCarthy just as Elizabeth had fallen in love with him. She didn't want this. But she could not control it. She knew to feel this way was foolish. It could do her little good to love this man, she told herself. But how was she to prevent it? She had not chosen this to happen. Elizabeth had chosen her. This house had chosen her. How could she fight this when her heart and Elizabeth's heart were as one? She knew what Elizabeth was feeling. She felt the rush of her heart each time he kissed her. She desired to know him in every way, just as Elizabeth did. She could resist only if Elizabeth could resist, and to Beth, it seemed Elizabeth didn't want to resist.

She realized this would stop only when the past was completely revealed to her.

She prayed silently to herself that Elizabeth's fate would not be her own. She did not know what had happened to Elizabeth, but in her heart, she sensed it was something very bad. Willow had tried to hide it from the world. She had secluded herself from everyone and drove herself insane because of what happened to her sister.

Beth wiped at the tears on her cheeks. She did not know how she could feel this way about a man that was long gone. She only knew that it was real. These feelings could only lead to heartache. But she did not want to fight against them.

She left the window and returned to her bed. She took the journal from her nightstand and turned to the entry of Elizabeth's encounter in the stables.

> Tonight Dillon stood outside my bedroom window, waiting for me to come down to him. I flew down the stairs and into his arms. We spent time together. I discovered tonight what a good man he is and that he truly loves me. How am I so lucky to have found a man such as him? I find myself needing him, as I have never needed anything in my life. Perhaps I am wicked to feel this way, but I want only to give to him what every woman who loves a man wants to give to him. I want to lie with him and feel his arms around me and his lips on mine. I want to feel his body next to mine. I know how that must sound, but I can't deny these feelings, nor do I want to. There is no shame in me when I am with him. If I am wicked, then so be it. I only pray that when he leaves me, God sees fit to bring him back to me. My life began on this night. I did not know what it was to feel real love. How could anything be so perfect and right? I can only pray that my father understands.

Beth laid the journal back on her nightstand and turned out the light. She lay there for a long time, reliving the events in the stable. Even remembering it caused her heart to race. She willed herself to relax and to forget. She needed sleep, and slowly it claimed her.

Beth rose early and dressed for breakfast. She had finally got some sleep that wasn't filled with dreams. She felt much better than she had in days, and she had a better outlook on the situation. She started from the room then remembered her mother had planned to work in the garden today. She wanted to plant flowers and till a place for some vegetables. Beth returned to her closet to pull out a sweater. It had rained last night, and she knew it would be cool until the evening sun hit the flowerbeds. Opening the door to the closet, she gasped and fell back against the bed. There hanging in the closet, among her clothes, was the Confederate uniform she had seen in the attic. Her hand shook as she reached out to touch the coarse fabric. It had a captain's insignia, the same as Dillon wore. It did strange things to her insides to think that Dillon had worn this uniform, that this fabric had touched his skin. She shook her head. She had to get hold of her emotion. She couldn't continue to think like this. It would do her no good. He was a phantom from the past. She removed the uniform from the closet. She didn't say a word as she wrapped it in her arms and carried it from her room and out into the hall. She pulled down the trapdoor and then the stairs to the attic. She climbed the steps with the uniform in one hand. In the attic, she hung the uniform on the nail where it had been before. She stood there a moment, looking at the uniform and thinking what it had meant to him to wear it. He had been proud to fight for what he believed, and Elizabeth had been proud of him. Beth shook these thoughts from her mind. She knew her mother was waiting for her, and she must hurry. She left the attic and raised the stairs and closed the door.

She would not mention this to anyone. She knew her mother was worried now. She wouldn't give her any more reason to worry. Besides, her mother would only think her insane. She was beginning to have doubts herself about her sanity.

In the kitchen, she joined her mother at the table for breakfast. "You look much better today." Joan reached across the table to squeeze her hand.

"Thank you, Mother. I slept better." She waited for Nell to fill her coffee cup, then added cream and sugar. She looked up at the servant and smiled. "You are spoiling us. We are not used to this."

Nell returned her smile. "It is my pleasure to serve such a nice family." She returned to her work and let mother and daughter talk.

"Nell has made some wonderful waffles, dear," Joan said to her daughter.

"Just toast. Thank you," Beth answered. She knew her mother didn't approve of her light breakfast, but she couldn't hold down a huge meal. Too many things were going on with her right at this moment. She needed to distance herself from Elizabeth, but she could not. She sipped at her coffee and tried to act normal in front of her mother. But how does a person act normal when they are in love with a phantom?

"I hope the ground isn't too soaked for planting today," Joan said as she took a generous bite of the waffles. She sipped on her coffee before praising the servant. "These are good." She turned back to her daughter. "Are you sure you don't want some?"

Nell came up to the table and poured more coffee into their cups. "After a good rain is the best time for planting, ma'am."

Beth finished her coffee and rose to follow her mother outside to the yard.

The air had a clean smell about it, and it revived her spirits. She looked up at the blue sky and felt her problems very insignificant compared to everything that was going on in the world. Somewhere across the ocean, men were fighting and dying in a terrible war. She could not compare her troubles to that. She took a deep cleansing breath of fresh air. It was such a beautiful day. She would enjoy it and not let the past interfere.

She knelt on the damp ground and began to cultivate the soil.

Working in the garden was backbreaking work. The sun was hot, and Beth had shed her sweater. After hours of physical labor, the ground was tilled, the flower plants and vegetable plants planted. Beth was hot, thirsty, and tired. She wanted only to take a shower and fall into her bed to rest before dinner. Lunch had been forgotten as they had worked straight through the noon hour. The only break they took was when Nell brought out lemonade for them to drink. Beth found a lawn chair and sat down, easing the ache in her back. Her mother joined her and stretched out her legs on an ottoman. She sipped on her lemonade and looked up at the sky. "It turned out to be a nice day."

"Mmm . . ." Beth nodded her head. She was too tired to talk and was enjoying the peaceful surroundings. Beth knew at that moment her mother was thinking about her father. She would not interrupt her thoughts.

After a half-hour break, Joan stood and returned to the garden. Beth could only groan. She didn't know how her mother worked so hard day after day. She suspected it was due to her great love of this place and the desire to see it restored.

Beth stood and stretched, rubbing her lower back. She turned toward the front of the house just as the truck pulled up to the front door. She watched as a uniformed man stepped out of the truck and started toward the door. It was the mailman, and he carried a letter in his hand. "Mother."

Joan stood and turned to her daughter. Her eyes traveled in the direction of Beth's gaze. She grabbed at her daughter's arm. "He has a letter to be signed for." Her voice was almost a whisper.

Beth tried to reassure her mother. "It's probably nothing. Let's go and see." She took hold of her mother's hand and had to force her toward the front of the house.

Joan's face was a deathly pale. "It's your father. Something has happened to your father!"

A few feet from the mailman, Beth released her mother and hurried on by herself. "Joan Mitchell?" he asked.

"No." Beth nodded in the direction of her mother. "I'm her daughter. Can I sign?"

Beth's hand shook as she took the pen and signed for the letter. Across the top was written, "War Department." A fear began in her heart and traveled throughout her body. She knew what the letter contained, just as her mother would.

Joan made it to her daughter's side and took the letter from her hand. An unearthly scream sounded from deep inside her, and her knees buckled beneath her. Beth grabbed at her mother to keep her from falling and led her into the house. She sat her down in the sitting room.

"Nell," she called out to the servant. "Bring me a cold wet washcloth, and hurry!"

Joan's head was leaned back, and she was so pale the sight of her frightened Beth. "Mother, let me read the letter. You're upset. It may be nothing."

"It's your father! I know it's your father!" Joan handed the letter to Beth and began to cry. Her sobs and wails echoed throughout the house. At that moment, Nell entered and applied the wet cloth to Joan's face. The servant looked as frightened as the rest.

"Nell, don't leave!" Beth said as the servant turned to go back to the kitchen. Nell returned to Joan's side. She reapplied the cloth after soaking it in cold water. There was little anyone could do to help. Nell thought, these were good people. Why did bad things happen to good people?

With shaking hands, Beth tore open the letter. She read silently to herself as tears ran down her face. She knelt before her mother and took her hand. "It says his plane was shot down. He's only missing, Mother. They don't know if he's died or not. There's still hope." But even as she said these words, she had real doubts that her father could survive this. She had to give her mother some reason to fight. There would be plenty of time for grief. Right at this moment, Beth wanted only to help her mother.

Joan began to laugh. "Hope! Don't you see? There is no hope! He's dead! He's dead!" Her voice rose with each word until she was screaming.

She grabbed for her daughter and pulled her into her arms. "You're all I have now. Your father loved you so," she cried as she rocked the young girl back and forth in her arms. But it was more to comfort herself than her daughter. Her heart was broken, and she didn't know if she could survive without her beloved husband.

Beth held on to her mother for a long while and let her cry herself out. When she began to quiet, Beth turned to the servant. "Let's get her upstairs to her room." Both women took an arm and half carried the silent Joan up the flight of stairs.

After laying her on her bed and pulling a blanket over her, Beth spoke to Nell in a whisper. "Call the doctor."

Nell turned, muttering to herself.

"What did you say?" Beth had only caught part of Nell's words.

"Nothing, miss," Nell answered.

"What did you say?" Beth's voice rose in anger.

The servant was visibly frightened. "That it is the same as the past."

Beth stood with unseeing eyes. Nell was right! It was just as the events of the past! Her father had been killed just as Charles Preston. She buried her face in her hands and began to cry. Would this nightmare never end?

"Miss, I'm so sorry." Nell wanted to take the young girl into her arms.

Beth shook her head. "No, you're right. It is the same. Hurry and call the doctor. I have to be strong for Mother." She wiped at her tears and turned to the bed. She sat down and took her mother's hand. Beth prayed, not only for her mother, but for her father as well. She felt in her heart that he was gone, but she would not give up hope. She had to hope for her mother's sake.

The doctor arrived a short time later and gave Joan a shot to make her sleep. He turned to the younger woman. "Are you all right? Do you want something to help you rest?" The concern showed in his aging face. In this time of war, he had witnessed many families in the same circumstances, and it never failed to make his heart ache for them.

"No," Beth said. "I have to be here for my mother. I'll be all right."

"Very well," the doctor said as he closed his black bag. "Call me if you need me. I'm very sorry, young lady. There's too much grief going on nowadays."

Beth didn't answer as he left the room, closing the door behind him. She could tell by her mother's breathing that she was asleep. Beth began to relax. She leaned back in her chair. Now she could grieve. She felt the warm tears roll down her cheeks. She would present a strong face to her mother, but she needed to grieve as well.

Beth sat staring at her mother for a long time. Her mind was wandering in the past. She knew there had to be a way to change things. If she changed the past, would the future also change? Could she save her father? She knew that Elizabeth's mother grieved herself to death. Could she prevent this from happening to her mother? She had to find a way! For some reason, this was happening to her. Was she to change things that had happened almost one hundred years ago? Was that why the past was being revealed to her?

She crossed the hall and entered her bedroom. She retrieved the journal from her nightstand drawer and hurried back to her mother. Seating herself in a chair, she pulled it close to her mother's bed then began to flip through the pages of the journal until she came to the entry of Elizabeth's father's death.

> The letter came at dinnertime while we were all seated at the table enjoying our lunch. Sara the maid brought it to Mother. At first, Mother chose to ignore the letter, saying it was of little importance. But upon Willow's urging, she opened it and began to read. Mother didn't read very far until a deep wail started erupting from her. It was a terrible sound, and I hope never to hear it again. Willow snatched the letter from her hand and read. She looked at me, her face as white as snow, and said, "Poppa's dead! Oh my god! Poppa's dead!" It seems Poppa was shot at some town called Gettysburg. We half carried her to her room. Mother tossed about the bed and tore at her face and hair. At that moment, Mother was quite mad. The doctor was sent for, but it seemed a very long time before he arrived. He administered a sleep aid and left the bottle for future use. There was no time for Willow or myself to grieve for Poppa. Our concern was for Mother. But after three days, there was little improvement. She refused to eat and cried continuously. We held a memorial service, although there was no body to bury. Many of the townspeople turned out for it. Poppa would have been pleased. When we came back from the cemetery, Mother's bedroom door was locked. A growing fear took hold of me. We begged and pleaded with her through the closed door. There was no answer, only the sound of her crying. We waited for several days, but after her food trays lay untouched in front of her door, I knew something had to be done. We sent for the locksmith in town and soon gained entrance to the room. Mother lay sprawled across her bed, large pieces of her hair torn from her head, her face and neck deeply scratched. Finally I allowed myself to cry. Willow was soon to join me. We posted a nurse at Mother's bedside so that we could find some rest. But for the most part, Willow and I took turns sitting with her

and reading to her from the Bible. She began to calm down, but there was no life in her eyes. She lay on her back and stared up at the ceiling. Nothing seemed to penetrate her mind. I prayed at those times as I never prayed before. I asked that God might grant me a miracle and allow me to live over those days before Poppa left for war. I would use whatever means it might take to see that he did not leave the safety of Brier Cliff.

Beth flipped forward in the journal until she found the entry of Joanna's death.

Mother died today. I sat with her until the end, holding her hand and trying to give her some comfort. She was a shell of the woman she had once been. She had not taken nourishment for days before her death, not even a sip of water. I think she was glad to go. Toward the end, she seemed to relax and held out her hand. It was as though she were reaching for Father's hand. She smiled, and then she was gone. I made the arrangements, and we placed her in the ground beside her beloved husband. It was a year to the date that father had died. We mourn her, but I know that she is happier were she is than in the world where there is no peace to be found. Willow and I are alone now. What will become of us? If this war continues much longer, I doubt that we will survive. I pray for peace, but there is no peace.

Beth closed the journal and wiped away her tears. She knew the pain Elizabeth had suffered. She mourned as Elizabeth mourned. The things written in the journal were similar to what was happening now. These two families lived almost a hundred years apart, but their lives were on the same course. Was this only a coincidence? She too had prayed for a way that she could save her father. She placed her head in her hands. There had to be a way. Things could not remain as they were. Something had to be done. But what? A thought came to Beth! She raised her head and took a deep breath. She could go back in time and save Elizabeth's father. If Elizabeth was sure she could persuade her father not to go, then Beth knew that she could do the same. She was going to go back! It was the only way! She was going to live out the entire thing. In doing so, she could, perhaps, save her own family. She wiped the tears from her face. She knew what she had to do. She was taking a big chance in going back to relive Elizabeth's life.

She stood and leaned over the bed to kiss her mother's cheek. Joan would sleep for a few hours. Perhaps in sleep she would find peace. Beth stood there looking down at her mother. "Rest, Mother. When I come back, I hope things will be different for all of us." She stood there a moment longer, wanting to put her mother's face to memory. She didn't know if she went back to Elizabeth's time, if she could ever return. The thought sobered her. Was this worth putting her life in danger? She knew the answer to that. She would do whatever it took to save Elizabeth's father. In doing so, she would save her own.

Chapter 7

Broken hearts cry for release, something that only time can give.

Beth called Nell to her mother's room to sit with her. She had something to do before she returned to the past, and she didn't want her mother to wake up and be all alone.

She hurried from the house and took the path that led through the woods to Cora's. She had to talk with her. She had to get the answers to her questions. She ran into the clearing and up to the porch.

Cora was sitting in her rocker on the porch, watching as she ran up to her. "I've been expecting you," the old lady said as she rocked back and forth, not taking her eyes off Beth. "I knew you would come to me. But there is little I can do for you."

Beth didn't respond as she climbed the steps to the porch and sat beside her. "I have to talk with you. You're the only one who can help me. Please, Cora, I need your help! Don't deny me before you hear me out." There was desperation in her voice.

"I know you need help, child. But I can't help you. Only he can help." She pointed toward the sky. The old lady's heart ached for this girl, but there was little she could do to ease her mind.

"I'm going back. Back to Elizabeth's time. My father is dead. I've go to do something," Beth blurted out her plan. She wanted Cora to know that she was desperate enough to take desperate measures.

"How in God's name, child, do you think that will help your father?" Cora reached for Beth's hand and held it in hers. "You are only endangering your own life. You should know that." She wanted to convey the importance of Beth listening to her.

"I've got this idea. If I can keep Charles Preston from dying, I can keep my father from doing the same. I know it sounds crazy, but my life and Elizabeth's are on the same track. Things that happen in her life are happening in mine. In her journal, she said she prayed that God would allow her to live over those days before her father left for war so that she could persuade him not to go. Maybe this is God's way of answering her prayer." Beth clasped Cora's hand tightly. "But I have to know what happened to Elizabeth. Maybe I could prevent it. Only you have the answers to my question about her. Don't you see, I am in danger only because I do not know."

Cora shook her head. "I wish I could, but I took an oath to a dying old woman that I'd never tell. And I've kept that promise. It would do no one any good to tell it after all these years."

Beth was angry. "That old woman was nothing to you! Nothing! She was selfish and mean to everyone. She tried to destroy her sister's happiness! Why keep a promise to someone like that?" She tried to calm herself. "I need those answers! You say my life is in danger. Then help me! Only you have the power to help."

Cora looked deep into the young girl's eyes. She was unmoved by her harsh words of Willow. It was important that she make her understand. There was only one way. To reveal something that no one knew. She had to tell a secret that she had kept for many years, a secret that had robbed her of a normal life. Wind whipped at her hair and blew it wildly around her face. She did not know if she had the power to say the words. She had kept this to herself for a lifetime, it seemed. She looked at the young girl beside her and knew she had to speak. She had to let this girl know that there was a reason for her silence. She spoke very softly. "She was my mother."

Beth's face paled. "Your mother! But how could that be?" She sat back in her chair and took a deep breath. That explained a lot. Beth was stunned to think that this old woman was the daughter of Willow. She would have never thought that possible.

"In the beginning, that was why she locked herself up in the house. She didn't want anyone to know about me. Everyone thought it to be grief, and part of it was. She grieved for all she had lost in her life. In only a few short years, she had lost her entire family. She almost lost her own life in giving life to me. She suffered for three days. She may not deserve my respect, but she was my mother, and I do owe her my loyalty. She didn't raise me, but she left me in Anna's care, her loyal and devoted servant. A woman I still think of as my mother. I was raised in a house full of children, and I had a good childhood. Anna was good to me. She was a good woman. Never did she tell me that I was not hers. I love her still for that.

"I didn't know Willow was my mother until she was ready to die. She then begged for my forgiveness. I gave her that, and I kept the promise to never tell her secrets.

"How could I not keep the promises I gave to my own mother? It didn't matter that she was insane and had ruined her life. She would have ruined mine if she had kept me. She did the only thing she could do. She gave me to someone that would take care of me and love me, as she never could." Cora lowered her head so that Beth could not see the emotion in her face. She still hurt to think that her mother could give her away and that she did not have an ounce of maternal love for her daughter. All her life, these things had been hard to accept. But she had been faithful to her word and had kept her promise to Willow.

"And your father?" Beth had to ask, knowing that question would only cause Cora more pain.

"I never knew. She never told me. It was unimportant by then. I had a good father, Anna's husband," Cora answered, trying to mask the emotion in her voice. "So now you understand why I cannot break my word to her."

Beth didn't know what to say. She had never thought that there was any kind of connection to her and Willow. She realized that she would never be able to make Cora tell what she knew. She carried some sort of false loyalty to a woman who did not care enough about her to recognize her as her daughter. She was wasting her time here. She had to get back to Brier Cliff and her mother. She had to get this thing over with so she could start to live her life. She stood and turned to walk away.

"Are you still determined to do this?" Cora's voice stopped her. The concern showed on her face.

"Yes. I have to do this. It's the only way." She turned and ran from Cora's house toward Brier Cliff.

"Then I can only say, God go with you," Cora said as Beth ran through the clearing and disappeared into the woods.

Beth stood at her window and looked down into the yard. The grass was green, and the trees were all in bloom. It was a beautiful spring day. Who would believe such pain and sorrow could dwell in such a lovely place and on such a nice day? Her heart ached for her mother, who lay in the other room sleeping. She didn't want to leave her. What waited for her in the past was still a mystery. That part troubled her more than anything else did. She could not let her fear of the unknown stop her from doing what she knew she had to do.

The voices from the past were pulling her toward her destiny. There was no way to stop what had to be. She knew that even if circumstances were different, she would still have to do this. Why delay what had to be? She turned to her bed and pulled down the blanket. She stretched out on the bed and closed her eyes. She whispered into the stillness of her room, "I am ready." Within moments, she was in the past.

Elizabeth spread out the blanket on the ground and set the picnic basket on it. True to his word, Dillon had returned, and they had ridden out over her property with Willow and a young man from town, Peter Derek, as companions. It was a beautiful day. The air was warm, and the sky was clear. Dillon joined her on the blanket and pulled her across his lap and into his arms. "Are you worried?" he asked as his lips brushed across her forehead then down to her ear. He loved holding her like this. She was his, and for the first time in his life, he felt protective of another.

She smiled and snuggled deeper into his arms. "No. Not now. Not with you here." She buried her face in his uniform jacket and breathed deep of the smell of him. She closed her eyes and listened to the steady beat of his heart. She thought again how lucky she was to love and be loved by this man.

"We'll have a wonderful life. I mentioned that my father taught at the University of Maryland. He teaches law. All my life, since I could read, he has pushed his law books in front of me. I've read and listened in on many of his lectures at the college. Father seems to think I'm ready to take the bar exam. If I pass, sweetheart, I can practice law." Dillon loved to speak of his future with Elizabeth. Before he had met her, he had delayed in taking the bar, not knowing what he wanted to do with his future. Now he could see the logic of his father's words and knew that he could make a good living for Elizabeth and the family that was to come.

She was looking at him intently. He couldn't help but smile. "Would you mind being a lawyer's wife?"

She wrapped her arms around his neck. "Not at all. Where will we live?" She softly rained kisses down his face to his neck. She smiled when she saw the gooseflesh rise to his skin.

He was trying to hold a conversation with her, and she was making it difficult. "Wherever you like. Here if you prefer. But of course, we'll have to visit my parents and let them meet you. They will love their new daughter-in-law. How could they not when they see how much their son loves her?"

At that moment, Willow and her companion rode up to them. "Come on, you two. Join us. We're having a wonderful time. The horses are loving the workout." Willow's face was alive with excitement. She loved to ride and had not had much opportunity of late.

"I've unpacked our lunch. Let's eat first," Elizabeth answered.

Peter Derek was a tall, slim man of about twenty years of age. He had curly dark hair and a nice smile. His smile was his best feature. He flashed it often. It was obvious he was taken with Willow. He dismounted and helped her from her horse. Gently he seated her on the blanket then joined her, crossing his long legs beneath him. They ate fried chicken and biscuits, prepared by the cook at Brier Cliff. They enjoyed every bite.

Elizabeth had to admit Willow was being very pleasant today. She knew the reason behind it to be all the attention she was receiving from her young man. After eating, Elizabeth packed away the remaining food. Dillon waited patiently until she was done before standing and offering her his hand. "Let's take a walk before we ride. I'm too full to sit on a horse right now."

Elizabeth took his hand and rose. She turned to her sister. "Would you two care to join us?"

"No, thank you," Willow answered. "We'll wait here for you."

Dillon led her through the woods until they were out of sight. He pulled her into his arms and held her tight. "I hate to share you with anyone. We need to talk, and we couldn't do that around your sister and her gentleman friend."

She tilted back her head and looked up at him. "What is so important that we had to be alone?"

He pushed a strand of blond hair from her cheek and looked down at her with all the love he felt in his heart. "Have you thought what we will do if your father does not allow us to marry right away?"

"I try not to think of that." A frown mired her lovely face. "What is this? You were the one that was so sure he would give his consent." Elizabeth did not like this new negative mood he was in. She wanted him confident when he faced her father. She knew her father could be a tyrant when it suited him. Dillon needed to convey his love and assurance that he was a good candidate for her future husband.

"I am sure, but the closer the time comes to talk with him, the more worried I become. I want to say the right things, to give the right impression. I want him to be as sure about this as I am. But he is your father. He has every right to be concerned. We have known each other for such a short time. And this will mean we will have to wait to start our life together. I would like to send you farther North to my home in Maryland, where you will be safe from this war. But I know he would never approve of that. He will want you here with your family. He thinks he can protect you, but I am not so sure any one person can protect another from this war. If the South prevails in this war, our way of life will be preserved, but if not"—he shook his head—"the South, as we know it, will cease to be."

"I have thought of all this. But it doesn't matter if we remain part of the Union or are an independent country, we will be together. That is all that truly matters." She pulled his head down to hers and kissed his waiting lips. She wrapped her arms around his neck and held him as close as she could. His arms came around her waist, and he returned her kiss with as much passion as she did. Long moments passed before he pulled away. He was visibly shaken. He looked down at her radiant face and had to smile. Her blue eyes were alight with passion. She was in love with him. The wonder of that filled his heart. She was as lovely as a spring day. She had an innocence that he adored. She had so much to offer a man, and she offered it to him!

"We had better join the others." He laughed aloud. "I don't think I need to worry you will be an unresponsive wife."

She joined his laughter as she took his arm and started with him back through the woods. He made her feel like she had never felt before. If she were to speak of it to her mother, she would think her wicked. Things of that nature were never spoken of between mother and daughter. But Elizabeth had seen the love and adoration between her parents and knew that her mother would know exactly what she was talking about.

As they rounded the trees that circled the clearing where they had picnicked, Dillon stopped short. Elizabeth followed his gaze. A gasp escaped her as she saw her sister leaning against a tree, her skirt pulled up, revealing her thighs and Peter's hands on her buttocks, pulling her tightly against him. They were embraced in a passionate kiss and were oblivious to what was going on around them. Dillon pulled Elizabeth back behind the trees. After a moment, he reached out and snapped a branch of a tree. Taking her arm, he led her back into the clearing. Willow was standing alone by the tree with her dress down around her ankles. Peter sat on the blanket toying with a strand of grass. They both looked up and smiled at Dillon and Elizabeth as they came up to them.

"Finally." Willow stepped forward. "Are you two ready to ride?"

"I think we'd better start back." Elizabeth could not look her sister in the face. "Mother will start to worry."

Dillon loaded the picnic basket then lifted Elizabeth onto her horse. Willow and Peter pulled their horses up beside them as he swung his long legs over the saddle.

They rode leisurely back to Brier Cliff in silence, each deep in their own thoughts.

That evening they sat around the dining room table enjoying a good meal and friendly conversation. War was the main topic, and Charles Preston was enjoying himself. He loved talking strategies and logistics. Dillon let him carry the conversation, interrupting only to add his point of view. He held tight to Elizabeth's hand beneath the table. She knew he was drawing from her strength. Peter Derek had been invited and sat beside Willow, paying little attention to the conversation.

He had eyes only for Willow. If Charles noticed the whispers between the two, he didn't let on. But Elizabeth couldn't help but remember the scene she had witnessed on their ride. She needed to have a talk with Willow. She knew it wouldn't be pleasant. Willow would not take reprimanding from her sister. Finally the meal was over, and they retired to the sitting room.

Charles poured each of the men an after-dinner drink and raised his glass in a toast. "The South," was all he said, but each knew the importance of that toast. It was a toast to all their futures. It was a toast to a lifestyle that they had known for hundreds of years.

Dillon set down his glass and turned to Charles. "Sir, I would like to talk with you in private."

Charles seemed disturbed but agreed to his request.

Charles led the way into his study.

Elizabeth's heart picked up its pace, and her hands shook. She knew this was one of the most important moments of her life. She could only imagine what was happening behind the closed doors of the study. She knew that her father would not be as easy to convince to let the two wed after such a short courtship. She could only pray that Dillon would be as convincing as he said he could be.

An hour later, her father called her into the study. He stood at the door and closed it behind her, then he returned to his seat behind the desk. She was visibly shaken at his stern face. She knew before he began to speak that he had some objection to what Dillon proposed.

"This young man," Charles began, "has asked for your hand in marriage. He assures me you are in agreement to his proposal." He studied her face and knew she was disturbed. But this was far too important to let that interfere with his decision.

"Yes, Poppa," Elizabeth managed to say. She clutched her hands together and waited for what her father was about to say. She prayed it would be different than she suspected.

Charles nodded his head and rubbed his chin thoughtfully. "I have no objections to your young man, Elizabeth. I find him an honorable and suitable partner for my daughter. But it is far too early for both of you to think of marriage. In times such as these, it is important not to rush into marriage. You two need to get to know each other. But I will agree to an engagement. You two can correspond and learn about each other. Within, let's say, a year, you feel the same, then I will agree to a marriage."

"Sir," Dillon interrupted, "in times like these, there is little time for the formalities of courtship. Elizabeth and I love one another. In less than three days' time, I am leaving for Atlanta. I don't want to leave her without knowing that she will be waiting for me when I return. I want her for my wife, sir." Dillon poured his heart out to Charles. He had to make him understand that Elizabeth meant everything to him. What difference did it make that they had known each other for such a short time?

Charles was thoughtful. His blue eyes searched the two young people's face. He could see the love the two felt for each other. But Elizabeth was his daughter, and he wanted to do what was best for her. She would suffer a long absence from Dillon when he left for war. What if she should become with child? How could she deal with that if he didn't return? No, he decided, he was doing the right thing in delaying the wedding. "I know what it is to love someone, son. Let us come to some sort of agreement. Do you think it possible to obtain a leave in a few months?"

"It is possible," Dillon answered, a ray of hope entering his heart.

"Then things will remain as I said. You will leave as planned and return in a few months. By that time, we will have the wedding planned, and Elizabeth can marry you respectfully. You two can correspond and get the date set. I realize that times demand we forgo tradition, so"—he slapped his hands on the desktop—"we are going to have a wedding."

Elizabeth began to cry as Dillon wrapped an arm around her waist. Her father joined them and wrapped his arms around the two in a bear hug. "Now let us go inform your mother and sister." His eyes glowed with tears, and Elizabeth realized he was as emotional at that moment as she was.

In the sitting room, Joanna rose as the three entered the room. She knew that something had happened. She saw the tears in Elizabeth's eyes, and she could not help but notice the arm Dillon had wrapped around her waist.

Charles walked up to the liquor cabinet and poured drinks for all in the room. He passed out the glasses one at a time then lifted his glass in another toast. Joanna held her breath, waiting for the announcement that she was sure to come.

"To Elizabeth and Dillon. May they have a happy life together, as happy as Joanna and I have had."

Joanna smiled through her tears as she hugged both her daughter and her future son-in-law.

Willow did not congratulate the couple. She stayed in the background, jealous of all the attention her sister was getting from her parents. She gulped down her drink and left the room unnoticed.

Elizabeth and Dillon rode out over her property. They both remained quiet. She couldn't trust herself to speak because she was so close to tears. Dillon was deep in thought. He was concerned about the well-being of the woman he loved.

He pulled his horse to a stop and came around Elizabeth's horse to help her down. Silently he took her hand and led her beneath a tree. He sat down and pulled her into his arms. Passionately he kissed her, marveling again at the passion she returned. Her hands went up around his neck and held him to her for a long moment. He released her and looked down into her beautiful face. "Elizabeth, you torture me so."

"There's no need to be tortured. We are engaged. There is no need to wait. I love you, Dillon, and I want to belong to you." She gently rubbed his cheek, feeling the stubble of his beard.

"I want you to belong to me too. But there is a lot to consider before doing something like that. We both don't know what tomorrow will hold. There's a war. What if I don't return? What if you should become with child? You'd be left alone to face the shame. I couldn't do that to you. I love you too much to do that to you." He turned away to look out over the meadow.

She pulled his face around to look at her. "There would be no shame for me in carrying your child. I would consider it a great honor. Besides, what if you didn't return? What would I have left of you? Nothing but these few days together. Don't you see? I want you to be a part of me. We have had so little time together. Give me something to remember on those lonely days and nights that I wait for your return."

He pulled her back into his arms. She rested her head against his chest and listened to the steady beat of his heart. "Believe, sweetheart, it is out of love that I deny you and myself. Our love is too perfect to ruin in any way. I'll be back. That I promise you. And when I do come back, no one or nothing will ever separate us again. You will belong to me in every way. Until then, you and I must be strong."

Elizabeth wrapped her arms around his waist and held to him tightly. Now that she had found love, she never wanted to be without it. She needed him, and she wondered what would become of her if he didn't return.

They spent the day together, sharing and holding on to each other. As evening approached, Elizabeth began to have a deep ache in her soul. She knew he would leave her, and with him would go her heart.

At the house, he held her to him, trying to ease the pain that he knew she felt. After long minutes passed, he leaned back and looked down into her tear-streaked face. "Don't cry. I can't bear to see you cry. You're my heart, and when you're sad, so am I. Have faith, Elizabeth. We will be together again. How could a just God deny us a life together? Don't you see?" He wiped a tear from her cheek. "He couldn't."

She could only nod her head in agreement.

He lowered his lips to hers and kissed her once again before he turned away and rode into the night.

Later that night, Joanna entered Elizabeth's bedroom and came to sit down on the side of the bed. Her daughter had been crying into her pillow since her young man had ridden away.

Joanna brushed the tear-dampened hair from her face and made her turn to face her. She looked down into her tear-streaked face and felt her heart go out to her. "Elizabeth, I know you think your heart is broken and that your parents are wrong to deny you a quick marriage before Dillon has to leave. But you have to understand. Your father has done this out of love for you. He doesn't want you to be left on your own to raise a child without a father or, in the least, to be a widow at the age of twenty. We love you and want what is best for you—"

Elizabeth interrupted, "But Dillon is what is best for me. We love one another. He is a good man, Mother. He will make me a good husband. What difference does it make if we marry now or wait a few months? We wouldn't love each other any more than we do now."

"I know." Joanna had to smile. She remembered how she felt so many years ago when she met Charles. She didn't want to wait either. But her father made her wait at least two months before he would allow them to marry. She thought it was the end of the world. But things had worked out. And she and Charles had a good marriage. "Your young man is going to be leaving in the morning. It is going to be hard on him. I want you to be strong in front of him. His men will be watching, and you don't want to shame him. Dry those eyes so your face won't be swollen and red tomorrow. You don't want his men to think he is marrying an unattractive girl now, do you?"

Elizabeth sat up in bed and dried her eyes on her nightgown sleeve. Her mother had to laugh. She had done that as a child. "Get dressed and come downstairs. We are waiting supper for you. Your father is upset now, thinking you are up here crying because of him. Why don't you try to ease his mind? You know that he loves you very much."

"All right, Mother. I'll be right down." Elizabeth rose from bed and poured water into her basin to wash her face. "And, Mother, I love you and Poppa too."

Joanna quickly left with tears in her eyes. She knew that Elizabeth was a good girl and would do what was right. Even if her heart did not tell her to.

Elizabeth waited on the front porch as Dillon rode up the drive. He was leaving and had only a few minutes to say his good-byes. He jumped from his horse and ran up the steps to take her into his arms. He lightly brushed his lips against hers. "I'm sorry I don't have a lot of time."

"I know. I know," she answered, holding back her tears. She wanted to be strong for him. She brought her hand up to lay it against his cheek. "You will come back to me?"

"You know I will," he assured her. "Nothing can keep me from coming back for you, sweetheart. I love you."

"And I love you." She circled her arms around his neck and pulled him to her. She didn't care that her parents and sister stood at the window and looked out at them. She kissed him with all the love she felt in her heart. He returned her kiss with as much affection. He finally pulled away. "Why am I always the one to pull away? Have you no shame?" He tried to laugh.

"Not where you're concerned."

"I don't have a ring to give you." He lowered his head close to hers, but I wanted to give you something that was important to me. My father gave me this when I left for war. It was his, and it means a great deal to me." He took the wide gold bracelet from his wrist and placed it on hers. "When I come back, I'll buy you the biggest diamond I can find."

Elizabeth could hold back her tears no longer. She reached out to him as the tears ran down her cheeks. She reached out to him, but he turned from her and ran down the steps of the veranda and threw his legs over the saddle. He raised a hand to signal his men to follow and turned, and the precession rode down the drive and out of sight.

She stood there until he disappeared from sight, then turned and entered the house.

Elizabeth walked from the house and out into the yard. It was late evening, and she had remained locked in her room, not wanting to face her family with a tear-streaked face. They were sitting down to supper when she quietly left the house. She wanted to be alone with her thoughts. Dillon had been gone twelve hours, and it seemed like a lifetime. She walked across the yard and into the trees. It was a peaceful and quiet evening. She came to the clearing where she and Dillon had picnicked and sat down on the ground beneath a tree. She sat there, remembering that day only a few hours before when they had been together. She longed for the time to fly so that he would return. How was she to go on without him? In the clearing, she spotted two young deer walking out into the field. They lowered their heads and munched on the spring grass. She had to smile at the lovely picture they presented. The trees were all in bloom, and the air was filled with their sweet fragrance. She looked up at the cloudless sky and prayed for the safety of the man she loved. An hour passed before she rose from the ground and slowly made her way back to the house. She stopped on the edge of the cliff and looked down at the ocean. The sun was setting and seemed to disappear into the water. A beautiful red orange sunset lit the evening sky. She took comfort in that beauty. How could anyone come in harm's way on such a lovely day? She reentered the house and climbed the stairs to her bedroom.

Chapter 8

Sorrow and pain wrapped
in the pages of time.

Elizabeth lay in her bed and cried. She tried to sleep, but no rest would come to her. She tried to think, to reason, but her heart was somewhere else than in this tiny bedroom and in this house. Her heart was on some lone battlefield with all the men who fought there and gave their lives. She tried not to think that Dillon may never return to her. He had given his word that he would. He had instilled hope in her soul. He had said that he would return and that they would have a good life. She prayed that night as she never prayed before. She asked God to grant this one thing, and she would be eternally grateful.

In the early hours of morning, she finally slept. But hers was not a peaceful sleep. She dreamed of dying men lying on the blood-soaked earth, reaching out for help, their bodies torn beyond repair. She dreamed of soldiers running, trying to find some safe place when there wasn't any to be had. She heard the sound of shots and shell everywhere. There was no escape from this place. She thought if there was a hell, then surely this was one. She smelled the smoke from the guns and the cannon fire. All around her was havoc and mayhem. She woke with a start and sat up in her bed. She was in a cold sweat, her heart racing in her chest. She began to cry anew. She realized that this was exactly what Dillon faced in this war.

She rolled toward the window and looked up at the early morning sky. She began to pray again. But she knew that her meager prayers could not save him if that was not to be his destiny.

Finally the sun came up, and she rose from bed and poured water into the basin from the pitcher and splashed it into her face. She looked into the mirror and thought how terrible she looked, but at that moment, she did not care. She dressed then ran a brush through her hair and pulled it back and wrapped it in a bun. She left her room to join the others downstairs.

Elizabeth remained aloof and quiet for days. She spent most of her time in her room writing in her journal. The few times she sat down to a meal with the family, she ate very little and refused all attempts at conversation with her. Everyone was worried about her, but there seemed to be nothing to bring her out of her depression. Charles offered comfort to his wife with his assertion that only time could help. Joanna did not think that time had anything to do with helping her daughter. She knew that only when her young man returned would she return to her old self.

That evening, Elizabeth wrote in her journal,

> Dillon has been gone for only a few days, and yet I miss him with every fiber of my being. I have cried and prayed, but nothing helps rid me of this terrible pain I am suffering. I know that I am worrying my parents, but this is something that I cannot control. I want to be able to act normal, but how do you go about your daily

routine when the one you love is off to war? I know that I can only trust in God that he will be fine. But there are times that even my faith is questioned. I wonder why there has to be such a war that places neighbor against neighbor. I think that some things are not meant to be understood. But that does not help me. I long for the time that he will be home and we can begin our life together. That time seems so very long in the future. But that is all I have to keep myself going. Tomorrow I will try and be better, if for no other reason than for my parents. Wherever Dillon is tonight, I send my love to him. May God protect him.

The next morning, she came downstairs with puffy red eyes. Joanna's heart went out to her daughter. She fussed and lavished attention on her in an effort to cheer her. But nothing seemed to bring her out of her depression. In desperation, Joanna came upon something that would cheer any young women on the eve of her wedding.

She came up to Elizabeth as she stood alone at the window looking out. "Dear, you and I have a wedding to plan. Instead of standing there all sad, why don't you and I go up to the attic and bring down my wedding dress? It's been in the family for a long time. My mother wore it on her wedding day, and I have always had hopes that my girls would wear it."

Elizabeth turned away from the window to listen to what her mother was saying. "It was at one time very beautiful. My grandfather sent all the way to Paris for it, and it cost a small fortune. We have time to restore it and make it beautiful again. It has a train that is yards and yards of silk and lace. You'll be the most beautiful of brides." Joanna's heart began to hope as she saw the light come back into her daughter's eyes. She thanked God that she had finally begun to reach into that dark shell of depression and draw her out.

A smile came to Elizabeth's face. Her mother continued, "Do you plan to have a lot of guests?"

"No. Dillon only wants family and a few friends," Elizabeth answered. She realized what her mother was doing, but she could not help but be interested in planning her own wedding.

"But that still means invitations and a reception afterward. We have a lot of planning to do. You can write up the invitations, and we'll take them into town to be engraved. I'm sure your sister will be in the wedding, and she will want a new dress. You and I can buy a pattern in town and some nice material to start on it. You know she is no good with a needle, so it will be left up to us to see that it is made." Joanna was really getting into the planning, and she found that she too began to feel better with her mind off the war.

Elizabeth's eyes began to sparkle. "Let's go now to the attic and get the dress. We need to see what has to be done to it. It could take us a long time to restore it. And tomorrow we can go into town and buy what we need in the way of material and thread and such." She hugged her mother and kissed her cheek, realizing what her mother was doing. And it had worked. She now had something to take up her time and keep her mind off what worried her.

The two women climbed into the attic and found the dress in a large trunk. It was placed in a box and then wrapped in tissue paper. Elizabeth knelt with her mother and stared in awe at the beautiful dress. "Mother, I don't think it will take much work to restore it. It is still lovely."

"I still want to replace some of this lace, and we'll have to fit it to you. We'll hang it up outside on a good windy day and let it air out," Joanna said as she wrapped it lovingly back in the tissue paper and placed the lid back on the box. Her eyes misted with tears as she remembered her wedding day. She too had been a beautiful bride. Her mother had worked with her to make the dress ready to wear on her wedding day. She would never forget those times with her mother. It had given mother and daughter a bond that had not been there before. She hoped that it would do the same for her and Elizabeth.

The days turned into weeks as mother and daughter worked each day on Elizabeth's wedding. The dress was transformed in no time. When she tried it on for the fitting, she was surprised to find that it fit almost perfectly. She loved the lace and silk and the beautiful long train that trailed for yards behind her. She did not fail to notice the tears in her mother's eyes. She hugged her more in those times together than she ever had in the past.

Elizabeth resumed her chores and afterward worked with her mother on the dress. In the evening, the two would sit and write up the invitations. The guest list began to swell, and Elizabeth was surprised at the many friends her family had. But she realized this didn't include Dillon's side. She had planned for only a few guests and the listed had somehow become two hundred. Her mother laughed. It had been that way for her wedding also.

Later that week, the two had made the trip into town to have the invitations engraved. The streets were teeming with Confederate soldiers. In every shop they stopped in, they heard the news that their boys were pulling out. A large division of Union soldiers were spotted not far from town, and orders had been given for all Confederate soldiers to depart immediately.

Elizabeth and her mother made the few purchases they wanted and stopped at the printers. They left town with a hoard of Confederates behind them.

Things did not look good for the little town. Civilians and soldiers alike were pulling out and leaving the remaining citizens to the waft of the Union.

Joanna knew that they could be right in the middle of a major battle. She and her daughter hurried home to inform Charles of the news.

Once they had returned home, the family seemed far removed from the effects of the withdrawal of the Confederate troops. But all knew that it was only a matter of time until Brier Cliff too would know what it was to be at war.

With the occupation of the town, Elizabeth did not expect to hear any news from Dillon. Her heart sank at the realization that he would not be able to return so that they could marry. But mother and daughter continued on with the plans for the wedding.

After six months, the plans were made and the dress put back into its box to wait until that day that Dillon would return and she could wear it for their wedding. She knew he would think it lovely, and she hoped he would find her as lovely as well.

Elizabeth took time every day to wait for the mail. She did not expect to receive any, but still she faithfully waited each day. She could not help but worry that he was not all right. She was keeping busy with her mother, and she was able to control her worry. They had begun to make Willow's dress for the wedding. Willow loved being fitted in the lovely soft pink silk they had chosen for the dress.

Each night she prayed for Dillon, that God would take care of him. And each night she would dream of what their life would be together.

The day was bright and sunny. Elizabeth was helping her mother in the sitting room with Willow's dress when a knock came to the door. Elizabeth's heart jumped into her throat as she ran to answer it. To her disappointment, it was only a young man, standing in a disheveled state on the other side of the door. He introduced himself as James Randolph and asked to speak with her father. Elizabeth held open the door to allow him to enter. She took in his tattered appearance. She forced herself to smile. He stood only as tall as her and had a head of long curly dark hair. He wore a suit, but it was in much need of cleaning. He looked like he could stand some nourishment. He was far too thin. His clothes hung on him as though they belonged to a much bigger man. Her father took him into his study and closed the door behind them.

Charles directed the young man to a chair then seated himself.

"What can I do for you?" Charles asked as he took in the man's disheveled condition.

"Sir, I am here to beg you for some compassion. I am destitute. I have no family to turn to. My parents are both gone, and there is no one else.

TIME AFTER TIME

But I don't ask for charity. I can repay you for helping me. I can paint. I used to do it professionally until the war came. I had my own shop, but it was burnned by the Yankees. In exchange for room and board, I will paint a portrait of any of your family. It will be something you can keep to remember for years to come. I am very good, sir. You won't regret letting me paint for you."

Charles was a generous man, and his heart went out to this man. He too could be in the same circumstances and need help. He readily agreed to let this young man paint portraits of his two daughters in exchange for room and board. Charles led him up to one of the guest rooms and told him supper would be at seven. He left the young man standing in the doorway to his room, very grateful.

Later that evening, Charles explained the arrangement to his family. "I want to introduce Mr. James Randolph to everyone. He is going to be staying with the family while he paints Elizabeth's and Willow's portraits. Since Mr. Randolph has no family of his own, he will do this in exchange for room and board. A very commendable undertaking, don't you all agree?"

Willow was very excited that she was to have her portrait painted. Elizabeth accepted her father's plans without much thought to it. She was too deep in her own worries to take notice of her mother's attitude toward the situation. Why the young man was not fighting for his country was never mentioned. But Elizabeth thought much and often about it. She resented the fact that he was safe and sheltered in their home while Dillon risked his life fighting for his beliefs. How was this man different than Dillon? Would he not reap the same benefits of victory if the South won this war?

Eight months after Dillon left, Elizabeth did not go to the window anymore to watch for the mail. When the knock came to the door, she didn't run to answer it. She had lost all hope of hearing from him. She had grown quiet and lost in her own thoughts. The servant walked to the door. The mailman stood on the other side with a letter in his hand. "Got a letter here for Miss Elizabeth Mitchell," the mailman said.

Elizabeth was in the sitting room with her mother and heard what was said. She didn't run to the door. She was afraid she would be disappointed again. She turned the letter over in her hand and looked at the return address. It was from Dillon! She began to cry. And didn't stop even when her mother drew her into her arms. "Open it, silly." Joanna smiled. "It's from your young man."

The mailman still stood at the door and heard their conversation. "Seems your letter was to be delivered sometime ago. It was sent from Atlanta by a rider that didn't arrive. The young man who was to deliver the letter deserted and left his mail pouch on someone's doorstep. We got it only today, so I rushed here because I knew you had waited a mighty long time for it. I slipped it in my pocket right under the nose of a Union corporal. He did not even know that it arrived. Don't worry that it will be discovered. This is between you and me."

"Thank you," Elizabeth managed to say. She wanted only to run to her room and read her letter alone. She sat down on her bed and looked at the envelope for a long time. She was afraid of what the letter might say. Did Dillon still love her? With a shaking hand, she tore open the envelope and began to read.

> Dearest Elizabeth,
> Sorry it has been so long. We arrived at the rail station as planned en route to Atlanta. Everything went as planned till we arrived at our destination. No wagons were waiting to transport the men. I sent two of my soldiers into town, but they arrived back empty-handed. So we made the long trip on foot, myself included, since there are no horses to be had in this war. The weather held out in our favor for the first three days. Then it began to rain. It rained steady and hard for the next week. We took shelter at night under any tree we could find. But during the day, we marched through the mud. I know that many of the men were downhearted. Many were away from home for the first time, and the rain only added to their misery. We arrived in Atlanta two weeks after leaving the rail station. The men were tired and hungry, so I released them to find food and shelter. After I was relieved, I went straight to my tent to write this letter. I know you must be worried since it has taken me so long to write to you. But now you understand why. I hope this letter finds you well and still believing in me. I long to see you again and to hold you in my arms. There was so much that wasn't said between us, but I want you to know that all those things a woman wants to hear from the man she loves is in my heart, and you will hear all of them upon my return. Elizabeth, I fear that I will not be returning as soon as we had hoped. Major Gage, my commanding officer, told me that we are to pull out soon for territory unknown even to him. We are to confront the enemy and stop him from entering the South. There will be no time to train the new men. They will face an enemy more numerous and better equipped. The new men are just farm boys who know nothing of war. God help us. I am sorry I sound so down, but I think I will remain this way until we are together again. So you see, sweetheart, there will be no way for me to secure a leave

at this time. But continue to trust that I will return and we will wed. One day, you will be my wife, and I will be most proud. As soon as I am in a town, I will write and send you an address. Until then, there will be no way for me to receive mail. You are forever in my heart.

Dillon

Elizabeth wiped at her tears and folded the letter and placed it on her nightstand, knowing this may be the only letter she would receive for some time. She was grateful that he was still alive and was thinking of her as she was of him. Now she had joy in her heart that the man she loved had not forsaken her or forgotten that she existed. She hurried downstairs to tell her family of what the letter contained.

It was later in the year of 1862 that her father announced his intentions to enter the war. They were sitting around the dining room table enjoying a meager meal of potatoes and greens when he made his announcement. Charles tapped on the side of his water glass with a fork. Everyone at the table came to attention. "I have something to say." He hesitated, knowing what he was about to say would disturb everyone. "I have given what I am about to tell you much thought. I know all the arguments against me going to war. Your mother has said every one to me. But I have decided I am going to join the South Carolina Regulars under Picket. That means I will be seeing combat. But don't think just because I am gone I will not be aware of what goes on around here. Your mother will keep me informed." He looked directly at Willow as he spoke. "Your mother will need a lot of help. So I am depending on you girls to give her a hand. There's plenty to keep you girls out of trouble. I am expecting a good report from your mother about your behavior."

Joanna pulled a handkerchief from her sleeve and wiped at her eyes. It was apparent she didn't want him to go.

"I know this will mean a big adjustment for everyone. But I have confidence in all of you." He cleared his throat, obviously filled with emotion at the thought of leaving home and family. "I have spoken to our lawyer, Mr. Miller, and signed all the papers necessary to make your mother the beneficiary of all my holdings in case of my demise. I know that is a morose subject, but it is one that has to be considered. Now"—he smiled at the stunned faces around the table—"let's continue our meal."

There were not many happy faces that evening around the table and a lot of lost appetites. Soon the table was emptied of its occupants.

The Beth side of Elizabeth came to attention. This was her opportunity to do what she had set out to do. After excusing herself from the table, she followed her father into his study and closed the door behind them. She didn't want the others to hear what she had to say.

"Poppa, I want to talk with you about what was discussed at the dinner table."

Her father, sitting behind his desk enjoying a cigar and an after-dinner drink, gave her his full attention. "Go ahead."

She took the chair on the opposite side of the desk and leaned forward, choosing her words very carefully. "Poppa, you can't go! You can't leave us. We need you!" She felt tears rise to her eyes. It was very important that he understand. She didn't want to cry, but maybe tears were in order at a time like this.

"Those are wonderful words to hear, but it is my duty to fight for my country. Can't you understand? Dillon fights for this new country, and I am no less a man than he." Charles tried to make her comprehend that it had not been an easy decision for him to make. "Your mother and I have discussed this, and she too shares your views, but she respects my decision to go. You can do no less." He leaned back in his chair and tried to ignore the pain he saw on his daughter's face. His mind had been made up many months ago, and no amount of tears would make him change his mind.

"I do respect you for wanting to fight for what you believe, but Poppa, this family is not strong enough to go on without you." Elizabeth reached across the desk and took hold of his strong hands. "You know Mother is not strong enough to live without you. She could go insane if something happened to you. And Willow, she can hardly be managed now. Without your authority around here, she will go wild. I surely can't manage her. You know you are the only one she will listen to. And for myself, I am to be married. I need you too, Poppa. A woman wants her father there when she takes her vows." She was trying to reach him with any means it would take. But nothing seemed to weaken his resolve.

Tears came to Charles's eyes. "I have thought of all this. But it didn't change my mind. Your mother will be fine. She assured me she could manage the short time I will be gone. I'll have a talk with Willow. She is a sensible girl. She will be on her best behavior in my absence. As for you"—he forced a smile to his lips—"your young man will wait until my return. With the Union occupying Hampton, it is impossible for him to get back to wed. But I don't look for the occupation to last much longer. These troops have more important things to do than to hold a town with such little importance. I do believe these men are just a renegade band of soldiers. There seems to be no leadership among them. All in all, I don't expect this war to last much longer. The South is whipping the Union on all fronts. I'll be gone for only a few short months. Six at the most."

"Of course, Mother would tell you she would be all right. What else could she say? She knows how stubborn you are. And she never argues with you over what you want. She is a good and faithful wife. As for the war being over in six months, that is what you said eighteen months ago. No one knows how long this war will go on, if it will ever end." Beth was fighting hard for Elizabeth's father. She had to make him know that the family would not exist without him. She had one more avenue to try. She would mix some of the truth with fantasy and try to convince him. "I had a dream last night. A dream of our family without you. I dreamed you were killed in this horrible war. I dreamed that Mother went insane and died shut up in her room alone. That Willow went completely wild and no one could manage her. The Yankees came and took over Brier Cliff, and we lost everything. I dreamed that the family completely fell apart, that there was no family, no Brier Cliff, without you. You, Poppa, are the stabling force behind this family. We all need you." When she was finished, tears were running freely down her cheeks. She didn't try to hide her distress from him. Let him see how important she felt it was that he remained at Brier Cliff.

But Charles was not so easily swayed. "So that is what is behind this." He squeezed her hand, trying to reassure her. "You can't let some silly dream upset you so much." He stood and came around the desk. He took her hand again and lifted her to her feet. "I'll take everything you have said into consideration. Maybe I need to give this some more thought."

He wrapped an arm around her waist and led her to the door. "Don't you worry. This family is strong, and Brier Cliff will stand forever. Your children and Willow's will play in its halls." At the door, he turned her to him. "Now I don't want to see any more tears. I depend on you, Elizabeth, to be the sensible one of the family." He kissed her cheek before she left him to his thoughts.

Charles stood at the door to his study and watched his young daughter walk away. He weighed her words very carefully and knew everything she had said was true. He knew that Joanna would suffer the most from his absence. But he had reasoned that she could manage in the few short months he would be gone. Willow was his biggest concern. But he would have that talk with her as he told Elizabeth he would. He would make her understand that it was important that she help out and obey her mother. He trusted the girl and was sure that she would do as he requested. Elizabeth would be the strong one. She would be of the most help around the house. He relied on her to take care of her mother and Willow. He was sure they would be fine with him gone. He knew he had another responsibility other than to his family. He had a responsibility to his country. How could he sit safely at home while his countrymen were dying by the thousands for what they believed in? He would not consider himself a man if he did so. He stepped back and closed the study door. His mind was made, and he would not change it. He sat down in his chair and closed his eyes.

Beth left the study, knowing that she had not persuaded Charles to not go to war. He would die just as the family Bible had said, and her father would die, almost a hundred years later. She was desperate and in a panic. She had so little time to change his mind. She began to think of ways to stop him, but nothing came to mind, short of holding a gun on him, and that she could never do.

There was only one other person who felt the way she did, her mother. So she turned to the sitting room and found her mother there alone with tears in her eyes. Elizabeth sat down beside her and took her hand. She knew her mother's thoughts were of her husband, and her heart went out to her.

Joanna wiped at her tears and drew her daughter into her arms. Together they cried for a man they both loved. Elizabeth held her tight in her arms. Her mother had helped her so many months ago, and she wanted to do the same for her.

Elizabeth pulled out of her mother's embrace and wiped away her own tears. She needed her mother's help and support, and she didn't think her mother was up to talking back to her husband. In all her life, Elizabeth could never remember a time that her mother disagreed with anything her father had to say.

"Mother, there has to be a way to stop him. You know him better than any of us. Tell me what would make Father not to go to war." She forced her mother to concentrate and listened to what she had to say.

Joanna shook her head and wiped the tears from her eyes with her silk handkerchief. "I've talked with him. I pleaded and begged. He is determined to go. Once your father gets an idea into his head, there is no way to stop him. He and Judge Brown sat and talked this over. They decided that they both would join the Confederacy. And Judge Brown is a man of sixty. His poor wife has been down sick with the lung fever for the last six months. I don't believe there is a way to make them change their minds. Why do men have to be so foolish?"

"I know. I just had a talk with Poppa, and he will not listen." Elizabeth stood and began to pace the room. "There has to be a way to make him see reason. We need him here. Can't he see that we will be three women alone in a time of war once he is gone?"

"I used that argument." She shook her head. "It doesn't work." Joanna blew her nose on her handkerchief. "It's his pride, dear. He sees most of his acquaintances going, and he feels it is his duty to do the same. Pride is a hard thing to overcome."

"Damn his pride!" Elizabeth was angry. "What good is pride when you're killed in this war! There has to be a way to stop him. Help me, Mother!"

Joanna buried her face in her hands. "I couldn't bear it if your father was killed in this war."

Elizabeth was instantly sorry for her outburst. She knelt beside her mother and pulled her hands from her face. She knew this dear woman would not survive once her husband was taken. She needed to know how much time she had. "When does he plan to leave?"

"Within the week. He's made all the arrangements. He's had this planned for a long time." Joanna found it hard to speak. She was so choked up with her tears. "He says he is taking the colored groom Joseph with him to tend to his horse and fetch and carrying. He cannot survive the hardships of a war, to sleep on the ground and endure the harsh weather that winter will bring. He has not thought out what it will be like to go without decent food or clean water. He thinks only of the glory in victory. I tried to make him see that to obtain victory thousands must die. He scoffs at death, as though his death would mean nothing. He does not realize that I could not survive alone in this world without him." Joanna looked up at her daughter with pleading eyes. She was begging her to find the answer.

Elizabeth stared at her mother for a long time before she leaned over and kissed her cheek. "Don't worry. We'll think of something. There has to be a way."

She left her mother alone in the sitting room and walked outside. The air was cool, so she wrapped her arms around herself to ease the cold. She looked up at the stars. The sky was so beautiful. Somewhere under these same stars Dillon lay. Was he looking up at them too and thinking of her? Was he suffering from the hardships of war that her mother spoke of?

She stepped off the veranda and walked out into the yard. The night was so still. In the distance, she could hear the ocean as it beat against the shore. She took the path that led down to the water and onto the beach. The smell of the salt water assaulted her senses. As a child, she had loved this place. She had spent many happy hours on this beach. She and Willow spent their summers playing here. They had swum and romped in the dunes. Her family had brought picnic lunches and spent hours lying on the sand trying to find relief from the sweltering heat that summer always brought. Her mother and her father had enjoyed the beach as much as their children had.

She removed her shoes and hiked up her skirt to walk in the surf. The water was cold, but it revived her spirit. She would not quit until she saved her father. She would think of a way. Elizabeth had been sure she could persuade her father not to go to war. But had she taken into account his stubbornness? She had used every argument that she could think of, but nothing helped.

She knew that she had been sent back in time for a purpose. And she would not stop till she had accomplished it. Charles Preston could not go to war. Of that she was certain.

She walked from the water and put on her shoes. She climbed up the path to the house. She needed to think.

Slowly she made her way up the stairs to her bedroom. Inside, with the door closed, she pulled off her damp dress and pulled her white nightgown over her head. She sat down at her vanity and began to brush her hair. Her mind began to drift.

Chapter 9

Time holds all secrets.

Beth slowly opened her eyes. She sensed something was not right. She rolled toward the window and blinked as the bright sunlight hurt her eyes. Then she saw it. Her electric alarm clock. Why had she come back to the present? She prayed aloud. "Please, not my mother." She threw off the blanket and pulled on her robe, which lay at the foot of the bed. She quickly made her way across the hall to her mother's bedroom and opened the door.

Nell looked over the top of her glasses. She had been sitting reading a book. "Miss?"

"Is my mother all right?" She came into the room and whispered to the servant.

"She's been sleeping for the last two hours," Nell answered. The look on Beth's face frightened Nell. She knew the daughter was under a lot of stress and refused to give in to the grief that she too was feeling.

"How long have I been asleep?" Beth said as she studied her mother's face for sign of distress. When she found none, she began to relax.

"Not long, miss." She held up her wrist to look at her watch. "Only about an hour."

Beth could not believe that so much had happened in an hour. But why was she brought back? If nothing had changed, was she fighting a losing battle? Was this something she could not change no matter how she tried?

Concern showed on Nell's face. "Are you feeling all right? I could call the doctor back. I'm sure he wouldn't mind."

"I am fine. It's my mother I am concerned about. She acts like a strong person. But I don't think she can survive this. She and my father had a special relationship. She was doing all this work on Brier Cliff to make him proud. Now with him gone . . ." She could not bear to think what would happen with her father no longer with them. She looked back at her mother.

"Has she awakened?" Beth moved to the bed and sat down on its edge. She couldn't take her eyes from her mother's face. She took her mother's hand in hers and held it tightly. She wanted to transfer some of her strength to her mother.

"No. But she should soon. Doctor Peters said the shot he gave her wouldn't last more than a few hours." Nell removed her glasses and rubbed at her tired eyes. The young girl's words had stirred her heart, but she did not want to weaken in her presence. Beth was trying hard to control her emotions, and tears would not help her.

Beth noticed that the servant was tired. How selfish of her not to think of this woman's feelings. She was instantly sorry. "I'll sit with her for a while. Why don't you go and get something to eat? I want to thank you for all you have done. Mother will be grateful as well. This has been hard on you too." Beth tried to smile, but it didn't reach her lips.

"Miss, I appreciate those kind words, but it is my pleasure to be of some help at this time. Your mother is a fine lady. I know no other that would have pitched in and helped with all the work that's been done around here. And you, miss, have been a good daughter. I have to say, I am proud to be working for this family." She left the room to give mother and daughter time to be alone.

Beth seated herself and leaned back her head. She had a lot to think about. Maybe she was being foolish to think she could change the past. But she had to try. This was her family, and like Elizabeth's, it too was falling apart.

"Charles?" Joan all but whispered his name. "Charles, is that you?"

Beth sat forward in her chair and reached for her mother's hand. "No, Mother. It's me, Beth."

"Beth? Help me out of this bed." Joan threw the blanket from her body. "Your father needs his breakfast. I've got to get up."

"It's all right, Mother. We have servants that can take care of that." Beth tried to pacify her. She would let her mother live out her fantasy. At least she was happy for a moment, thinking her husband was still alive. Soon reality would take that away from her.

"No . . . no. Your father says no one can cook like me. He expects it, and I enjoy doing it for him." She tried to rise from the bed.

Beth rose and came around the bed to make her lie back. "Mother, I want you to take this medicine the doctor left for you." Beth took a pill from the bottle sitting on the nightstand and placed it in her mother's mouth. She held the glass of water to her lips and helped her to drink.

Joan took the medicine without protest then lay back and closed her eyes. "I didn't know I was so weak. Thank you, dear."

Joan opened her eyes and turned to her daughter. "I think I've been working too hard on this house. I just don't seem to have any strength left. You know, there is something strange about this house. I always thought it appreciated my restoring it. And the more I did to it, the happier it made me. I knew deep in my heart that Nell is right about this house. It does have a soul. It longs for joy beneath its roof, the happiness a family can bring it. There is a deep sadness in its halls, and I thought my making it over would remove that sadness." Joan smiled a weak little smile. "I've always worried that you would not love this house as I do. I wanted you to be happy. You have always been a special child. Your father loves you more than you will ever know. He bought this place for you. He wanted you to know the happiness that he felt as a child. He knew you would never find that happiness in Baltimore. He wrote me that he worried that you would never let yourself be young, that you were too concerned with others to let yourself enjoy your life. He had hoped that this beautiful place would give you that happiness. Do I sound like I am rambling? I don't mean to. It's just important that you understand why we uprooted you to bring you here."

Beth returned her smile. She felt tears rise to her eyes. She realized how much her parents loved her. Now her father was gone. Her mother wanted her to remember that love. "I always knew how Father felt, Mother. I appreciated all you and he have done for me. And for this house I too believe that it has a soul. It knows how much you love it. You have loved it from the very beginning. I see the beauty of this place. I know what it can be. I am not unhappy. I just have to find my place here. It will come. In time, I'll fit in. How could I not when it makes you so happy?" Beth took her mother's hand and held it tightly.

Tears ran down Joan's cheeks. "Tomorrow we will have to rest. We've been working too much. Your father will not allow me to work you so. Now that he is home, we will have to take time for him. We can do something as a family. Won't that be nice, dear?"

Beth wiped the tears from her own face. She nodded her head, afraid to speak.

Joan closed her eyes. "I have to rest now. Tell your father I'm sorry. He'll understand."

Beth sat with her mother and tried to think of happier times. Of times when she was a child and the family had been all together. There had been no hint of this war that claimed her father's life. And her mother and her father had shared a special bond that few married people shared. Beth wiped the tears from her eyes. She was trying to be strong for her mother's sake, but it was so hard. She had loved her father very much. She had always been so proud of him. He was a handsome man, and together, her parents had made a handsome couple. She could still hear her parents' laughter and see their bright smiles. It would be that way again, she promised her mother. She would do all she could to undo what fate had brought about. The light tapping at the door brought her out of her thoughts.

"You need to eat too. Let me take over for you," Nell said as she came into the room.

"Thank you, Nell." Beth stood and stretched away the pain in her back. "She was awake for a few minutes. I gave her medicine. She should sleep for a few hours. If she should wake, call me. I'm going back to my room."

"Yes, miss." Nell took her seat and opened her book.

Beth paced about her room, deep in thought. She could not reason why she was back from the past. She walked to the window and stared down into the yard. In the distance, coming through the path, was Cora. She walked stooped over, leaning on her cane, her gray hair flying in the breeze.

Beth ran from her room and out of the house. She met Cora as she entered the yard. Beth led her to a lawn chair and seated her in the shade beneath a tree. Beth sat down on the ground and looked up into her wrinkled face. She waited for Cora to talk.

"I came because I had to," she began. "After you left me this morning, my heart was breaking for you. I wanted to help you, but I could not. The sun was hot, so I went into the house and turned on the fan and lay down on the sofa. Within minutes, I fell asleep. I began to dream. I saw Willow, as she was when she was very old. She was a tiny lady. Tiny and very mad. But she did not look mad in my dream. She spoke in a quiet voice. She said, 'I release you from your promise to me.'" Cora paused a moment, thinking of her dream. Slowly she continued, "Then I saw her as a young girl. Her hair was long and dark, flowing as though she was standing in a wind. Her eyes were alive, and she was smiling. She was lovely. A beautiful woman-child with a promising future ahead of her. Beside her stood her sister, Elizabeth, and she was just as lovely. Together they stood with their hands held out to me. They were both saying the same thing. 'Help us! Help us!' I said to them, 'How can I help you?' Then Elizabeth said something I couldn't understand. In a voice that was as soft as a whisper, she said. 'I brought her back so you can tell her the truth.'"

Cora turned to Beth. "Do you understand what she was saying?"

Beth shook her head. "Yes. I do."

"So," Cora continued after a deep breath, "I came over here to tell you what you want to know. I hope in the telling that it will do you some good. I know I have held the secret for a long time. She was my mother, and what blackened her name blackened mine. So I thought it was in my best interest to keep her secret, but now I know that by telling her story, I am freeing her soul to find peace."

Beth wiped away her tears and reached out a hand to take Cora's in hers. "You're doing the right thing."

"Well, that's to be seen." Cora shook her gray head. "But to tell it, I have to tell it her way. The way she told me so many years ago. It has to be told in her words, not mine." Cora leaned back in her chair in order to get comfortable.

Beth agreed. "I understand."

"At first, when I went to work for her, I thought her ravings to be nothing more than her madness. I paid little attention to them. But when she was close to dying, she told me that she was my mother. That changed everything. I went to Anna and asked her to tell me the truth. She lowered her head and told me that it was true, that Willow was my mother. She said she never wanted me to know. She had loved me as her own, and as far as she was concerned, she was my mother.

From that moment on, I wanted to listen to Willow's ramblings. I wanted to know of the rest of her family, now my family. I wanted to know what had driven her mad. I listened intently, trying to make some sense of it all. But it was no use. She went from one thing to the other. And when she grew angry, when someone in the past had angered her, she threw things. Those times were the worst. She tried to hurt anyone that got in her way and only hurt herself.

Near the end, she grew very calm and began to talk in a way that I could understand. She took my hand and said that she had always been proud of me. She would stand at her window and watch me play in the yard, but she would never allow herself to hold me, to tell me that she loved me. She said she thought in doing so, she would harm me. That her madness would in some way rub off on me. She never wanted me to know that my mother had been a madwoman. A madwoman and worse. Then she asked if she could tell me what she had never told another, and could she trust me not to tell a soul? She said that she could not die in peace until it was told, and I was the only one she could tell that she could trust. She made me swear. And I did. Now she has released me from that oath. It is time to let the past die." Cora shifted in her chair to make herself more comfortable.

Beth waited in silence for her to continue.

"You asked me if I knew my father's name, and I said I did not, but that was not true. I thought in telling his name, I was revealing part of what she had told me. His name was James Randolph. A young man who came to Brier Cliff to paint the portraits of Willow and Elizabeth. He stayed at the mansion even after Charles had gone away to war. He was supposed to be working on the portraits, but that was not all he did. He and Willow were having an affair.

"At first it was just kissing and touching. She allowed this because she enjoyed it, and she enjoyed the attention he gave her. She said, at first, he would let his hand linger on her breast as he arranged her dress. When she allowed this, he took more liberties. He would touch her with his hands and his lips. She said it was very enjoyable. Soon it was not enough for him. He wanted more. Once he laid her hand on the front of his trousers to let her feel what she was doing to him. She said she could have laughed at the misery she saw in his face. She said she was playing a game with him and had no intention of doing what he wanted. She was saving that for the man she would marry. She had no intention in marrying this man. But she didn't know how deep the feelings were between a man and woman. She said she let him undress her. Alone in her father's study, which had been used as his studio, with the door locked, they had no fear of being caught. He kissed her passionately, and she liked the kiss. He knelt in front of her and kissed her breasts. It gave her a feeling of power to have him on his knees before her. Then he lifted her into his arms and carried her to her father's desk. He spread her legs and knelt again. He kissed her thighs. She said that nothing had ever given her such pleasure. And she wanted more. She said the pain was nothing. Then after the pain, there was only pleasure. She had discovered what a man could do for her, and she only wanted more. And he was more than willing to give it to her.

"He began to come into her room at night, and they would spend the night making love. She said she finally found something she was good at. At first, he was careful, but there were times that he lost control and was not. But she didn't become pregnant.

"Finally, after a year, the portraits were done, and Joanna and Elizabeth asked him to leave. He did so reluctantly.

"After he was gone from the house, the affair continued anywhere they could find to be alone. But Mr. Randolph was in need of money, and there was no money. Willow gave to him what she could, but in those times, no one had much to give.

"Then the letter came of her father's death. Her mother went insane and left Willow and her sister to fend for themselves. There was no one to tell her she could not do something, so she did what she pleased. And it pleased her to have James Randolph in the house where he could be at her service anytime she needed him.

"Elizabeth objected, but she was too busy taking care of her mother to see what was going on with her little sister. A year after her father's death, her mother died.

"Willow said she starved herself to death. But she felt no sadness. As far as she was concerned, her mother died the day her father did. They buried her beside her beloved husband and quickly forgot her. Or so Willow did.

"The sisters found it hard to find enough food to eat. There erupted huge fights between Willow and James. She wanted him to find work, to try and help. He was not one for hard labor.

"When the Yankees came, Willow knew she would do whatever it took to feed what was left of her family. She would leave the house early in the morning and return late in the evening. She always returned with baskets full of food. She did not say how she came about this food, but one can guess. James did not like this, but he ate the food and sat back and did not say a word after the first time.

"Willow's appearance began to change. She did not take care of herself as she once did, and nothing Elizabeth said could change things. She hated herself yet continued to do what she pleased and justified it by thinking she was saving her family. But she was only killing herself. The beautiful young girl was no more and, Willow feared, would never return. She said often she thought that if the war did not end soon, she would die beneath the body of some unknown Yankee. The Northern invaders were everywhere. And many Southern ladies were doing the same as Willow to survive. It made her proud that she was the one feeding the family.

"Elizabeth might not like what she was doing, but that did not stop her from eating the food she brought in. Willow and Elizabeth had many arguments about this, but that did not stop Willow. She was headstrong and stubborn. She did what she pleased now, and it pleased her to lie with the Yankees. She did not feel remorse. Remorse, she said, was for weaklings; and she was no weakling. She was a survivor. There were times that the shame of what she was doing crept into her mind. But she quickly pushed it away. She had turned her heart to stone. And she liked it that way. She would never be the one used by a man. She would use men and walk away. But she did not consider the consequences to her actions. Everyone has to pay a price for sin. And she paid dearly for hers. I think even then, she was going mad. She did not rant and rave as she did when she was older, but the seeds to insanity had been planted; and with all the attention she gave to her sins, insanity began to grow.

"Late one night, the two sisters were awakened by a knocking at the door. Elizabeth called out to the visitor, frightened at who it might be, without opening the door. It was Dillon. After three years and only as many letters, he had returned for her. He looked much older and had a full beard. But he was still the handsome man that Elizabeth loved. He took her into his arms and held her for a very long time before he released her. Tears ran freely down his face. Elizabeth could only stare at him, thinking him unreal, something she had dreamed. But he was real, and he wanted to take her with him, away from Brier Cliff, to his home. Elizabeth finally began to sob when she realized he was flesh and blood, that he had returned for her. Their tears ran together as he gathered her back into his arms to rock her gently back and forth. 'My poor dear,' he said to her. 'My love.'

"Willow was not happy for her sister. Elizabeth had not suffered. Willow had suffered to keep the family together. Who was it that went out and used her body to obtain food so that the family could survive? Not Elizabeth. She had saved herself for the man she loved and did not do the things that Willow did. But, Willow reasoned, everything she did was necessary. How else could a woman survive in this war? She had made all the sacrifices. She had worked to bring food into the house. She had blackened her name along with her soul to see that the family survived. Elizabeth had reaped the rewards of her labors. Now she was planning to leave, and Willow would be all alone. She could not bear the thought.

"This stranger was here to take away the last thing Willow had. The only person who loved her unconditionally. To leave her with no one to care if she lived or died. She was furious. How dare he, she thought. After all she had done to keep them together. He had no right to think he could ride up to Brier Cliff and take Elizabeth from her."

Cora turned to Beth. "I think she was very close to the edge with the thought that she could lose Elizabeth. Everything began to accumulate in her. The loss of her family. The war. And what she did to survive drove her to madness.

"Dillon had only a few days to get Elizabeth back across the Yankee lines and into Maryland. The town was overrun with the enemy, and if he was caught, it would be his death. There would be no time for a wedding before they left. Elizabeth knew how dangerous it was to be caught traveling with a Southern soldier, but she would not let her happiness ride away from her this time. She hurriedly packed a few belongings and went to find her sister to tell her good-bye. But Willow was like a statue when Elizabeth took her into her arms and kissed her cheek.

"Willow's fury mounted with each moment. She would not stand for this. She would not let her sister ride away and leave her. A plan began to form in her sick mind, a plan that would ruin everyone's lives. But she was determined. She found her father's pistol and hurried to the stables to confront Dillon. She entered as he was saddling the two horses for their trip. His back was to her, and he didn't see her enter. She had the revolver hidden in the folds of her dress.

"Elizabeth entered the stable and saw what was taking place. Willow said she didn't hear her come in until it was too late. Elizabeth stepped between the two just as Willow pulled the trigger. Dillon grabbed the gun and stood over Elizabeth as James Randolph walked into the stable. Willow by that time was on her knees at her sister's side. Elizabeth was dead. Shot in the chest. Her worn traveling dress slowly staining a dark red.

"Willow screamed when she saw James and turned to Dillon. Why? Why would you do such a thing! Dillon was in shock, first from the death of the woman he loved, then from being accused of her murder by the very murderer. He did the first thing he could think of. He mounted his horse and galloped away.

"James had to drag Willow off of her sister's body and take her into the house. He left her in the sitting room and ran up the stairs to his room to pull a blanket from his bed. He returned to the stables and covered Elizabeth with it. Later that day the undertaker arrived to take Elizabeth's body away. When he returned to the house, Willow was not where he had left her. He found her sitting against the wall in her bedroom, covered in her sister's blood. She had tried to wash the blood from herself and had smeared it everywhere. It covered her hands and face and was smeared on the walls and floor. She was not aware that he carried her to her bed and undressed her and washed her and put her nightgown on. He went to the kitchen and carried a bucket of water up to the bedroom to wash down the walls and stairs. He told Willow later that one bloody handprint took many attempts at washing before he could get it off. Willow lay in her bed that night and did not speak a word. When he climbed in beside her, she rolled into his arms and cried into his chest. She was like a small child, whimpering and sobbing uncontrollably. Sometime in the night, she fell asleep still wrapped in his arms. The next day, he woke to find her not in the bed. He hurried downstairs and found her sitting in the room staring into the fire the servant, Anna, had built in the fireplace. He tried to make her eat, but she refused. When the military police came, she was able to rouse herself enough to give a statement. She told them the same story she had told James—that Dillon had shot and killed her sister. Later that same day, she dressed and went into town with James to make the arrangements for Elizabeth's funeral. Willow wore all black with a wide-brimmed hat and a veil pulled down over her face.

"In the funeral home, she asked to see her sister. Elizabeth was dressed and laid out, ready to be put in her coffin. Willow leaned over and kissed her sister's cheek. She cried and tried to gather Elizabeth into her arms. James had to force her away. She jerked out of his arms and turned to the undertaker and asked him for a pair of scissors. She cut one small curl from the bottom of her hair and placed it in her handkerchief and put it in her dress pocket. Later, she told me she placed it in the family Bible. She would take it out every once in a while to look and caress it. She missed her sister and was truly sorry for what had happened.

"Elizabeth was buried beside her mother and her father in the family cemetery. Willow, James, and Anna were the only ones to attend. Long after the last shovel of dirt was thrown on her grave, Willow stood beside it and looked down. She was far away in the mind, reliving past times with her sister, when they had been happy. The undertaker came up to her and interrupted her thoughts. He told her he would get right to carving her name on the family stone. Willow was furious. She didn't want her sister's name put on a gravestone. If her name appeared on a stone, that meant she was dead. Willow could not stand the thought. She told him she would contact him when she was ready for that. She never did.

"The same day of the funeral, the military police returned to inform Willow that her sister's murderer had been captured and hung for his crime. She remained calm until they left, then she began to moan and scream out in terror. She ran through the house, beating her hands upon the walls and scratching at her face. Just as her mother had done in her time of grief. All efforts from James and Anna to stop her and calm her down were fruitless. She could not be controlled. She told me she went on like that for hours until she finally wore herself out. James found her in the upstairs hall sitting on the floor. Her hands were bloody and bruised. He again carried her to her bed and washed the blood from her body. He dressed her for bed and sat with her for many hours until he too became tired. But he did not sleep in the same bed as her. He went across the hall to Elizabeth's room and locked the door. I imagine he was frightened of Willow. He was well aware of the fact that she was capable of anything.

"The next day, he left his room to find Willow's bedroom door open and her bed empty. He hurried down the stairs and found her sitting in the sitting room dressed and looking as though nothing had happened the night before. She was very pleasant to him. They shared breakfast and carried a second cup of coffee into the sitting room to enjoy. I imagine he thought her well. But soon after coming to the sitting room, she turned to him and, with a smile on her face, told him she wanted him to leave. He looked like he was in shock. He told her she could not mean that. Had he not taken care of her? He said he was under the impression that they were in love. Was that not the truth? Why send him away when she needed him most? She continued to smile. She told him she needed no one. And she loved only one person, and that person was buried in the ground. She said she wanted no reminders of the past, and with him there, it would be a constant reminder. She rose from her chair and walked to the door and opened it. Again she told him to leave. He asked if he was permitted to gather his things together. She gave him five minutes, and if he did not remove all his belongings in that amount of time, she would burn all that was left behind. She returned to her chair and waited.

"A few minutes later, she heard the front door close behind him. She smiled. She was alone now. That was how she wanted it. She deserved to be alone. She deserved to be punished for all that she had done.

"She remained in the house with only Anna, Nell's grandmother, to care for her; but she didn't know to handle her wild behavior. Willow was pregnant, and she tried in every way she knew to rid herself of the unwanted child. She would go for days without eating. She would throw herself against the walls and beat upon her stomach. But nothing would rid her of the child. Finally she accepted the fact that she was going to have this child. She made arrangements with Anna to take it right after its birth.

"When she went into labor, she suffered terribly. Anna was at her side and tried to give her comfort. But there was little she could do to ease the pain. After three days, she gave birth. She refused to look at the child and told Anna to get it out of her sight. Anna wrapped me in blankets and took me to her home. Her eldest daughter watched me while she returned to Brier Cliff. Willow could not be left alone.

"Willow had no human contact except for Anna. She grew more mad with each passing day. At times she would disappear and go to the cemetery and lie upon Elizabeth's grave. She would beg her to forgive her. Anna always knew where to find her. She would bring her back home, change her clothes, and try to talk to her. But there was no way to reach her. She was in her own world, and she wanted no contact with any other person. That was her way of punishing herself.

"She was to be felt sorry for. She never knew what it was to love another person. I guess the closest she came was her love for Elizabeth and she had destroyed that.

"Anna took me in as her own, fed me and clothed me, and gave me as much love as she did her other children. I grew up a happy child and never knew that Willow was my mother. When I found out, it destroyed any chance of me living a normal life. I was afraid of the madness she possessed. I too locked myself away in that little house she gave to Anna and never ventured out into the world. I worked here, at Brier Cliff, helping to take care of an old woman that had hurt everyone she came in contact with.

"Anna died in 1886, and that left Willow completely alone except for me. I lived in the main house and saw that she was fed and properly clothed. It was as though she were the child and I the mother. But she needed someone, and there was no one else.

"She died in 1906. She had said the strangest thing to me right before she died. She took my hand, and in that tiny voice that she had, she said, 'Elizabeth is not dead. Don't you see her?' She looked around the room, and her eyes settled on a corner and remained there. She was quiet for a long while as though she were listening, and then she turned to me and said, 'She says to tell you that she is coming back. That you are to wait. You will know when she has returned.' A smile came to her wrinkled face, and then she breathed her last. I saw that she was properly buried in the family cemetery. I didn't understand at the time, but I do now. I moved into the cottage, and I waited.

"The main house was always a strange place after all the death it had seen. But I could rest well beneath its roof because I was not the one it was waiting for. That first day I saw you, I knew that you were the one. I tried to not interfere, but it was hard seeing all the trouble you were going through. I wanted to tell you the truth, but how does a person tell another that their mother was a madwoman and killed her own sister? I thought in time all would be revealed to you. I never thought your father would die in order for you to seek the truth. I am truly sorry about that. But maybe you can help. There is some reason all this is happening." Cora sighed. "That's the story I've kept hidden all these years. It feels good to finally tell someone."

This answered many questions for Beth. She now could explain the bloody handprint on the wall and many other things that were meant to lead her to this place. This was what Elizabeth had been trying to tell her all along.

She was stunned that anyone could be as evil as Willow. She tried to understand, but there was no way. But perhaps Willow was not evil, but only sick. It was better to think of her in that way than to think of her as insane. She had loved her sister. Even though she was the reason for her death, there was no doubt in Beth's mind that she did care for Elizabeth. Was there any salvation for Willow? Maybe all this was not intended to help Elizabeth but to help Willow. That thought sobered Beth. Willow was in more need of help than any member of the Preston family. Could this all possibly be happening because her soul needed saving more than anyone else's? Whatever the reason, or for whatever person, Beth had been chosen to do this. And in doing so, she would save her beloved father.

She finally turned to Cora. "Thank you, Cora. You don't know what this means to you and me."

She rose from her chair and, without a backward glance, hurried through the woods to the house. Her mind was in a whirl. This was what she had wanted to hear for months, and now it filled her with dread to think that sweet, honest Elizabeth had come to such an end. She knew that only she could rectify what had taken place. She would not only save Charles, she would save Elizabeth as well; and in saving Elizabeth, she would save Willow from a life of hell. She prayed as she ran that this would be so. She had something on her side that she did not have before. She had the truth of what had happened, and that could make all the difference. She ran up the steps to the house and hurried up to her mother's room.

Chapter 10

Time heals all wounds.

B eth went into her mother's room and spoke quietly with Nell. "Stay with her. No matter how long I am gone, stay with her."
Nell had a strange look upon her face. "Miss?"
Beth smiled. "It's all right. Everything is going to be all right." She left for her bedroom with a feeling of anticipation. She knew what she had to do. And as Elizabeth said, she would use whatever means it took. She lay down on her bed and closed her eyes. Within seconds, she was in the past.

Elizabeth rolled over in her bed. Something had awakened her. She listened for a moment more before she heard sobbing in the hall. She knew this to be her mother. She crept to the door and opened it an inch and peeked out. Her father's back was to her, and he was dressed in his uniform. He held Joanna in his arms, her head buried in his chest. She was crying, and he was trying to comfort her with soft words that Elizabeth could not understand. The scene before her made her heart jump erratically. She realized that her father was leaving for the war. He chose to leave in the middle of the night so he would not have to face the tears and pleading from his daughters.

Beth took over. She knew it was now or never. She had only minutes to do something to stop him. She waited—her mind racing, her heart jumping in her chest—by the bedroom door until she heard his footsteps on the stairs. She was dressed in her white nightgown but had no time to change. At that moment, she did not care how she was dressed. This was her last chance, and she was going to make the most of it. Quickly she followed. On the stairs, she saw him through the window as he adjusted the stirrups on the horse and gathered the reins in his hand. He paused a moment and looked toward the house before he swung his legs over the saddle. She began to run through the dark house, arms flying in the air. She stepped through the front door and continued to wave her arms. She screamed out his name in a terrifying loud voice. "Poppa!"

The sight of her coming out of the dark—dressed all in white, her arms waving frantically, her scream loud and shrill—frightened the horse. It gave a cry of panic and rose in the air, flaying its hoofs at the object running toward it. Rider and horse fell to the ground. Charles lay still, not moving. The horse lay on top of him, desperately trying to rise to its feet. Its hoof continued to thrash in the air, and its eyes were wide with fright.

Elizabeth screamed. A cry that echoed in the still of the night and woke both family and servants. Soon a group of people had gathered on the porch to see what had happened. Joanna screamed and fell into a dead faint. Willow joined in with a scream that rivaled them all.

Elizabeth gained control and took over the situation. She called out to the groom, who stood wide eyed, his mouth hanging open in shock at the scene before him. "Joseph, help get Father up to his room. Sally, send someone for the doctor. Hurry!"

She turned to Willow. "Help me get Mother to her feet." They knelt down, and each took an arm and all but carried Joanna into the house. They sat her in a chair and watched as two men servants carried their father up the flight of stairs to his room. He was unconscious, and a droplet of blood ran from the corner of his mouth. To Elizabeth he looked more dead than alive. A fear took hold of her. She had not meant for this to happen. She never wanted to harm her father.

Willow looked down at their mother. "Who would think that such a little thing could be so heavy?"

Beth had to laugh. It all seemed so funny at this moment. Her dear sweet mother lay in a dead faint while her father was unconscious from an accident she had caused. She had succeeded, but not in the way she had planned. Elizabeth's father would not go to war. She only hoped he would live through this.

Willow gave her a strange look. "I don't think laughter is in order at a time like this."

"I'm sorry." Elizabeth lowered her head. "I guess I am just in shock. Poor Poppa. Now he can't go off to the war." She raised her eyes to look at Willow.

Willow stood there a moment contemplating what Elizabeth had just said. Then a smile came to her lips. She understood. But a thought sobered her. "Yes, but he is going to be mighty angry when he recovers. You not only kept him from going to war, his finest horse will probably have to be put down. Joseph said he thinks its leg is broken."

Elizabeth had not given the horse a second thought. Now she realized he had been her father's finest and was worth a great deal of money. But the horse was a small price to pay if she managed to save her father's life. She only hoped, in time, he would see things that way.

Elizabeth had servants carry her mother up the stairs and lay her out in Willow's bedroom. A maid stayed with the elder Preston, applying cold compresses to her forehead. Willow and Elizabeth stood outside their father's room waiting for the doctor to come out and give the news of his condition. Both girls grabbed for each other when a terrifying scream came from inside the room. Willow clung to her sister. "Poppa is in terrible pain."

"He'll be fine." Elizabeth tried to reassure her sister as well as herself. Long hours passed, and still the doctor had not come out of the bedroom. Elizabeth was very worried. She prayed that her father would be all right. She would not be able to look into her mother's eyes again if something terrible happened because of this accident.

When finally the doctor came out, the two girls had sat down on the floor in the hall and leaned back against the wall. Willow was close to sleep. Elizabeth shook her awake. The doctor walked up to the two and offered a hand to help them up off the floor. He pushed his glasses back off his nose before he began. "You father is going to recover, but he will be bedfast for several months. His leg is broken, along with his hip. It will be a very long time before he can walk properly, if ever. Along with the broken bones, he has a deep cut in his right thigh that was most likely caused by hitting his leg on a stone when he hit the ground. It is a very deep wound, almost to the bone. At this time, I am more worried over that laceration than his broke bones. The bones will mend, but that cut can become infected. It seems to be the most life threatening. He is not out of the woods yet, but he is a strong man, and it will take a lot to do him in. He is going to have a long recovery, and you two girls are going to have to help your mother."

Elizabeth had to ask. "What of his desire to go to war?"

The doctor shook his head. "There will be no fighting for him. I told him so, in no uncertain terms. I doubt he'll ever sit on a horse again without extreme pain."

The wrinkled, gray-haired doctor turned his full attention on Elizabeth. With a finger pointing into her face, he spoke. "And you, young lady, should know better than to run up to a horse screaming and waving your arms. You frightened the animal and caused your father's injury."

Elizabeth lowered her head. She was truly sorry she had caused her father pain and injury, but the Beth side of her was overjoyed at the news that he would never go to war.

"Here now." The doctor took her in his arms. "I shouldn't have spoken so harshly. I know you were only trying to say good-bye to your father. And he is as much to blame as you. He should not have tried to go off without saying his good-byes to his two girls." He patted her shoulder affectionately as he spoke. He cast a feeble smile in Willow's direction. He released Elizabeth, and once again, he was all business. "How is your mother?"

"She's been asleep for hours," Willow said dryly.

"Then let her sleep. It can only do her good. At least she doesn't know the pain he suffered when I set his leg." The doctor removed his glasses and wiped at them with his handkerchief. "I'll be back tomorrow. I gave him something to make him sleep. He'll be in a lot of pain when he wakes. I left a bottle of pills in his room. Give him one when he wakes and as often as he needs for pain, not to exceed six a day. Do you understand?" He looked over the top of his glasses at the two girls.

Both girls nodded their head. They waited till he walked down the stairs and started for the door before turning to their father's room. Charles lay in the dim light of the lamp on his nightstand, his leg wrapped from ankle to hip. He looked very pale and frail at that moment. Elizabeth's heart went out to him, and she began to cry. Willow placed an arm around her shoulders and tried to speak words of comfort. "You heard what the doctor said. Poppa is a strong man. He's going to be fine. Besides, Mother will be pleased that he won't be able to go to war."

Elizabeth wiped away her tears. "Yes. Yes, she will."

The next few days were hectic around the house with Charles's constant pain and Joanna running up and down the stairs to care for him. Everyone was at his beck and call. Elizabeth was surprised at the strength her mother displayed in this situation. After she came to from her faint, she took over care of her husband and was constantly barking orders at the servants and her two daughters. This was something the two sisters had never seen before. Her mother was a fighter, now that she had something to fight for. Beth was very pleased with the way the situation had worked out.

Two days after the accident, Elizabeth was asleep in her room when the sound of the door opening caused her to awaken. She opened her eyes and saw her mother creeping up to her bed. She quickly closed her eyes and pretended to be asleep.

Her mother knelt over her and softly kissed her cheek. Her words were so low they were hard to hear. "Thank you, my sweet daughter. Thank you for saving my husband."

Elizabeth was awakened by loud voices in the hall. She pulled on her robe and opened her bedroom door. Joanna was standing in the hall shouting orders at a servant. "Bring me cold water and hurry!"

Elizabeth walked out into the hall and looked toward her mother. The worry on her face was evident. "What is it?" she asked, afraid of the answer.

"Your father. He is running a high fever and is out of his head." Joanna turned back to her room. Elizabeth followed. Charles lay in the middle of the bed, tossing and turning, talking incoherently. Joan wrung a cloth out in the basin and applied it to his forehead. "Sssh . . . you're going to be all right." It was obvious that she was very concerned. She turned to look at her daughter. "We need the doctor. I'm afraid it can't wait until morning. Someone will have to go now."

Elizabeth knew there was no one to go for the doctor at this hour. They had only the two old servants left, and neither was capable of riding that distance into town. Joseph had been sent into town earlier for the vet and had not returned. He was in hopes of saving Charles's prized horse.

At that moment, Willow and James appeared from their separate bedrooms. Willow came quickly to her parents' bedroom door. She saw what was transpiring in the room. She turned to James Randolph. "You must ride for the doctor."

"Me?" He backed away, trying to reenter his room. "At this hour with Union troops on the road? I'd be shot."

"No," Joanna said with disgust in her voice. "I'd not trust him to go. It has to be one of you girls." She turned to her daughters.

"I'll go," Elizabeth spoke up. She knew she had little choice. Willow couldn't be trusted to go either. There was no one else. She could do this, she reassured herself. She was frightened of the long ride into town in the middle of the night. She knew soldiers patrolled the road and shot first and asked questions later. She mustered her courage and took control of the situation. It had to be done.

"Hurry and change." Joanna gave no argument to her daughter.

Elizabeth reentered her room and quickly changed into a spite skirt used for riding and a pair of riding boots. She pulled on a coat and hurried from the room. Her mother waited for her downstairs in the foyer.

She took her hand and looked intently into her eyes. "I've had Mr. Randolph saddle you a horse. Be careful and return as soon as possible." She wrapped her arms around her daughter and held her close. "I don't know what I'd do without you." She released her and hurried her out the door.

Elizabeth felt tears rise to her eyes, but she quickly blinked them back. Joanna stopped her. "Thank you again." She forced a smile to her face.

Elizabeth jumped astride the horse and turned it toward town. The night was very dark, and she could not make the time she wished for. But luck was with her. The horse took the lead and ran the road it had often traveled.

She slowed the horse as she saw movement ahead of her and a light in the darkness. She thought it to be a lantern. She pulled her horse off the road and into a group of trees. She waited for long moments before the two soldiers came alongside the place she hid in. They had obviously been drinking and were talking among themselves of a woman they were to meet that night. She willed her horse to stand still as they passed by. She knew in their condition they would not hesitate to shoot her. She waited. Finally they passed and walked on down the road and disappeared over a rise. She pulled her horse out of the trees and continued on her journey. She galloped into town and pulled her horse to a stop at the doctor's house. He and his wife were in bed, but after much pounding, he answered the door. "Sir," she said breathlessly. "My father is ill. He is running a high fever. Mother says to come right away."

After seeing the look upon the young girl's face, he turned without a word and hurried to dress and grab his doctor's bag. The doctor's gray mare joined Elizabeth's black stallion as they rode back down the dark road.

The sun was just coming up over the ocean as they started back toward Brier Cliff. They traveled several miles without mishap until they rode over a rise and encountered the same two soldiers Elizabeth had come across on her way to town. One was a sergeant, and he forced Elizabeth and the doctor to stop. His dark eyes traveled slowly over Elizabeth and came to rest on her lovely face. "What are you doing out this late? Did you meet some man on the road and your pa is come to fetch you?" He smiled and grabbed the reins to her horse.

"Let go of my horse," she demanded. "This is Doctor Wilson, and we are going back to my home to tend my father. He is very ill." She tried to jerk the reins from his hand, but he would not let go.

"Easy there. I have every right to stop civilians when they are suspicious. The horse was nervous and was pulling against the restraint the sergeant was putting on it. "What's your name, little lady? And where do you come from?"

"That is none of you business, and we are in a hurry." She kicked the horse in the ribs and jerked again on the reins. This time the horse bolted and ran down the road. The doctor took her lead and followed quickly after. The two soldiers stood looking after them.

The sergeant removed his hat and ran a hand through his thick black hair. "I plan to meet that little lady again. She sure is a looker." The two turned and continued down the road toward town.

Joanna met them at the door and hurried the doctor up to her husband. The doctor examined Charles and began to unbind his wound. He took water, as hot as Charles could stand, and washed out the deep cut in his thigh. He rebound the wound. "The cut on his thigh is what is causing the fever. We will have to keep cleaning his leg and try to keep his fever down. I can't tell you if he'll make it. But we need hot and cold water."

Joan hurried from the room and started barking orders to the servants. Elizabeth and Willow helped as much as they could, but there was little they could do but sit and wait. Willow and Elizabeth fell asleep as before outside their parents' bedroom door.

It was past noon when the doctor finally walked from the room. Joanna was at his side and closed the door behind them. She turned to her daughters, who rose to their feet when they saw their mother and the doctor. "His fever is down." A weak smile came to her face. Joanna looked like she was ready to drop. Her face was ashen, and her eyes were red rimmed. She was in much need of sleep. "I am going to go home and get some rest. I'll be back in a few hours. He should sleep for a while. Just keep checking his fever and pray it doesn't return." The doctor walked slowly down the stairs and out of the house. It was obvious he was very tired.

The next few days, they battled Charles's fever. It would disappear for a few hours then return to cause more panic in the house. No one found much sleep. Joanna stayed by her husband's side and kept administering the cold compresses to his forehead. She had to save her husband. Without him she would have no life. She often felt tears come to her eyes, but she fought them back. She would be strong for him. After this was over, she would take the time to cry. Hours turned into days, and still his fever raged. She felt at times as though she could not go on. But from deep within her, she found the strength. On the third day, her vigil ended.

Willow and Elizabeth tried to relieve their mother, but she would not give up her post at his bedside. When she emerged from the room after three days, the girls waited for her to speak. "He's going to be all right." She slumped forward and would have fallen if not for Willow and Elizabeth. They helped her to back into her bedroom and laid her on the bed next to her husband.

"Rest, Mother," Elizabeth said to her very tired mother. "You did a good job. Father is going to be fine." She removed her mother's shoes and pulled the blanket over her. They left the room to find rest of their own.

Joanna slept through the next day. When she woke, she admonished the two girls for not waking her. Elizabeth assured her that she and Willow had taken turns sitting with their father and that he was resting without any sign of the fever. Joanna was grateful to her two girls and cast them the first smile they had seen from her in many days. She took back over her charge. She saw to it that Charles received round-the-clock care. Which meant that Elizabeth and Willow would take turns in sitting with him. But the two sisters didn't mind. They were only glad to have their father alive. They knew that their mother wouldn't rest until he was well.

Charles grew steadily better and soon began to behave like his old self. When Elizabeth brought his meals up to him, he laughed and joked with her as he had done in the past. She was so happy to see him in good spirits. She knew that it had been an ordeal to overcome the pain he suffered from the accident. Everyone in the house was extremely grateful. Joanna had a smile on her face now and was much easier to get along with.

Elizabeth and her father had not spoken of the accident. But she knew that sooner or later, he would bring up the subject. Two months after the accident, when she brought his supper tray up to him, he stopped her as she started to leave the room. "Come sit with me and talk. You seemed to be always running from this room." He was propped up in bed with his tray on his lap.

She came up to him and took a chair at his side. She didn't know what to say. She had been afraid of this these two months. But now she knew she had to face her father's anger.

"You and I are long overdue for a talk," he said, looking down at her. She sat with her head down, and he knew she was frightened.

"I know what you want to say to me." She raised her head to look him in the eyes. "I deserve whatever punishment you want to administer. I was to blame for your accident. It almost cost you your life. I am truly sorry. I was trying to stop you. I didn't want to see you die in this war. Please forgive me." She again lowered her and began to cry.

Charles was instantly sorry for his hard tone of voice. He knew that his daughter loved him very much. She was only trying to save him from what she thought was his death. How could he be angry with her now? He looked away and blinked the moisture from his eyes. "Well, that is in the past. I'm not going to punish you. But you must promise me never to run at a horse in that manner again. The horse could have killed you. We were lucky that the horse survived. So there is nothing for me to be angry about. I should have not tried to leave in that manner. I just couldn't stand to see you and Willow cry. Your mother's tears were bad enough."

She nodded her head in agreement.

"You go on down to your supper now." He smiled at her. "And be sure to tell your mother I gave you a severe tongue-lashing."

Elizabeth rose from her chair and leaned over to kiss her father's cheek. She was so grateful to have him back. He was his old self again. She could not help but love him all the more for his words of forgiveness.

Three months after the accident, Charles was able to walk with aid from Joanna down the stairs. He hobbled on one leg, holding his injured leg in the air, to a chair and sat down. He was very grateful to Elizabeth for all the time and work she put in to make him comfortable. She would fetch and carry for him, bringing him his pipe and pouring him an after-dinner drink, reading to him after his eyes grew tired from reading for himself. She wrote letters for him and helped him explain why he was not fighting in the war as so many of his friends were. Once she even made him laugh. He was making remarks about how he was to explain his injury when she said, "You can always tell your grandchildren that it was a war injury. After all, you were on your way to the war. And didn't it happen during the war?" He had laughed till tears ran down his cheeks.

Charles noticed a difference in the family. Both of the girls worked alongside their mother to care for him. He watched Joanna as she ran around the house barking orders and working tirelessly from first light to dusk. She was constantly at his side seeing to it that he wanted for nothing. He had never seen this side of her. He was very proud of the way she took over running the house. She had always been the one to be comforted and taken care of. Her husband would spoil her and not let her lift a finger for herself. Now she was in charge of the servants and of the two girls. She ran the house like a general, and no one questioned her authority.

Of late, she noticed that Willow was spending far too much time locked in the study, the makeshift studio, with James Randolph. It took him far longer with Willow than with Elizabeth. And less seemed to be getting done on Willow's portrait than on Elizabeth's. Joanna had gone so far as to say something to her husband about this. He had dismissed the matter, saying, "Let the boy take his time. He has no home, no place to go. And we can well afford to feed another mouth." But Joanna could not dismiss it so lightly. Once she had stood at the study with her ear to the door. She had heard nothing until she had rapped on the door. Shuffling and moving came from inside the room. Finally, after a lengthy wait, the door was opened. She looked over the room and its two occupants but could not see anything amiss. She realized that soon their guest would have to leave.

She knew her daughter's nature, and she was not going to stand by and let that shiftless no-good take advantage of her.

Elizabeth was busy in the yard, taking down clothes from the line, when Willow came up to her. It was unusual for Willow to be anywhere near work, so Elizabeth stopped what she was doing so she could listen to her. Willow appeared nervous. She kept twisting the fabric of her dress as she talked.

"Elizabeth, tell me the truth. What do you think of James Randolph?"

Elizabeth was surprised at the question. Never had it mattered to Willow what others thought. She turned back to the wash. She had no desire to start a disagreeable conversation with her sister.

"Why would you ask for my opinion? It never mattered before what I thought of your men friends."

"Because this one is different. Do you think I am wasting my time with him? I know Poppa has a low opinion of him, but Poppa has a low opinion of all my young men."

"Maybe Poppa is right about him. Have you ever thought that might be the case?" Beth folded a sheet and placed it in the basket at her feet.

"Do you not wonder why he is not fighting in the war? All the young men were called to duty. How did he get out of going?" Beth asked.

"He doesn't go because he doesn't want to leave me," Willow said in a small soft voice. "He says that I would be left to the mercy of the Union army if he were to leave. He has taken a lot of abuse from the whole family because of his love for me."

"He could better serve you if he was fighting for your liberties." Beth could not keep the anger from her voice.

Willow was visibly angry. "You don't like him because he cares so much for me that he would take abuse from others to remain at my side while your man left you and doesn't find it necessary to write. You're afraid he used you and discarded you like a dirty rag."

Elizabeth's face turned white, and tears came to her eyes. But she was determined not to let Willow see her cry. Often she had questioned Dillon's love when he failed to write. But she never thought that others felt that way also. She realized that Willow had not sought her opinion of James Randolph; she used him to stab her in her heart with her cruel words. She turned away and continued her work. She could not answer her sister.

Willow laughed aloud. "I am right. Am I not? You do fear he used you to take up some lonely days before he went off to war." Willow had struck a nerve with her sister. But she did not feel proud when she saw the pain on her sister's face. She was jealous of Elizabeth. She had always been the good daughter to her parents while Willow had been mischievous and of late very bad.

Elizabeth did not turn from her task. "You know nothing of him. We love one another. You don't even know what that means."

"And I don't want to know what that means." Willow laughed. "I don't want to be shackled by that word *love*. No man will ever use me like yours has done to you." She turned and walked away.

Elizabeth watched her go. She could not help but feel sorry for her sister. She prayed that one day Willow would find a love as strong as hers for Dillon.

Elizabeth carried the laundry basket back into the kitchen and began to fold the towels and wash clothes. She turned as her mother entered the room. Joanna reached into the basket and began to help fold the clothes. She said nothing for a long time, but Elizabeth knew something was on her mind. Finally she spoke. "Dear, I am very worried about your sister and Mr. Randolph. I've tried to talk to your father, but he is blind to anything Willow does. She can do no wrong where he is concerned. I'm afraid I am going to have to take matters into my own hands. It's not something I am good at, but if your father refuses to say anything to the man, then I will have to." She took a stack of towels and walked to the linen closet and placed them into it. She turned back to her daughter. "Do you think I could be wrong about this? I don't want to do anything if there is no cause."

Elizabeth was not one to talk about someone else, especially her sister, but she knew the importance of this. "Willow is far too engrossed with that young man. I fear for her too. I think you would be within your rights to say something to him." She returned to the folding, knowing that her mother was weighing her words. Elizabeth could have said a lot more, but she did not. She did not want to be the one that caused her sister any pain. Willow would not have hesitated to bring her mother's wrath down on her sister's head. But Willow was far different than Elizabeth. Elizabeth knew that Willow was simply Willow. You either hated her or loved her. And Elizabeth loved her sister.

Joanna could only nod her head. She knew what had to be done, and the sooner the better. She finished helping Elizabeth and went into the sitting room to speak with her husband. She would try one more time for his assistance in this matter.

"Charles." Joanna seated herself beside him on the settee. "I know you get tired of me saying this, but we have to talk about Mr. Randolph. He has to go. He and Willow have gotten too close, and I am afraid of the outcome."

Charles removed his glasses and laid down his book. He reached for his wife's hand before he began. "Dear, Mr. Randolph is a homeless young man. We can't throw him out into the cold. Both of his parents are gone, and he has no other family to turn to. Be patient, and I will talk to the young man after he has finished with the portraits. Willow has been infatuated before. She knows how to handle herself. I think you are worrying for no reason. Besides, he has done a lot of work for no pay except room and board. I think we owe him more than he could ever owe us. We are Christians, and is it not our duty to help others?"

She was defeated, and she knew it. She tried to smile as she rose to her feet. "I'll give him more time, but I tell you now, if I discover anything going on between those two that shouldn't be, I'll tell him myself. I won't wait for your permission." She left Charles sitting alone, thinking of her words. He had never seen her like this. He smiled as he picked up his pipe and filled it with tobacco. He had to admit he liked the new Joanna. She had spirit.

Elizabeth began to watch her sister and the young painter. She saw the constant touching and witnessed the long hours they spent together in the makeshift studio. She began to worry that already things had gone too far. At night, unable to sleep, she would hear the floorboards creak as though someone was walking across the hall. She wondered if her mother heard it too? If so, her mother never mentioned it. But Elizabeth saw something in her mother's face each time she looked at the man. She saw a growing hatred.

Joanna waited patiently for the right opportunity to rid the house of Mr. Randolph. She was not the fool Willow took her for. She knew that more was going on between the two than anyone suspected. She had a great dislike for the man. She knew he was using her daughter to make a home for himself. That thought sickened her. The man probably didn't even love Willow. Charles insisted that Willow knew how to handle herself. She had been raised properly and would do nothing to bring shame on the family. But Charles did not see what Joanna saw. She had protected him from that. Something had to be done. Joanna was only biding her time.

Chapter 11

Time and death wait
for no man.

TIME AFTER TIME

It was well into the fourth year of the war, and things were going badly for the South. People were starving, and families were homeless. Everyone had lost some loved one to this war.

The Prestons were luckier than most. They had food to eat and wood for warmth. The family thanked God each day for these blessings. Winter had arrived, and the family suffered more than normal. The big house was cold. There was not enough wood to keep all the fires going. Fires were kept only in the kitchen and the sitting room. Elizabeth rose early and left the house to gather wood. She did not mind this task. It gave her time to be alone, to think of what was and what could be. She filled her mind with thoughts of Dillon and dreams of when he returned.

Her father still suffered with much pain from his accident. He was unable to walk any great distance and could not hunt for any game for the table. They ate the vegetables and fruits her wise mother had canned and preserved in the fall.

All the black slaves had run off when Lincoln had delivered the Emancipation Proclamation. Only a few white servants remained. They stayed without pay. They stayed out of loyalty and devotion to the family.

All the stock had been stolen or run off by the Yankees. Men that were not part of the regular army roamed the countryside, stealing from and terrorizing the people of South Carolina. They took everything of value. They left nothing for the civilians. A group of about a hundred soldiers had taken over the town of Hampton and remained because this was a safe haven for them. But steadily their number was growing. They were mainly deserters and ne'er-do-wells whose only purpose was to take all they could from the South. They had no authority over them and did what they pleased. No one was safe from these men. Charles was in hopes that the Confederate army would return and run them out of the town. But all reports had the Confederate army in the North trying to take the capital of Washington.

The only horse that remained was an old swaybacked mare that no one wanted. But she served a purpose. Once a month, she pulled the buggy into town.

Their days were filled with struggles and hardships. They fought to survive. Charles cursed his injured leg daily. He was of little help to the family, and he felt useless. But each day, he improved, and he had hope that soon he would be able to hunt and bring some meat to the table. Although shells for his rifle were in short supply, he had stockpiled them at the beginning of the war to keep at Brier Cliff. He knew he would not always be there to help in case of emergency, and he wanted his family protected. Now with the Yankees so close, he thanked God he had the foresight to do so.

Each evening, they gathered in the sitting room to play a game of cards or to read. Elizabeth would read out loud to her family. Each night they would crawl into their beds, piled high with blankets, and try to sleep.

The Yankees had stopped all mail deliveries, but that was of little importance to Elizabeth. She had received only a few letters from Dillon since he left. She had not been able to send him any. He was always on the move. But she wrote often. She stored her letters in her dresser drawer so he could read them on his return. She poured her heart into those letters and could only hope that one day he would get the chance to read them.

Soldiers passed often on the road in front of the house. Every once in a while, a stray soldier would stop at the house and ask for a dipper of water. Charles had instructed his wife and daughters to give to them what they wanted but not to be too friendly. He didn't want them returning, expecting favors from his girls. If Charles knew any Yankees were close, he ordered the girls to stay indoors. Willow agreed but didn't like it. She did not fear the Yankees. They were only men, and there wasn't a man she couldn't control.

On one occasion, Willow had not taken her father's words seriously and had disobeyed him. She had been standing in the kitchen by the stove warming her hands when she saw a Union soldier coming up the driveway in front of her home. She looked around and did not see her parents, so she opened the door and walked out onto the back porch. The soldier came up to her and stopped. The smile on his face told her he liked what he saw. She beamed back a smile at him. This one was young, she thought, and handsome. She looked down his tall frame and back up over his clean-shaven face and encountered a pair of gray-blue eyes. His hair was sandy colored and fell forward onto his forehead. He removed his cap and ran a hand through his thick curly hair. He could not help but think that this girl was his for the taking. The smile she gave him was more invitation than he had received in months from any of the Southern ladies. "What's a pretty little thing like you doing standing there in that tattered old dress? You should be dressed in silks." He reached out a hand to take her hand and lead her down the three steps from the porch.

Willow looked down at the old dress she was forced to wear now and blushed with embarrassment.

He laughed when he saw the rosy glow of her cheeks. "If you belonged to me, I'd see that you were dressed properly, fitting your beauty."

Willow had men talk like this before, and she knew it was just a ploy to get to know her better. But she didn't care if it was true or not, she was enjoying his flattering words and strong Yankee accent. "Thank you, kind sir." She curtsied in front of him.

"Is there someplace I can rest my tired feet? I've been walking for miles trying to reach Hampton. Am I getting close?"

"You are," she answered. "It's just three miles up that road." She pointed in the direction of town. She looked back toward the stable. "And there is a stable where you can rest, and I'll bring you a cup of my mother's coffee. If you'd like?" she added.

"That sounds good to me." He smiled again, and Willow noticed how white and straight his teeth were. She liked his looks, and she was not afraid to let him know. She returned his smile then pointed toward the stable. She watched him a moment as he walked away then hurried into the kitchen to pour him a cup of coffee.

In the stable, she found him lying in the hay with his eyes closed. She came up to him and cleared her throat in case he was asleep. He came to his feet and took the cup from her hand and set it down on the railing to one of the stalls. Then he reached for her, pulling her into his arms. She allowed him to hold her and did not fight when his lips came crushing down on hers. But she did not like this rough treatment of her, and she protested in a loud voice.

"Stop, you are hurting me!" She struggled to get out of his arms, but he would not let her go. She placed her hand on his chest and pushed with all her strength. He was too strong for her. Then suddenly he released her and stepped back.

"Stop playing games, little lady. You know you want me as much as I want you."

Willow tasted her own blood from where he had kissed her. She was furious and did not want any more to do with him. But he was not going to let her get away that easily.

He grabbed her as she started toward the door. He pulled her roughly against his chest and wrapped his arms around her so she could not get away. "Relax. This can be good for the both of us," he said before lowering his mouth to hers once again.

This time Willow was ready, and she bit down on his lip as hard as she could.

He swore and grabbed at his mouth. Blood ran through his fingers. She had scarred him for life, and he wanted to hurt her as well. He came at her and grabbed at her arm, but she pulled away and ran for the door. He caught her before she made it and slammed her body against the wall. She wanted to scream, but she knew not to. She did not want her father to see the dilemma she had gotten herself into. She did the only thing she knew to do. She brought her knee up and connected hard with the area between his legs. He moaned and leaned forward clutching at his groin.

She now had the advantage. She could run from the stable, and he would never catch her, but she wanted to let him know just what she thought of him. "You get your scurvy self off my father's property and don't set foot back on it. I'd rather lie with a dog than the likes of you. And if you do come back, I'll see that my father shoots you. Do you understand?"

He could not speak. He was in too much pain. Tears came to his eyes. But one thing he knew—he didn't want to encounter this young lady again.

Willow left him in the stable and returned to the house. She stood watch at the kitchen door until she saw him leaving the stable and going back down the driveway. He was not walking as good when he left as when he came. She had to smile. She turned away from the window with a satisfied feeling running through her. She had handled that well, she thought.

James Randolph remained at the house. It seemed his only purpose was to eat their food and take up all of Willow's time. Joanna was beginning to be wary of his actions. She didn't like the fact that he did not help with any of the chores. He had begun to paint a picture of the house. She knew this was only a ploy to stay.

The day was extremely cold. Rain fell at a steady downpour. Charles had called Elizabeth into the sitting room to give her a few coins. She was to make the trip into town for supplies. "This is all there is left. God help us!" He pulled her into his arms. "It's bad outside. You can wait until tomorrow if you like."

"I'll go. Maybe the weather will force the Yankees inside." She returned her father's hug.

"You be careful." He smiled down into her upturned face. He knew that she was the one that took care of the family. She was the one that saw that everyone in the family did not go cold and hungry. Even Joanna had commented that she did not know what they would do without Elizabeth.

"Don't worry. I'll be back early." She turned and hurried to the stable to harness the horse and hitch up the buggy.

She hated this task because the Yankees were always standing along the storefronts and insulting the Southern ladies. She had no protection from these men. It was a game to them, and a woman had to present a strong face or was an easy target. She had experienced their vile tongue on many occasions, but she knew to give them any recognition was only adding fuel to the fire. On one such occasion, she had been pulled into a group of soldiers as she was leaving the store with her supplies. They had circled her and taunted her with pinches and rude remarks. She had stood her ground and did not say a word. She knew that the order had been given that if any Southern lady insulted a Union soldier, she would be subject to prosecution and could face jail. They had soon tired of her lack of response and let her go. She had suffered only hurt feelings and a sore bottom from the many pinches. But she could suffer that if it meant her surviving. But today, she hoped it would be different. The rain was heavy and cold. The soldiers would probably be inside out of the weather. This might give her some protection from them.

She climbed into the buggy and cracked the reins. The old swaybacked horse walked slowly away from the house. Her mother stood in the doorway with a worried look upon her face. She raised a hand to wave at her daughter as the buggy disappeared down the driveway.

Joanna reentered the house and turned to where Willow sat by the fire. Of late, her laziness was starting to bother Joanna. Everyone lent a hand to keep the family going. Everyone except Willow and James Randolph. "Can't you find something to do? You have been sitting there by the fire all morning while your sister has gathered wood for the fires and is now on her way to town for supplies in this cold rain. You should be ashamed." At that moment, she did not care if she upset Willow or not.

Willow began to pout. "Poppa doesn't want me going into town. He lets Elizabeth go because he knows none of the men will bother her. And I am sitting by this fire because it is cold in this house." She began to cry. "I am tired of the cold and the food we have to eat because there is nothing else. I am tired of being locked up in this house with only you and Poppa for company. Elizabeth hardly speaks to me, and since James has started his new painting, he has no time for me. What do you want me to do?"

Joanna was disgusted. She walked to the stove and placed the metal pitcher on it to heat the water. "I am going to start lunch. Elizabeth said she should be home by that time. She will be cold and hungry. You could help with that."

Willow began to cry harder. "You know I can't cook. Poppa always said he didn't want me getting my hands soiled with manual labor. Is it my fault that he never wanted me to do anything?"

Joanna only shook her head. There was a time when it was proper for a young lady to not know how to cook or care for her family. That was left up to the nanny and the servants. But those times were gone and would never return. Charles had always encouraged his girls to comply with tradition. Willow would be the one to suffer from her lack of knowledge in such things. "Then get out of the kitchen and out of my way. Go sit in the sitting room with your father. He needs some company."

Willow hurried away before her mother thought of anything else for her to do. The rain began to slow and turned into a drizzle. The wind died down, and the air was slightly warmer. Elizabeth pushed down the hood to her cape and gave the reins another crack. The roads were muddy, so she took her time. The sun was bright but gave off no warmth. She pulled her cape tighter around her shoulders and let the horse walk on her own. There were no troops on the road. She knew this to be because of the weather. She looked up at the sky and saw only black clouds trying to obscure the sun from view. She knew she was likely to get in another downpour before she returned home. In the distance, she could hear the roll of thunder. She prayed the rain would hold off a few more hours until she made this trip.

It was a three-mile ride into town, and with the old horse, the journey was slow. As she came upon a grove of trees, she slowed even more as she saw movement in the brush. She pulled her horse to a stop and stared for a long time before jumping down and walking over to see what was making the grass move. There, lying in the thick brush beneath the trees, was a Confederate soldier. She ran back to the buggy and pulled out the canteen from the bed. She ran back to him and knelt down to lift his head and pour water into his mouth. He was a young man. There was not a trace of a whisker on his dirty face.

"Please, ma'am," he moaned. "Don't turn me in. I'm dying. Just let me lie here. The Yankees will be hard on me, and I can tell them nothing."

"How did you get here?" she asked as her heart went out to him. He was shot in the right shoulder, and blood covered his chest. His clothes were worn and dirty and gave no protection from this weather. The boots he wore were full of holes and offered no insulation from the cold. She too thought he was dying. But she could not leave him out here alone. Even though it meant death to anyone harboring a Southern soldier, she had to take him home and see that he was cared for.

"I rode until my horse threw me. I walked until I couldn't walk anymore. The rest of the way, I crawled. I only want to get back home to see my maw before I die." He looked up at her and pleaded with his eyes for her to understand. "I left my company, ma'am. If my own troop finds me, I will be shot. So you see, I am a goner no matter what. Just give me some water and let me die."

Elizabeth knew to stay here would mean certain capture. Yankees traveled this road often. "I'll do no such thing. Can you walk?"

"I don't know, ma'am. Maybe if you help," he said as he began to pull himself up off the ground. Blood began to pour from his wound.

She supported his weight as much as she was able, and in that way, they made it to the buggy. She laid him in the back and covered him with the blanket she carried in the front of the buggy. She climbed back into the seat and turned the buggy and headed back to Brier Cliff. She whipped the old mare into a trot and tried to hurry before any Union troops came across her. With every bounce, the buggy made the young man groan in pain. She knew if she happened across any soldiers, they would surely find the man. She would be shot, and more than likely, so would every member of her family. She was taking a big risk to help this man, but she would not let any human, be it Confederate or Union soldier, die in this manner.

The sky opened up again, and it began to rain in earnest before she had traveled a mile. She looked back often to see that the soldier was covered with the blanket. She knew how miserable he must be and what pain he must be suffering. She tried to hurry the horse, but there was no hurrying it. They plowed through the muddy roads very slowly, and with each turn of the wheels, she lost more and more hope for the man's survival. She had pulled the hood to her cape back up over her head, but it gave little protection from the rain. And to make matters worse, it was beginning to freeze. She was soaked from head to toe, and chills were overtaking her body. She cracked the reins again in an effort to speed the horse. As Brier Cliff came into sight, her heart began to lighten. She was almost home. She could see her mother standing in the doorway watching her approach.

Joanna remained standing in the rain until Elizabeth pulled the buggy up to the kitchen door. "What happened?" She knew Elizabeth would not return unless something was wrong.

"Help me, Mother. I have one of our boys in the back of the buggy. He's wounded and bleeding badly," she said as she ran to the back of the buggy and removed the blanket from over his body.

Oh my!" Joan could only say. "Let's get him in the kitchen." Together the two women pulled and tugged him along until they got him into the house. Carefully, they laid him in front of the cooking stove. Elizabeth ran for her father. Only he would know what to do.

Charles knelt down and looked at the young man's wound. "We have to move you one more time. There is no way we can leave you here on the kitchen floor. Yankee soldiers are always coming this way."

Elizabeth looked at her father with concern in her eyes. "But where can we hide him?"

"In the attic. I prepared it long ago for just such a time," Charles said as he pulled the man to his feet. Elizabeth quickly took the other shoulder. The boy was near to unconscious, but she tried to make him hear. "You have to help. We can't do this on our own." Her words reached into his pain-ridden mind, and he helped as much as he could.

With the young man helping, they were able to get him up the steps of the attic and lay him on the cot her father had prepared. Immediately Charles began to remove his filthy clothing. "Bring me hot water and tell your mother to tear up some sheets to use for bandages." She turned to leave. "And bring me that last bottle of brandy." Elizabeth hurried down the steps.

Joanna returned with her daughter, helping to carry the supplies. She turned to her daughter. "You go downstairs and watch for Yankees. You don't need to be here to see this. And you get out of those wet clothes before you catch your death of cold."

Elizabeth didn't argue. She hurried away from the terrible scene being played out in the attic. She was wet and cold, but she gave it little thought. Her mind was on that young boy who fought for his life.

When she returned to the kitchen after changing her clothes and towel-drying her hair, she found Willow and James standing by the fire.

"What is going on?" Willow asked. She had heard the noise and came out of her bedroom to see her mother running up the attic steps.

"I found a Confederate soldier along the road to town. He has been wounded. Mother and Poppa are tending to him now," Elizabeth answered.

"You brought a Confederate soldier here? You know what that means if he is discovered? These are not regular Union troops in town. They will not show us mercy. They will shoot us for harboring an enemy," Willow said with fear in her voice. Elizabeth could only agree. "I knew all that when I brought him here. But what would you have me do? He is only a boy. And he was in a lot of pain. I could not leave him in the cold rain to die."

Willow surprised her sister with her answer. "You did the only thing you could. You couldn't leave one of our boys to die. We will have to be extra careful in case any Yankees come this way."

James Randolph did not give his opinion. He feared only for his own safety.

Joanna knelt beside the cot and looked at the wound in the boy's shoulder. It was very bad, and he had lost a great amount of blood. She took warm cloths and wiped away the blood. The hole in his shoulder made her heart sink. She turned to her husband. "You're going to have to take this bullet out. Do you think you can do it?"

Her husband did not answer. He turned and left the attic. He returned a few minutes later with his hunting knife. It was the sharpest in the house and was the only knife that could do what had to be done.

Charles held the knife over the flame of the lantern. He looked worried over the procedure he was about to attempt. But he knew he had no choice. It was either this or let the boy die. With the wound clean, he dug the tip of the knife into the boys flesh. Joanna held him as best she could, but after a while, there was no need to hold him down. He passed out from the pain.

Sweat formed on Charles's forehead and ran down into his eyes. After twenty minutes of probing, he found the bullet and was able to remove it.

Joanna wiped away the blood and wrapped the boy's shoulder in the clean sheets she had torn for bandages. Minutes later, the boy awoke. He was in a lot of pain. Charles lifted his head to help him drink some whiskey.

He shut his mouth and turned his head away from the bottle. "My maw don't hold with strong spirits, sir. I'd rather not drink that stuff when I am so close to my maker."

Charles tried to reassure him. "You'll go when your time comes and not a minute sooner. This whiskey will deaden the pain."

"No, thank you, sir. I want a clear head. There's plenty that I have to repent for. I want to make things right with him." He raised one finger toward the sky.

Joan wiped the sweat from his forehead. "What could a boy like you do so wrong?"

The boy began to cry. "Plenty, ma'am. I've kilt my share in this war. And I'm none too proud of it."

"That's war, boy." Charles felt his heart go out to the young man. "The good Lord doesn't hold that kind of killing against you."

"I just want to be sure." He wiped his face with the palm of his hand. "There are some things I need to tell you. My name is Thomas Winters from Macon Georgia. I'm the youngest of three boys. My maw is widowed and is all alone on our farm. I was the last son to leave for the war. She begged me not to go. But I didn't listen. I wish to God I had." He got a faraway look in his eyes. "My maw is a good Christian woman. She raised me right. If God sees fit to let me live, I'm going home, and I'll never leave again. There ain't nothing romantic about killing another man. I'll never raise a gun on a human being again. Let my maw know that I went right. That I asked him to forgive me. Her name is Betty Winters. You'll find her at South Fork, Macon, Georgia. Make sure she knows where I'm buried. And, ma'am, I'm seventeen. Make sure you put that on my marker."

Joanna had tears in her eyes. "Your mother should feel proud to have a son such as you. I'll let her know. But we won't talk like that now. We're going to ask the good Lord to let you live."

"Thank you, ma'am. I think I'll sleep now. I'm mighty tired." Thomas closed his eyes and slept.

An hour passed before Elizabeth's parents retuned to the kitchen. Both were covered with the young man's blood.

Elizabeth poured hot water into the basin so her father could wash his hands. "Is he going to make it?"

"I don't know." Charles was solemn. "He may have a chance, but only with God's help." Charles scrubbed away the blood from his hands and took the towel that Elizabeth offered to dry them.

Joanna poured fresh water into the basin. "He told us his name is Thomas Winters from Georgia. He was trying to make it home before he died. He said he wanted us to see that his mother knew where he was buried. He lives on a farm, the youngest of three brothers. His mother didn't want him to go to war. He said she cried and begged. There was no one left to help on the farm. His father had died long ago, and his two older brothers had left to join the Confederacy. He's only seventeen. Too young to be talking of dying." She lowered her head so her family won't see the tears that came to her eyes. She could only imagine how his mother must feel with her young son off fighting in this war.

Elizabeth began to cry. "Will this war never end? So much pain! So much sorrow! How much more can the South take?"

Charles took her into his arms. "There there. Don't cry. Remember you're supposed to be the strong one." Charles knew at that moment that Elizabeth had been right to not want him to go to war. War was a terrible thing.

Elizabeth buried her face in her father's chest and took comfort in his arms around her. She pulled away to dry her eyes. "I am sorry. It just seems to be so wrong. Why do young boys like this one have to die? He hasn't even started to live yet."

Elizabeth helped take care of the man as much as her mother would allow. Joanna didn't want her to get attached to the young soldier for she held out little hope for him. On one visit, he motioned her near so that she could hear what he had to say. "Thank you, miss. You're family has been good to me. Your maw reminds me of my own. You have given me some rest and peace before I have to go. What more could I ask? To not lie on some battlefield and rot under the sun or be eaten by wild animals was one of my greatest fears. All the boys fear that. All I want now is to have a descent place to be buried and a marker to show that I was here. Please don't forget to let my maw know where I am buried. She's a good woman. She'll want to visit my grave once this war is over."

Elizabeth could only nod her head as she fought back her tears. Once out of the attic, she ran to her room and buried her face in her pillow. She prayed that Dillon was safe and that he would not come to the same end. She turned and wiped away her tears. She looked toward the window and felt the winter sun coming through the pain. The way things were going for the South, she sometimes doubted he would return.

Joanna worked hard to save the young man's life. She was constantly going up and down the steps of the attic to tend to him. She dressed his wound every day and tried to get him to eat the broth she made especially for him. On days that he was conscious, she would sit and talk with him, telling him of how good things were going to be after the South won this war. She read to him out of the Bible and held his hand to pray with him. She gave her word to tell his mother what happened to her youngest son. And to let her know his last thoughts were of her.

Emotion ran high those days at Brier Cliff. Everyone was silent and was close to tears. Only Willow refused to help with him. She said she could not stand a sick room. But Elizabeth noticed Willow was helping more than usual to lessen the burden from her mother. She began to help with the family's meals and with the cleanup. One day she went out into the woods to help her sister gather wood. Elizabeth's heart warmed toward her sister. Willow cared.

Three days later, the young man died after a twenty-four hour battle with a high fever. Joanna walked slowly down the attic steps. She wiped her hands on her apron and turned to Elizabeth, who stood waiting at the bottom of the steps. "Well, he's gone to his maker. God rest his soul." She turned and walked away to grieve in her own way.

Elizabeth could only stand there and look up the attic steps where he still lay. Tears ran freely down her cheeks. She was crying for this lost boy, but more, she was crying for the South.

Charles washed and dressed him in one of his own suits. He ran a comb through his hair and made him look presentable. He was a fine-looking boy, he thought. His mother was probably very proud of him. Charles had never had a son, but he thought, *I'd want him to be just like this boy.* He lowered his head so the family would not see his tears.

They held a service late at night and buried him in their family cemetery. It was a solemn group that stood in the dark of night in the pouring rain and prayed for a boy they barely knew. All the family was present, including Willow and James Randolph. Charles prayed over the grave.

"Dear Lord, take this young man home to be with you. Where there is no war. Where there is no pain and suffering. Give to him what he could not find in this world. Give him peace. And give to his mother comfort in the fact that she raised a good and decent boy."

The family solemnly returned to the house and blew out the lamps so that they could go to bed. Few slept that night. Their minds were filled with thoughts of a young man who gave his life for his country. Of a mother who still waited for her sons to return. And of the many more who would die before this thing was over.

Chapter 12

Lost somewhere in the passages of time.

Elizabeth and her mother cleaned the attic the next day. Both women were close to tears as they removed the bloodstained sheets from the cot and scrubbed away the blood from the floor.

Their thoughts were troubled. Both knew that there were many boys suffering the same fate as Thomas. Elizabeth's sweat and tears ran together as she scrubbed the floor on her hands and knees. She wished she could remove the pain and suffering this war caused as easily.

After everything was washed down and the sheets laundered, Joan sat down and wrote a letter to the young boy's mother. She praised the woman on raising a wonderful boy and assured her they had done all they could to make his end as comfortable as possible. She sealed the letter in an envelope and laid it on the mantel of the fireplace to mail at a later date.

Later that evening, as they sat at the dining room table eating their supper, they heard horses approaching the house. Charles rose from the table and motioned for everyone to remain seated. He made his way slowly to the door.

He opened the door to Union soldiers. A young sergeant pushed past Charles and entered the foyer. Three others followed him. The smell of liquor followed the men into the house.

"What do you mean barging into my home?" Charles did not hide the anger from his voice. He wanted these men out of his house, but he knew they had the advantage. He had to show a strong face to these men, or else they would overrun his home and family.

The sergeant looked around the house. He turned back to the older man. "Look's like you're doing well for yourself in this fancy house." He picked up a gold cigarette box and carelessly tossed it to one of the soldiers. "What do you think that will bring us? Looks like it might be real gold."

"Sergeant, if you and your men do not leave immediately, I will inform your commander of your actions." Charles tried to take the cigarette box out of the hands of the soldier, but the soldier only laughed and tossed it to his companion.

Charles did not try again. He knew it would turn into a game, and he would be the loser.

At that moment, the women entered the room. James Randolph was not with them. He had hurried up the backstairs to lock himself in his bedroom.

"Well, what do we have here?" The sergeant walked up to Elizabeth. He twisted her hair around one of his fingers. "I knew I'd see you again. I said to my friend"—he nodded in the direction of one of the soldier—"that night I met you on the road that you and I could be real good friends." He leaned closer so that his breath was directly in her face. "I thought you were something then. But you're better-looking than I remembered. I bet you'd like to spend some time with a Union soldier. I can take care of you. You'll not go hungry when you're mine. Name's Sam." He was standing too close, but there was nothing Elizabeth could do. She tried to back away, but he held tight to her hair, pulling her back to him. "Don't try to get away. It will do you no good. I always get what I want."

Elizabeth remained still. She recognized the man as the one she had met on the road with the doctor. She knew to fight would only anger the man more. She had been through this type of treatment before from the Union soldier.

"Sergeant," Charles' voice boomed in the room. "Let go of my daughter! And get your men out of here, at once." Charles took a threatening step toward the man when he saw the sergeant tighten his grip on Elizabeth's hair.

The corporal held out his foot, and Charles came crashing to the floor, landing on his injured leg. The men all joined in laughing at him. Charles tried to rise, but the corporal put his foot on his chest and held him down. "Stay right there, old man," he warned.

Joanna saw the pain her husband was in and rushed to his side. She pleaded with the man. "Please let him up! He's leg has been injured, and he is in pain. Please!" She was close to tears as she knelt and tried to remove the boot from her husband's chest.

The sergeant laughed with his men. "Let him up. Can't you see he is injured?" he mocked Joanna.

The corporal removed his foot, and Joanna helped her husband to his feet.

The sergeant released Elizabeth and walked up to Charles. "I don't like the tone of your voice. I think you owe my men and me an apology. Don't you boys agree?" he asked his men, not taking his eyes off Charles. "Let's hear it. Let's hear you say you're sorry."

Charles wanted to spit in the man's face, but he was not a fool, but he'd be damned before he apologized. Charles looked into the man's eyes and did not respond.

The sergeant removed his pistol from its holster and pointed it in Charles's face. "The old man's got spunk. I admire that in a man. But not in an enemy of my country." He pulled the hammer back on the gun and positioned it beneath Charles's chin.

Elizabeth could remain silent no longer. "Please don't hurt him," she pleaded.

The sergeant came around fast at the sound of her voice. "I almost forgot about you. Let's see what your daddy will do when his daughter is in danger." He walked back to her and took her in his arms. "You smell good. I knew you would. I've thought about you since that time on the road. You thought you were too good for me then. Let's see what you think with a gun pointed at you. Do you think you will change your mind about ole Sam?" The sergeant raised the gun to point it at Elizabeth. He moved closer until there was not an inch between them.

Charles jerked free of his wife's hold on him and advanced toward the sergeant. "You bastard. Let her go!"

The sergeant didn't turn around at Charles's command. He spoke to his men with his eyes still locked on Elizabeth. "Tie up the old man and gag him. I don't want to hear any more out of him. This little lady and me are talking, and we don't want to be disturbed." He smiled down into her face, and Elizabeth could smell the liquor on his breath. "What do you say, pretty lady? You willing to let old Sam give you a tumble? It will be good. I promise you that. Ain't no woman left my bed that wasn't satisfied." He placed his gun back into his holster and pulled her closer to him. His lips descended toward her and meant to capture hers.

All reason fled Elizabeth. Now she was frightened. She tried to get away from the man's grip, but he held her close, pulling her even tighter against his chest. She tried to scream, but his foul mouth captured hers. She could only struggle against his assault. She freed one hand and brought it up to dig deep into his cheek. He swore and pulled away. He raised his hand and backslapped her across the mouth. She fell against the wall and remained there, unconscious.

Willow and Joanna screamed and ran to their daughter and sister. Charles could only watch helplessly. He struggled against his bonds, but it was no use. There was nothing he could do. These men would ravage his daughters and destroy his home. If only he had his pistol, he thought. But that was upstairs in his bureau drawer. He pulled against his bonds until he felt blood run down his hand and drip on the floor. But he could not loosen them.

The sergeant turned to his men. "Ransack the place. Take anything we can sell. Then burn down the house."

Willow stood at his words. She was determined to save her home and family. "Sergeant, couldn't we find a better way? My sister isn't the woman for you. She is inexperienced and would not satisfy a man." She walked up to him and began to toy with the buttons on his jacket. "Now I, on the other hand, am more than willing to try and help out a good-looking man like you." She looked up at him with warm dark eyes, and he could see the invitation there. She smiled, and that smile told him everything he wanted to know.

He leaned back his head and yelled. His voice echoed through the halls. He picked up Willow and twirled her around. "You are a damn fine-looking little girl. I like my women young." He set her down on her feet and turned to his men. "We're going upstairs. You watch the old man and women."

A corporal reached up on the mantel and pulled down the letter Joanna had written earlier. "Wait, Sarg. Look at this. Might be something important."

Willow snuggled in his arms. "That's a letter my sister wrote today to her finances mother. It is far from important." Willow and the sergeant were standing by the hall desk. She reached behind her and picked up the letter opener lying there and slipped it into her dress pocket. She knew if the sergeant read the letter, it would be certain death for all of them. She had to get the letter away from him. She would use whatever means it took.

He took the letter from the corporal and placed it in his jacket pocket. Then he turned and led Willow to the stairs.

"Are we still going to burn the place?" a soldier asked, stopping the sergeant. His voice held an air of anticipation. It was evident that he and his fellow soldiers had done this many times before.

The sergeant looked down into Willow's face. "That depends. I'll let you know when I get back." He wrapped an arm around her shoulders and followed her up the stairs.

Willow led the sergeant to her bedroom and opened the door. He followed her into the room. He pulled her into his arms and crushed his lips down on hers. She pulled away and tried to smile. The smell of this man was enough to turn her stomach. He pulled her back into his arms and again brought his mouth down on hers. She endured his touch and even let him think she was enjoying it. But she could barely control the shudder that ran through her body. His hands roamed her body and cupped her breasts. He pulled back and looked into her face. "You sure do have nice ones." He grinned and picked the nipple.

A pain shot through Willow's breast. She tried to smile. She raised a hand to his cheek. "Not so fast," she purred. She pulled out of his arms and moved to the bed and lay down. She cast him her most inviting look. She knew the danger she faced, but she would not let this man destroy her family and home. She held out her arms in an invitation for him to join her.

A laugh came from the sergeant. He tore off his shirt and joined her on the bed. His rough hands roamed her body. His chest was pinning her down on the bed. She could not move. She knew she had to free her arm so that she could get to the letter opener. Fear took control of her. She would not be raped by this man. She would not allow him to have his way with her.

She pushed against his chest. "You're hurting me. Let me free my hand so I can touch you."

He rose up on one arm and looked down at her as she ran her hand down his bare back.

"You sure are a sweet thing. Let me see what you got." He jerked the material of her dress, and the buttons flew across the room. He had the look of a hungry dog. She could have sworn she saw salvia drip from the corners of his mouth. He lowered his head to her exposed breasts and began to kiss her roughly. Willow could stand no more. She reached into her pocket and pulled the letter opener out. With as much force as she could, she drove it into his throat. She heard a gurgling sound, and his eyes seemed to bulge out of his head.

Blood spilled from the wound onto her face and chest. She pushed at him to get away, but he was falling forward and onto her. She wanted to scream, but she knew she could not. She squirmed from beneath him and stood beside the bed. He didn't die fast. He struggled for long minutes for air. Blood soaked the bed and dripped onto the floor. He pulled at the letter opener until it released from his neck. He held out his hand to her. She moved back as far as she could so he could not touch her. The look on his face filled her with terror. She had never seen a man die before, and she could not take her eyes off him. Willow stood there as though in a trance. Her eyes never left his face. Time seemed to stand still as the sergeant struggled for his life. Willow's heart jumped with every drop of blood that ran from his wound. She was afraid he would make a sound and the others would come to check on him. She pulled the pillow from under his head and held it over his face. Long minutes passed before he was finally still. She removed the pillow and looked down at him. His eyes and mouth were open, and his face was contorted in a gruesome pose. She dropped the pillow and backed away from the scene until she came in contact with the wall. There she stood, staring at the dead man.

The three soldiers found a bottle of Charles's liquor and sat down to drink and wait for their sergeant to be finished with the young girl. One young soldier turned to his friend. "Some people have all the luck. What I wouldn't do to be between that pretty little thing's thighs." He lifted the bottle to his mouth and took a generous swig.

They passed the bottle between them until it was empty, then one rose to search for another. Joanna saw what was taking place and rose to her feet and ran to the liquor cabinet. She pulled out a bottle and handed it to the young man. She wanted these men as drunk as Charles's liquor would make them. They would be easier to deal with. She returned to Charles's side and slid down the wall to sit on the floor beside Elizabeth. Already Elizabeth's jaw was swollen and turning dark with a bruise. Joanna propped her head on her lap and brushed the hair from her face. She cooed softly, "My poor sweet dear. Everything is going to be fine." Joanna looked up the staircase and prayed for her other daughter. God only knew what was happening to her.

Elizabeth had come to. Her mother helped her to a chair to sit down. They huddled together beside Charles. Hours passed, and still the sergeant did not return. At midnight the three soldiers were drunk and wanting to leave, but they were too afraid of the sergeant to do so.

The corporal turned to the other two. "He's asleep up there, and we won't get back until morning. You know what that will mean for us? A week in the brig. I say let's go and let him face the captain. I have no wish to do so."

The other men agreed. They stood on wobbly legs and left the house without taking a thing.

Joanna untied her husband and fell into his lap in tears. He soothed her as much as he could, but his thoughts were on what was going on upstairs.

At the sound of the front door closing, Willow appeared at the top landing. Her dress was torn and covered with blood. In one hand, she held the letter opener and in the other the letter she had taken from the sergeant's jacket. Her face was as pale as death. She had remained in her room with a dead man for hours.

Charles grabbed his daughter and held her tight. Elizabeth came quickly up to the two and wrapped her arms around them. Joanna stood in the background, crying.

He handed Willow off to Elizabeth. "Take care of her. See that those clothes are burned. I am going to take care of our sergeant."

Charles had forced the young painter to leave his bedroom and help in the digging of a grave. An hour later, the body of the sergeant was carried down the stairs wrapped in sheets and deposited in the cold ground.

Charles stood long after the chore was done and looked down at the graves of the soldiers he had buried. Both were young men. Both should have lived many more years. They lay side by side in ground that was foreign to them. What sense did this war make? *Aren't we all just men?* he asked himself. He walked away from the gravesites with a new hatred for this war. War made men do things they wouldn't normally do. War made some men into animals, and the sergeant had become one of them.

Joanna and Elizabeth gained enough control to go to Willow's bedroom and wash down everything in it. Elizabeth thought this was the second time in just days that she and her mother had washed away the traces of blood from a young soldier that had died in their home. How ironic that these men had been bitter enemies and yet would be buried side by side in the same ground by the same hand.

In no time, there wasn't any trace of the sergeant. Charles and his family retired for the night. All were exhausted. Willow slept with Elizabeth for the first time in years. She could not bear to go back into her room. Elizabeth wrapped her arms around her sister and held her.

Late that night, Elizabeth awoke to a sound in her room. She rose in bed, realizing Willow was not beside her. The sound was like a whimpering child. She reached out and turned up the lamp sitting on her nightstand. Willow was standing against the wall in a corner, her eyes wide and her face was a deathly pale. She was brushing at her nightgown, trying to remove something she imagined was there. A whimper came from her open mouth.

Elizabeth leaped from the bed and ran to her sister. "Willow, what is it?"

"Get it off me!" she screamed. "The blood. Get it off me. Can't you see? It is everywhere! On my hands!" She held out her hands. "On my dress!" She began to violently brush at her gown again. A deathly scream erupted from deep inside her.

Elizabeth tried to talk to her, but it was no use. She was in a world all her own. Nothing could penetrate her fear.

Joanna bolted into the room followed by her husband. "Willow, dear, listen to your mother. Everything is all right. Come back to bed." She took her arm and motioned for Elizabeth to take the other. Together they led her to the bed. Joanna continued to talk in a low, soothing voice. Willow began to respond. She followed the two to the bed and lay down. Her mother covered her with a blanket and sat down on the side of the bed. She gently pushed the hair from her face and continued to talk to her. "There is nothing to hurt you. You're safe now."

Joanna looked to her husband. "Get my laudanum from my nightstand. It will calm her down and make her sleep."

She turned her attention back to Willow. "There there, sweet child. Your mother is here, and I'll not leave you."

Willow began to cry and call out for her mother. Joanna took her into her arms and rocked her back and forth. She began to sing a lullaby, one she sang many times when her girls were small.

Elizabeth stood with tears running down her face. Her poor sister had relived the nightmare of the sergeant's death. *Dear God,* she thought, *it must have been terrible.* She wanted to help her sister, but she didn't know how. Elizabeth had no idea what it meant to kill another human being. She knew Willow would live out this nightmare for a very long time to come.

Charles returned with the laudanum and a glass of water. He stood staring down at his daughter. Remorse filled his face. He blamed himself. He was supposed to protect his family. But then he thought what if he hadn't been here? Far worse could have happened, and then he would have been responsible. He could have ridden away and left his family without any kind of protection. The thought was more than he could bear. He had Elizabeth to thank that he did not go the war. He would be grateful to her for the rest of his life.

Joanna was able to get her daughter to take the medicine after much pleading. Within a few minutes, she began to calm down and appeared sleepy.

Joanna turned to Elizabeth. "She'll sleep until morning. You can rest. There will be no need to remain awake to watch her." She leaned over the bed and kissed her daughter's cheek. "Sleep will heal you, dear." She took Charles's arm, and together they left the room.

Elizabeth turned down the lamp and crawled into bed beside her sister. But she could not sleep. She kept reliving the events of the last few hours. Were all soldiers like the sergeant and his men? Did none have any concern for others, or did they just take and take until there was nothing left to take? That was all she had seen in this war. There was no compassion. There was no remorse. *At the end to this war,* she wondered, *how could these two peoples live together again?* She rolled toward her sister and listened to her even breathing. She wrapped an arm around her waist and held her close. Slowly sleep claimed her.

Willow remained in bed the next day. Elizabeth carried her a tray of food up to the bedroom and tried to make her eat. She ate very little. She lay on her back and stared up at the ceiling with unseeing eyes. She was breathing. Her eyes were open, but she could not see or hear what was going on around her. She was still in that place where nightmares lived. Elizabeth sat with her and took her hand. She began to talk of trivial things. She wanted to reach her sister, but she didn't know how. Finally, after an hour, she rose and left the room. Willow had not moved or responded in all that time.

That evening after supper, Elizabeth went up to her bedroom to check on her sister. She found the bed empty. Elizabeth turned from the room and ran downstairs. Both her parents turned in alarm at the sound of her screams.

"Poppa, Willow is gone!" Fear gripped Elizabeth as never before. She knew Willow was not herself. She worried that she might do something to harm herself. But she would never voice this fear to her family.

Charles was on his feet immediately. Joanna began to cry. "My poor baby. Find her, Charles."

"We will." He turned to Elizabeth. "Help me look for her. I'm not so fast with this leg." He grabbed Elizabeth's hand and started for the door.

The night was very dark with no moon. Everything was still; not even the sound of a cricket could be heard.

Both called into the darkness, but there was no answer. She was nowhere to be seen. Father and daughter headed toward the barn and stables. After a thorough search of both buildings, they still had not found her.

Elizabeth turned to her father. "Where can she have gone?"

Charles stood silent and listened. Faintly he heard a sound coming from the direction of the graveyard. Elizabeth heard it too. Without a word, they hurried in that direction.

They found her kneeling on the ground dressed in her nightgown, digging at the earth over the sergeant's grave. She was babbling something they could not understand.

Elizabeth was the first to reach her. She knelt at her side and tried to force her up and away from the grave. "Willow, please. We have been so worried about you." She pulled away from her sister and continued to dig with her bare hands.

"Willow!" Charles's voice was firm. "Come away from there and go with us back to the house."

That seemed to penetrate her fog-ridden brain. She looked up at him. "But Poppa, he's not dead. I have to get him out of there. Can't you see? He'll die if I don't." There was a wild look in her eyes, and the sight frightened both father and daughter.

Charles leaned down and took hold of her arm to pull her up to her feet. "There is nothing you can do for him. He's dead, child."

Tears ran down Willow's cheeks. "Yes, and I killed him." She buried her face in her dirty hands.

Her weeping tore at Charles's heart. But he knew he had to talk firmly to her, or his words would not reach her. He held her against his chest. She buried her dirty face there and continued to cry.

"Listen to me. You did nothing wrong." He looked down at her and tried to make her understand. "He meant to kill us. You did the right thing. He got what he deserved. If not for you, child, the whole family could have been killed." Charles tilted up her face and looked into her eyes. "You saved us all. And that is nothing to be ashamed of. I'm proud of you. It took courage to do what you did."

He turned with her still in his arms and began to walk back to the house. Elizabeth followed at his side with tears running down her face. She thanked God that they had found her.

They got her back into bed. Joanna washed her and put a clean gown on her. In some way, she seemed better. Joanna kissed her cheek and pulled the blanket up over her. Willow closed her eyes and slept.

The next day, a troop of Union soldiers rode up to Brier Cliff and dismounted. A Captain Hollis led them. He stepped up to the door as

Charles opened it. He removed his hat at the sight of Joanna and Elizabeth standing behind Charles.

"Sorry to bother you. I am Captain Hollis. I've been looking for a man for a long time. His name is Sam Davies. He was one of my sergeants, but he deserted about six months ago along with two other men." He pointed toward two men sitting on horseback with their hands tied in front of them. "They killed a sentry in the process. These men tell me they last saw Davies here. Is that true?"

Charles opened the door for the captain to enter then closed it behind him. "This is my family, Captain. My wife, Joanna, and my daughter Elizabeth.

"Please to meet you." The captain nodded his head toward the ladies.

He was of medium height with a handlebar mustache and wide sideburns. His hair was a sandy gray, and he appeared to be about forty years of age.

"Captain, are you aware that a band of renegade soldiers have taken over the town of Hampton? They have been terrorizing the citizens for months," Charles asked.

"We are aware of it, but there is little I can do. We are under orders to report farther South. I wouldn't be here now if we had not come across these two men on the road, and they led us here. I mean to capture this man. Can you be of any help?"

Charles looked directly into the face of the captain. "Sir, I can tell you he and his men came here to rob and assault my family. As you see, my oldest daughter has a bruised and swollen jaw where he attacked her."

"Then he was here?" the captain said. Then turning to Elizabeth, he continued, "I'm sorry for what my man did. I assure you, he will pay for this assault against you."

Willow appeared on the top landing of the stairs. She had dark circles under her eyes and looked unwell. Her hair was a tangled mess around her face. "Captain, your man was here. He beat my sister, but he did far worse to me. He assaulted me in the worst way a man can assault a woman. He left soon after and never returned."

The captain was visibly upset by her words. "What can I say to apologize to you and your family? I want you to know that not all Union soldiers are such scoundrels." He turned to Charles. "I know that nothing can make up to you for what has been done to your daughter, but I would like to see that you and your family receive something to show how truly sorry my government is. I will see that a wagon full of supplies is delivered here today."

He took Charles's hand and shook it. "My government does not uphold this sort of thing. Once Davies is captured, he will be jailed then shot at my orders. I wish you and your family a good day."

The captain left the house and mounted his horse. With a farewell salute, he turned his men and rode away.

Charles closed the door behind him.

Willow grew steadily better and, within a month's time, was her old self. But at times, there was a look in her eyes that reflected the horror that she had been through. She seemed to laugh more now, but Elizabeth thought it was to cover the pain she must still be feeling deep inside. All members of the family had always spoiled Willow, but now she held a special place in all their hearts. If not for her, their home could have been burned down; and far worse, they all could have been shot for harboring a Confederate soldier.

James Randolph had remained out of the picture in all Willow's troubles. But now he hoped to resume his affair with her. She had not been near him in over a month. But she had moved back into her bedroom, and he hoped she would allow him to make the journey between their two rooms. Willow was a different girl than the one he first met, but he knew her nature all too well. She would need him soon, and he would be there for her. He tried often to make eye contact with her, but she remained aloof. He thought he might approach her after dinner some evening and see if she still cared for him. But he was afraid of her parents hearing. They would not hold with him making advances toward their daughter, and he would soon be put out of the house.

He waited until one of those rare occasions when Charles and Joanna retired early for the evening to approach her. She was sitting in the sitting room doing a crossword puzzle when he walked up to her. She didn't acknowledge his presence when he sat down on the arm of the sofa and leaned over her. He gently tickled her ear. She brushed his hand away and continued with what she was doing.

He leaned down and whispered in her ear. "Willow, I have missed you."

She looked up at him and then rose to her feet. "I presume you would like to continue with our affair?"

He was shocked at her abruptness. "Why, yes." He too rose to his feet to stand in front of her. "I was wondering if you were still interested. You haven't spoken to me in a month."

She sat back down on the sofa and picked up her puzzle. "Tonight. And don't make it too late. I'm tired this evening." She dismissed him without another word and continued with her crossword puzzle. He quietly left the room. But his feelings were not hurt. At last she would be his again, and he could work on making it permanent.

Later that evening, he made the journey over to her room. She had left her door unlocked, as she always did when she was expecting him. She was lying on the bed completely naked. He approached her slowly. She had never received him like this before, and he did not know what to make of it.

She smiled and held out her hand to him. He quickly undressed and joined her on the bed. She was the aggressive one this time. She wanted to have her way and be done with the whole thing. She seemed in a great hurry to get what she could out of their meeting and be done with him.

It was over far too quickly for James, but she had been so forceful he could not contain himself. When they were through, she rolled over with her back to him and dismissed him. He was surprised. She had always wanted to talk and hold one another afterward. She was different. But he put it down to her encounter with the Union sergeant. He thought that she would be her old self in time. He planned to wait for that. He dressed and made his way back to his room.

Willow was very different. She spent more time alone and seemed distant when she was with the family. Her mind was often miles away. But everyone knew what she had gone through and didn't press her for answers to why she was acting the way she did. There were times that she seemed her old self. She would laugh and talk with her father. But that would last only for a few minutes then she would turn back into that dark mood.

As time passed, she seemed to be less the happy cheerful girl she had once been and was more angry and demanding. Especially with James. He took her mood as they came, grateful that she allowed him near her. He was the only one she seemed to want to spend time with. This pleased him. What he didn't understand was that with him, she could stop pretending and let the dark mood envelop her. She didn't have to worry that someone in the family would question her behavior.

She became very good at pretending. As time passed, the family thought she was well. But alone with James, she would retreat back to that place that frightened even her.

Chapter 13

Time has no heart,
but time remembers.

It was Christmas 1864. The weather was cold, and food was scarce, but the little family continued to work hard each day to survive. Elizabeth had given up hope of hearing from Dillon. She had received only a handful of letters in the last three years. She knew it was hard for him to write, but she only wanted word saying he was all right. She knew he could be killed, and she would never know. The little town of Hampton was ravaged by the Union troops, and most of the people had deserted the town. The only thing that grew in the town was the graveyard. Thousands of young men were killed each day in this war that seemed to never have an end. The Union soldiers had pulled out of the town, but they left behind a skeleton of what the town used to be. Rumors were rampant among the community. Some said that a bigger force was coming to completely destroy the South, while others said the troop withdrawal was a sign of victory. No one knew the truth. News was nonexistent in the little town. The Prestons hung on to the only thing they had left. Brier Cliff and the family circle.

The cold weather made things that much more miserable for the family.

There was no food to be had in the town and no money to buy food, if there had been any. Every evening the Prestons huddled around the sitting room fire in an effort to keep warm. They ate what they could find. Sometimes a stray rabbit would get caught in one of Charles's traps, and the family would feast on it for a day. Elizabeth scavenged for roots and plants that had not perished in the cold, and Joanna would cook up a soup.

But still, with all their misery, they planned a Christmas celebration. For weeks Elizabeth and her mother had unraveled shawls and sweaters to knit gifts for the others. They had knitted gloves, hats, and socks for everyone in the house. Even Mr. Randolph was included in their gift giving.

Elizabeth had taken the axe to the woods and chopped down a small tree to decorate. She and Willow had made paper ornaments and placed candles on the branches.

Charles had taken his rifle and the few shells he had left and walked out into the woods to kill something for their Christmas dinner. He had returned a few hours later with a turkey. He had been so proud that Joanna could not reprimand him for walking on his bad leg. She kissed his cheek and took the bird to the kitchen. Along with the vegetables and the last jar of canned fruit, they would have a somewhat meager but hearty meal for their Christmas dinner.

Charles suffered for days because of that hunt into the woods, but he was very proud of his accomplishment. Joanna and Elizabeth fussed over him and made him rest in his favorite chair in front of the fire until he felt like getting up and moving around.

The meal could not compare to the usual holiday fare, but to the family, it was wonderful. Everyone gathered around the table, and Charles said a prayer. He prayed for the South and for his loved ones and hoped for the war to end. Elizabeth said a prayer of her own for the man she loved. She hoped that he too would have a meal this Christmas. She could only imagine how the soldiers must be suffering in this cold and so far from home on this special holiday. When Charles was done with his prayer, Elizabeth looked up to see tears in her family's eyes. Even Willow brushed at her eyes and tried to hide the fact that she too felt such emotion. She tried to smile. But there was little to smile about. They ate and talked and enjoyed each other's company. Then all retired to the sitting room to exchange gifts.

Everyone seemed pleased with the gifts Elizabeth and Joanna gave. Even Willow seemed to appreciate the work that went into the gift. She apologized for not having anything to give them and promised next year would be different. This was a far cry from what she had been used to in the past. But gloves and a hat would come in handy in these cold days. James Randolph thanked the ladies for his gift, but he had little use for them since he rarely ventured outside in the cold. Charles had hidden under his chair his gifts for his family. He pulled them out and handed each of them a package wrapped in brown paper. All were surprised to see yards of beautiful material. He explained that on his trip into town with Elizabeth so long ago, he had purchased the material to give to them. But he seemed never to have had the chance. He had forgotten completely about the material until he was searching through his closet and found it on his top shelf. What better time to give it than Christmas? The ladies were pleased, and each gave him a kiss on the cheek for being such a thoughtful husband and father. They knew that the material would give them something to work on during the long days of winter.

After the gift exchange, they sat around the fire in the sitting room as Charles read the Christmas story from the Bible. They had heard it many times before, but this Christmas, it held a special meaning. They had a lot to be thankful for. They were all alive and all together. Brier Cliff was safe for the time being, and they had hope that the war would soon be over.

Later that evening, Elizabeth walked to the window and looked out. She was surprised to see snow falling to the ground. She marveled at the sight. It had been many years since snow fell on their home. She knew in the morning it would be gone, along with their cheerful mood, and the struggles to survive would begin again. She walked away from the window and rejoined her family in the sitting room.

Charles pulled out his last bottle of brandy and poured a small amount into five glasses. He raised his glass in a toast. It was simply "The South." But this toast had a far different meaning than the one he made so many years ago. The South was in danger of extinction. The traditions they lived by and protected with their lives was gone. The South, as they once knew it, would never exist again.

Elizabeth helped her mother in the kitchen clean up after the dinner. Joanna seemed in a cheerful mood and began to hum a hymn Elizabeth had heard often in church. She joined in and began to sing along. Soon the two were both singing. Afterward they broke out in laughter at their feeble attempt to carry a tune. Elizabeth excused herself and went to her bedroom. She quickly undressed because the room was very cold and pulled on her nightgown. She climbed under the stacks of blankets on the bed and tried to sleep.

Later that night, as Elizabeth lay in her bed, the blankets pulled to her chin, trying to keep warm, she heard the floor creaking as someone walked across the hall. She knew it to be James. She had heard it many times before.

Elizabeth came downstairs early the next day to find her mother and her father locked in his study. She couldn't explain it, but once they emerged from the room, she saw something in both their faces that set her heart to racing. She stayed out of the way as her mother marched up the stairs and rapped loudly on James Randolph's room. Her words could be heard loudly downstairs.

"Mr. Randolph, you have remained in my home three years now. You have eaten our food and enjoyed the warmth of our fires, but in all that time, you have not lifted a hand to help with any chore. You did a fine job on the portraits, and I wish to thank you. But the portraits are done. You are no longer needed here. You have been paid tenfold what you deserve. Please pack your bags and leave Brier Cliff immediately." She turned and marched back down the stairs with a satisfied look upon her face.

Willow was standing beside her sister when her mother came into the room. Joanna gave her a look that sent a chill up Elizabeth's spine. "And you, young lady, will stay away from that young man. Or else your father will take a strap to your backside. Do you understand?"

Willow could only nod her head that she did. The family went into the dining room for breakfast and did not bid James good-bye when he left a few minutes later.

Everyone was quiet around the table. Charles was determined to break the silence. "I heard today that the Dawsons pulled out late last night. Seems Mary Ellen has family farther South, and the entire family packed up what they could carry and left everything behind." He shook his head. "I hope it doesn't come to that here. We have no place to go. Brier Cliff has been our home for a long time, and I wouldn't want give her up."

Joanna finally answered. "Mary Ellen has family in Florida. Does she think that is far enough away to elude the Union Army? I don't think there is such a place. I plan to stay right here. Let them come. They were here before, and we survived them. We can again. I don't plan to give up my home." She passed her husband a plate of potatoes. "Luke Dawson never did have a backbone. He left during the war with Mexico, afraid he would have to serve. He's a coward and has put Mary Ellen through hell all through their marriage."

Joanna did not mean a word she said. She was angry, and she was venting her anger on her neighbors. She was instantly sorry, but she would never let her husband know that.

Charles was surprised to hear his wife talk like this. "Well, I do think he did not serve in that war because of a back injury that happened when he was young. And as for putting Mary Ellen through hell, I have heard it said that she has caused him some grief."

Joanna scuffed at that and continued with her breakfast. No one directed any conversation toward Willow. She sat eating in silence, waiting for the axe to fall and was surprised when it didn't come.

Joanna was upset with her daughter. She didn't raise her to behave in such a manner. She had been pampered and spoiled all her life, but it was time she grew up and took responsibility for her actions. She planned to have a long talk with her, and if she refused to change her behavior, she would take the strap to her. That was her problem anyway. No one in the house would say a word to her or raise a hand to correct her. But this was different, and Joanna planned to see that things changed with her daughter.

The day progressed as usual. Everyone went about their daily chores, and nothing was said to Willow about the night before. Willow tried to stay out of her mother's way. That was not too difficult. Joanna made a wide diversion around her daughter. She was afraid of what she would say, and she did not want the rest of the family to hear. But as evening approached, Willow became nervous. Her mother had not talked to her all day, and she knew that sooner or later, Joanna would have her say. She excused herself early and hurried up to bed. She hoped to be asleep before her mother came up to bed, then maybe she could stall the inevitable.

But Joanna was more determined than even Willow imagined. She followed her daughter up the stairs to her room. Once inside with the door closed, Joanna began, "I want to talk to you about what happened last night and this morning. I know that Mr. Randolph has been visiting your room. I have known it for some time but did not say anything because of your father. He would have me believe that it was nothing more than my imagination. But you and I know different." She didn't pause to give Willow a chance to answer. "Your behavior has been a thorn in my side for some time. You are lazy and self-centered. I know before the war it was fashionable and proper for a young lady to do nothing all day but entertain and do needlepoint. I too indulged in this, letting the servants do the work. But this war has changed all that. From now on, you will get out of bed and help Elizabeth gather the wood. You will help me in the kitchen. I know that you say you don't know how to cook, but it is time you learned. There are many other chores you can be doing. I'll make a list for you in the morning, and you can start right away. If you fail to do as I tell you, you will be punished, and I don't mean sent to your room. You will be punished in the old-fashioned way. With the rod."

Willow gasped. She had never been struck by either one of her parents. She could not believe that her mother would threaten to do so now.

Joanna took a step toward her and pointed a finger in her face. "And if I ever see you around that man again, you will be punished. Or behaving in that matter with any man again, you will feel my wrath. Don't think your father is going to protect you. I've had a long talk with him, and he has agreed to let your discipline be left up to me. He has promised not to interfere with whatever means of punishment I decide to administer." Joanna paused to catch her breath. Willow was in tears and had covered her face with her hands. But Joanna would not let up now. She was going to make sure Willow understood that she was serious. "There's going to be a lot of changes made around here for you. I am going to make a proper young lady out of you or die trying. When this war is over and things settle down, your father and I are going to find a young man for you to marry. If he'll have you. But we can only pray that nothing comes of your encounter with Mr. Randolph. Heaven help you if something does. No young man will want you." She started for the door then turned back. "Get some sleep. Tomorrow you are going to do your fair share around here." She walked out of the room, satisfied that she had gotten through to her daughter. But Joanna was not aware of how determined Willow was to have her own way.

As soon as her mother was out of the room, she wiped the tears from her eyes. She would do the chores her mother assigned her. She would even learn how to cook. She would be the proper lady when with her family, but she would stop seeing Mr. Randolph when she wanted to stop seeing him. And as for her parents choosing her a husband, she'd be damned first. She would choose whom she was to marry. She would not be told what to do by her mother and father or anyone else. She dressed for bed, already making plans on how she was to see her love.

With James out of the house, it was harder for the two lovers to continue their affair. But Willow could always find ways to see him. She would wait until all the family had gone to bed then sneak out of the house to meet him in the barn or stables. Their lovemaking continued, but something was different this time. James knew that to obtain a permanent residence, he had to marry Willow. And to marry Willow, he had to make her pregnant. He began to make mistakes. At first the two just laughed off his lack of self-control until it happened too many times. Willow began to realize what was happening, and she was not happy about it. After one such time, she pushed him from on top of her and stood up to rearrange her clothing. She turned on him as he still lay in the hay, relaxing. "You bastard! Do you think I am a fool? I know what you are trying to do." Her eyes turned dangerously dark. "But I won't have your baby! I'll kill it first! Just as I killed that Yankee. I'll slit its throat." She laughed, and the sound of it sent a chill down James's spine. She had a look in her eyes that he had never seen before. He thought at that moment that she was close to insanity.

He rose to his feet and pulled up his trousers. He had not seen her like this before, but he knew to be ready to take flight. "What are you talking about? You know that I won't do such a thing. I love you."

She looked at him and smiled. "Love me? Do you?" She advanced toward him with that mad smile on her face, and he backed away.

She clinched her teeth. "I want you off this property and out of my life. If you ever come around me again, I will have Poppa shoot you."

"Willow!" He held up both of his hands to hold her off. "You know you don't mean that. You enjoy our times together as much as I do. What will you do with me gone?"

"I'll find someone else." She smiled in his face. "Someone worthy of my marrying. Not some shiftless no-good such as you. Why don't you go fight for your country instead of trying to live off my family? You'll never use me again to try and make yourself a home. My mother was right about you. She had your number long before anyone else. She'll have her way now. I'll never see you again. And all I can say is good riddance."

She left him there, determined not to give him a second thought. Her mind was already thinking of someone to take his place.

Days turned into weeks, and Willow began to worry. All the times she had been with James, he had made many mistakes, but she had never gotten pregnant. This time was different. She was late. And she was beginning to be concerned. She shouldn't have sent him away so quickly. Perhaps she should have waited to be sure it was safe for her to do so. But it was too late to bring him back. He was gone. He had ridden out of town, and no one knew where he had gone. She wasn't so sure she wanted to bring him back. She could find someone else to blame this baby on. She knew she didn't have money or the means to get rid of it. That would be the best solution. But that was out of the question. No one had the kind of money she needed, so she would have to have the little bastard. She laughed aloud at the thought. That was exactly what it was—a little bastard.

When word reached Brier Cliff of Sherman's march to the sea, everyone was in a panic. Even Willow forgot her own troubles as the realization that her beloved home could come under the torch by the Yankee invaders. Everyone knew that the war was all but over for the South. But still they fought on, but at a great cost. Sherman left a trail of destruction that spread through the South like a plague. Families began to pack their precious belongings and load them in wagons and leave their homes to distance themselves from the advancing troops. Reports were slow in coming to the citizens, so no one knew for sure where Sherman would strike next. Charles began to prepare his family for what was inevitable. Only what they needed would be packed and taken with them when the time came for them to flee. Hope still held them together, but with each day and with each report, that hope slowly vanished.

Elizabeth stuck to her routine of gathering wood each morning. Even though the Union army was bearing down on them, they still needed wood to keep warm.

Willow had taken to her bedroom, buried under the covers to keep warm. She was in constant fear now. She knew that the Yankees would not show mercy, even to a woman. She had little hope for the outcome. Joanna allowed this. She knew that Willow had faced the Yankees once before, and she knew firsthand what they could do to a young lady. Joanna was also in great fear. She wanted to protect her daughters and home, but there was little anyone could do to stop the advancing soldiers.

Charles sat alone in the sitting room reading from the Bible. It seemed to be his only source of comfort in these troubled times. He pulled his glasses from his face and rubbed his tired eyes. Silently he prayed for his family and his home. He knew he would not be able to protect them from what was happening all over the South. He prayed it wouldn't come to that.

It had rained for three days, and fog hung heavy over the house. A young boy from the neighboring estate had ridden up to Brier Cliff only hours before. He was spreading the word that the Yankees were at their doorstep. They were only five miles down the road and advancing fast toward the town of Hampton. The Prestons sat together in the sitting room, not making a sound. Sherman's troops would be upon them soon, and still they did not leave. Joanna still held out hope Brier Cliff would escape from the horde of troops. As darkness fell, the family was afraid to light a lamp. If a Yankee saw the light from the lamp, they would come and destroy all they had worked for so many years.

They had heard stories of renegade troops raping and killing all over the South. The stories were so horrible they were hard to believe, but Charles believed every word. He had seen war before and knew that victory turned troops into less than humans. Man was capable of doing things that could turn the stomach of the strongest. And everything and everyone was a target to this less-than-human behavior.

The knock at the door sent shock waves throughout the group of people. Charles was the first to react. He stood and hobbled to the door. With his revolver in hand, he called out. "Yes?"

"Sir, it's Dillon MacCarthy. Let me in."

Charles swore beneath his breath. He quickly came to the door and opened it to the welcomed visitor. He pulled the man into his arms and gave him a huge bear hug. "It's so good to see you! We lost hope that we'd ever see you again."

Elizabeth heard his voice and came running. She threw herself into his arms and held on for all she was worth. Their tears ran freely down their faces as they embraced. "Dillon! Dillon!" was all she could say. He looked older, with a full beard on his face, and his hair was long and shaggy. He was dirty and smelly, but he was a most welcome sight to Elizabeth. He kissed her cheeks, her eyes, and her nose. His lips found hers. He held the kiss for as long as he possibly could. He realized her family was standing behind her watching. He laughed as he pulled away. "You are always the last to let go."

She looked deep in his eyes. "I have never let go. And I never will."

He pulled her back into his arms. "I love you, Elizabeth."

"And I love you, Dillon MacCarthy," she returned.

Charles was the one that finally made them part. "Tell us, boy, what is going on. Have you seen any of Sherman's troops?"

Dillon wrapped an arm around Elizabeth's waist and held her close to him. "Yes, sir. They are everywhere. Sherman has sent out scouts to look for property to destroy. If they find Brier Cliff, it could mean all of you could die. You have to get out of here. And do it quickly!"

"We are ready. I've had everyone pack only what is necessary and load it on a wagon. It is in the barn, hitched to a horse and ready to go," he answered.

"Sir, if you go with me, you must leave everything. A wagon cannot sneak through the Yankees' lines. Our men are camped not far from here. If I can get your family there, you will be safe. I've already made arrangements for Elizabeth to be taken to my home in Maryland. You are all welcome to go with her."

Willow stepped forward. "Then we won't go with you if it means leaving everything behind. We'll take our chances on our own. And tell us why are your men so close and are doing nothing to protect us from these Yankees?"

Dillon looked at Charles. "There are only a handful of my men left. They have been through hell. There is nothing we can do to protect you from such a large number of troops. I wish to God there was." He lowered his head as though he felt shame at not being able to protect this family. Then he looked to Charles and asked, "Sir, does Willow speak for you? Will you and your family not leave Brier Cliff?"

"Yes, she does. We'll take our chances on our own. We'd only slow you down, and if you are caught, it will mean your death. You are better off without us," Charles answered.

"Then I want your permission to take Elizabeth with me." Dillon still held on to the young girl.

Willow stepped forward, visibly angry. "We are a family and will not be separated. If we are to go through hell, then we'll go through it together."

Joanna had stayed in the background. Now she stepped forward. "We can't speak for Elizabeth. It is her choice, not yours, Willow."

"I love you all." Elizabeth looked toward her family, begging them to understand. "But I can't be separated from Dillon again."

Dillon pulled Elizabeth around to look into his face. "Be sure, because once we leave, there will be no way to come back."

She threw herself into his arms. "I want to go with you. I never want to be away from you again."

Dillon turned to shake Charles hand. "I wish you luck, sir. And may God go with you." He turned back to Elizabeth. "Say your good-byes and gather together a small bundle of clothing. We travel light and fast. We'll have to ride double, but we will make it. This fog is on our side. It will make us hard to detect. Meet me in the stables. I left my horse there." He knelt and kissed her lightly. He reached for the door then turned back to the family. He didn't say a word but turned and disappeared through the door into the fog and darkness.

Elizabeth turned to her family. She saw the tears in her mother's eyes and the painful look upon her father's face. She could only give in to her own tears. But Willow stopped her. "You're not really leaving us? Not after everything we've been through as a family. You're going to run away to safety and leave us in the hands of the enemy. Father"—Willow turned to Charles, wide eyed and in a panic—"stop her. You can't let her go. Dillon has been gone close to four years, and you're going to let him come here now and take her away? What right does he have? And what right does she have to leave when a crisis is at our doorstep?"

"Elizabeth has every right to make up her own mind, Willow. We'll manage. It will be just as dangerous for her to cross the enemy lines as for us to run in the opposite direction." Charles knew Willow's outburst was more than a concern for her family's safety. She depended on Elizabeth to be there in times of importance. She could manage crisis when Willow could not.

"Mother." Willow turned to beg her mother to take her part in persuading her sister to stay.

"Your father is right. You sister has to follow her own heart. She delayed her wedding at your father's insistence. It is not fair of us to demand that she remain with us and let her young man go without her." Joanna could well understand Willow's persistence that her sister stay in the family fold. Joanna didn't know how they would manage without her.

"Now go, dear. Your young man is waiting." Her mother forced a smile to her face.

Elizabeth hurried to her room to change into a riding skirt and a shirtwaist top. She threw a few things into a shawl and tied a knot in the shawl to hold it secure. Willow walked into her room and watched her silently. Finally she spoke. "So you are really deserting us. Leaving me to care for Mother and Poppa. How could you be so selfish?"

Elizabeth turned to her sister. "Mother and Poppa are more than capable of taking care of themselves. You helped only when Poppa was injured."

"Yes, he was injured. Thanks to you." Willow returned, her voice growing sharper with her anger.

Elizabeth tried to push past her sister, but Willow would not allow it. "One minute." Willow grabbed at her sister's arm. "You leave now, and you realize it will be the last time you will see any of us. The enemy is all around us, and you are like the rat that deserted the sinking ship."

"Please." Elizabeth pushed past her sister. "I want to talk with my parents before I leave."

She left Willow standing there, smoldering in her anger and rage. Willow lifted the revolver from her skirt pocket. She had taken it when her father had laid it on the hall stand, and it had not been detected. She had no intentions of letting Dillon ride in here and take Elizabeth away when she, Willow, needed her most. Looking down at the gun for a long moment, she knew what she would do. She turned and hurried down the back stairway that led to the kitchen and out the back door.

Elizabeth said a tearful good-bye to her parents and turned to leave. But she hurried back to her mother's arms. Her father circled them both in his arms. Together they stood, a family. But a family for only a few moments more.

She ran through the darkness, part of her heart in pain at leaving her mother and her father and the other part overjoyed to be reunited with her love. She could see the light coming from the closed stable doors, and she hurried toward it.

She pulled open the doors and stood there in shock at what she saw. Willow was standing with a shaking hand, pointing her father's revolver directly at Dillon. It took only a second for Beth to take charge of the situation. Slowly she approached Willow. Willow glanced in her direction. "Stay back, Elizabeth. I'll not let him separate our family. I'll not let him take you away from me."

Beth was only a few feet from Willow. She could feel her heart racing in her chest. She knew what fate held for Elizabeth if she did not approach this the right way. She had only one chance to stop Willow. She began to speak in a clear, calm voice. "Willow, you know you don't want to do this. How do you think you can explain it? Poppa and Mother will know. What if the Union soldiers hear the shot? You could bring them down on our heads." She was walking slowly, closer with each word.

Willow began to wave the gun from one to the other. "I told you to stay back. I don't want to hurt you, Elizabeth. He's the one I mean to kill. And as for getting away with it, I'll tell Poppa he was shot by a Union soldier he came across in the stable. They'll not know unless you tell them. And you will not tell, or else I'll kill you the first chance I get."

"Then you'd better kill me with him because I will tell Poppa and Mother what you have done. Do you think you could kill your own sister?" Elizabeth shook her head. "I don't think so."

"Don't come any closer. I can kill you, Elizabeth. You know I can. I'll not let you leave me now when I need you the most. You're the only one I can depend on to help me. Please." Tears came to Willow's eyes. "I don't want to do this."

Elizabeth lunged for the gun. A deathly scream echoed in the stables; a loud report and a puff of smoke, and Elizabeth fell to the ground.

Chapter 14

Awake to where time has
no hold on your heart.

July 1942

Beth woke slowly and looked around her. Where was she? She tried to raise her head; her mother was quickly at her side. "Lie back, dear. You are all right. We were in an accident. Do you remember? You're in the hospital."

"No!" Beth closed her eyes and tried to sort her thoughts. "The house? What happened to Brier Cliff?" Her mind was all a jumble. She couldn't be in the hospital. Only moments ago, she was at Brier Cliff ready to leave with Dillon. Then she remembered the events in the stable. She opened her eyes and looked at her mother. She didn't say a word, but she felt like the hand of death had just passed over her. She tried to relax. She needed to sort things out before she began to ask questions.

"Brier Cliff is fine." Her mother pushed the strand of sweat-dampened hair from her forehead. "You're just confused. That's all. You've been in a coma for a very long time. You sustained quite a head injury when that car ran into us on our way to Brier Cliff. Now do you remember?"

Beth opened her eyes and stared up into her mother's face. "No, that's not right. I was at Brier Cliff. We made it to the house. And you and I worked so hard to restore it. I know every corner of that house. I can tell you anything you want to know about it." She felt tears rise to her eyes, but she quickly blinked them away. Brier Cliff was her home, and now her mother was telling her that she had never seen Brier Cliff. That was ridiculous.

Joan laughed. "All right, dear. Have it your way. We'll talk of it later. But do you think you're ready for a surprise?" Joan pointed toward the door. "Look over there."

Beth's eyes followed Joan's. Through the door, walking on crutches, came a tall man dressed in an army uniform. It was her father! "Daddy!" She began to cry. He took her into his arms and held her against his chest. "Daddy! You've come back to us!"

"Yes, sweetheart, and I'm never going to leave you and your mother again." He kissed her cheek and wiped away her tears. He leaned back and smiled down at his daughter. She thought how handsome he was. He was thinner, but he was still her father. His smile made her heart fill with joy.

Beth wrapped her arms around his neck and held on to him. Tears gathered in her eyes. He was alive! That was all that mattered. She knew everything she had gone through was worth having him home. No one could tell her she had not gone back in time and saved her father and Elizabeth's. She held on to him for a long time before she could let him go. She released him and wiped away her tears.

"What happened? Why are you on crutches?" she asked. She could hardly believe that he was sitting beside her. She reached out a hand and took his in hers. She wanted to touch him, to ensure that he was real and not some dream.

"My plane was shot down. When I hit the water, I broke my leg and hip. A ship picked me up an hour later and took me on board. I was in a hospital when I received word of your and your mother's accident. The army flew me home to be with you," he said as he rose and pulled his wife toward him to circle her waist with his arm. "Your mother was not injured but you, little girl, have been in a coma for the last three months."

"Three months," she whispered. She had lived a lifetime in three short months. But how could that be? she asked herself. She did not have an answer to her own question. She wanted to get out of the hospital and find out what had happened to Elizabeth and Dillon. She turned to her parents. "How long do I have to stay here?" She needed to get home and talk with Cora. She could tell her what she wanted to know.

Both her parents laughed. "You'll be here quite a while longer. I doubt you can walk after lying in that bed for so long," her mother answered.

"Then I want to speak with Cora," she said without thinking. Cora was a figure from the past. She should not know of her. Perhaps there wasn't a Cora now.

Surprise and shock showed on her mother's face. "How do you know of Cora? You have never met her. I met her only after coming to South Carolina."

Her father leaned forward to whisper in his wife's ear. "They say the unconscious hear everything. We have probably mentioned Cora in one of our conversations."

This seemed the most logical explanation, but still Joan couldn't help but wonder.

"Please, Mother. I want to speak with Cora," Beth said again. Only Cora could help her sort out this mess her mind was in. She would have the answers to the new history of Brier Cliff.

"I'll speak with her and see if she can come with me on my next visit." She leaned over Beth to fluff the pillow beneath her head. "How's that? Do you agree?" Joan was trying to pacify her daughter. But she was very worried over her insistence that she had been to Brier Cliff.

The doctor entered. He was a young man with jet-black hair and dark eyes. He flashed his most professional smile at the parents. "Sorry to interrupt, but Beth has only just awakened. She needs to rest. You can come back tomorrow. We don't want to overdo the first visit."

Charles shook the young man's hand. "Thank you for everything you have done to help our daughter. We are very grateful to have her back with us."

Joan leaned over and kissed her cheek. "See you tomorrow." Tears moistened her eyes. "Get some rest. We love you."

Charles followed. "See you tomorrow, baby. Love you."

Beth smiled. "Thank you, both. I love you too."

With her parents gone, Beth relaxed and let her mind relive the events of the past. Rest was far from her mind. She thought, after three months, she didn't need to rest. But in spite of her assumption that rest wasn't what she needed, she closed her eyes and was soon asleep.

Beth opened her eyes and looked up into her mother's smiling face.

"Good morning," Joan said. She looked intently at her daughter. She seemed better today, but she looked very tired and thin. She needed time to heal, and Joan would give her that. She loved her daughter and felt the accident was her fault. She had been the one to insist they move to South Carolina. She was the one who would not pull the car over in that terrible rainstorm. She had spent many months blaming herself, and now that she had her daughter back, she was going to shower her with love and understanding.

"Good morning," Beth returned then looked behind her mother to see another woman. For a moment, it was hard to recognize Cora. She stood straight, not leaning forward on her cane. Her hair was done up in a stylish bun, and her smile was as bright as the sunlight. She was dressed in a very nice pantsuit. Beth felt tears come to her eyes. "Cora," was all she could manage. This was not the same Cora, but yet again, it was. Her heart filled with joy. She was happy for this new Cora.

The older lady stepped forward and took Beth's hand. "Your mother said you wanted to meet me. I thought it a great privilege to meet the daughter of such a fine lady as your mother," she said as she seated herself in a chair close to the bed.

Beth could only stare at the change in this lady. She smiled as one tear ran down her cheek. She was so different, and yet the same.

"Tears? What is this?" Joan leaned forward to wipe at her daughter's face.

Beth didn't respond to her mother's question but continued to stare at Cora. "I'm so glad that things worked out for you. You deserve to be happy."

Joan and Cora didn't know what to make of this, but they thought it part of her injury and didn't comment.

Beth shook off the feelings that had overtaken her and tried to have a pleasant visit with her mother and Cora. She listened intently when Cora began to speak of Brier Cliff.

"You are going to love your new home. These months you've been in the hospital, your mother has been working so hard to restore the house. I knew when I sold it to your father that it was going to take a special family to love that house as much as I do. But I think I chose the right family to own Brier Cliff."

"You sold it to Father?" Beth asked. "Then you received your rightful inheritance?"

Cora looked at Joan. They both considered this a strange question. But neither said a word. Cora answered, "Yes. It was left to me by my mother."

"Willow," Beth half whispered her name.

Cora was visibly shaken. She stood. "I think I'll let you and your mother visit without me. I have so much to do. It has been good meeting you. When you're home, we'll become great friends." She nodded to Joan then quickly left.

Beth stared after her for a long moment. Why did she leave so suddenly? What had she said to upset her?

Joan came around the bed and took a seat in a chair. She tried to bring Beth out of the mood she was in. "Your father didn't come with me today. He is having a lot of pain when standing on his leg. He said to give you a kiss for him and that he would try to visit soon."

Beth turned her attention back to her mother. "I'm so glad Father is home from that war. He's safe now."

Joan agreed. "And he'll never have to go back. The doctors say he'll never walk again unaided and that he will always have some pain. It's a terrible price to pay, but I'm happy to have him any way I can."

Beth smiled. It was the same with Charles. He too could not walk without pain. She changed the subject. "Tell me about the renovations you have done to Brier Cliff. I am so anxious to see it again."

Joan ignored that and began to tell of the renovations to Brier Cliff. She loved to talk of their new home and was very proud of the way it was beginning to take shape. "When you get home, we are going to renovate your bedroom. It is very dark wood, nothing a young lady would like. I thought to do it before you got out of the hospital, but you and I have different tastes, and I thought you might like to choose the colors yourself." A blush came to her cheeks. She had talked for a full thirty minutes. "Sorry, dear. Once I start talking about the house, I don't know when to stop."

Beth laughed. "That's all right. I love Brier Cliff too." She couldn't wait to see Brier Cliff again. She longed to find out about the Preston family and their new history.

Beth felt proud that she had accomplished what she had set out to do. Because of her, the Prestons went on, she hoped, to find happiness. She relaxed back in her bed and smiled to herself. She knew she had to concentrate on getting better so she could get home.

After an hour, a nurse entered and said it was time to leave. Beth was due her medication and would sleep after taking it.

Joan bid her daughter good-bye and promised to return the next day. After kissing her daughter, she hurried out of the room.

Beth remained in the hospital for another month. Her days were filled with physical therapy and a lot of rest. Her mother visited every day and talked of the renovations to the house. Her father came only when he was able. But each time he did come to visit, Beth's heart filled with joy at the sight of him. Cora didn't visit again. Beth knew that once she was on her feet, she would seek out Cora and talk with her of her family's past. Never again did she mention to her parents that she had already seen Brier Cliff, and this seemed to make them happy. The doctors assured her parents that Beth was doing well and could leave soon.

It was a gray, rainy day when she was released from the hospital. Joan wheeled her out to the car in a wheelchair and helped her in. She hurried around to the driver's side and climbed in. She cast a quick smile to her daughter before turning the car and pulling away from the hospital. Beth rode along the road, thinking how familiar it was. Even the smell of the ocean was familiar to her. She smiled to herself as the clouds rolled back and the sun peeked out its head. It was so like the first trip down this road that led to Brier Cliff.

Suddenly Beth screamed. "Stop the car."

Joan looked over at her daughter. "What? What is wrong?"

Beth grabbed at the wheel. "Stop the car, Mother."

Joan slowed the car and pulled off the road. Beth felt tears come into her eyes. "It was here, wasn't it? This is where we had the accident." She could see it clearly in her mind. She could smell the smell of burning tires and gasoline just as it was so many months before.

Joan looked around the area and turned back to her daughter. "Yes, I think it is. Things were not that clear after the accident. I didn't give the location that much thought, but I think you're right. In fact, this is my first attempt at driving down this road by myself. I have always had a fear of it since the accident. Your father usually drives. But today his leg was giving him a lot of pain."

"I remember it well. You were driving in a terrible rainstorm. We were going very slow when a car came around that turn up ahead in the middle of the road. It tried to get over and ran off the road and came back across to hit us. Our car spun around and turned over close to the edge. What kept us from going over into the water below?" Beth did not know why or how she remembered the accident. But suddenly it was very clear to her.

"Only the good Lord," Joan said in a low voice. "We were both very lucky. If our car would have gone into the ocean, we would have drowned.

I was unconscious for several minutes. When I came to, an ambulance was here loading us into the back. I was only bruised and had minor cuts, but you were in a coma. The doctors didn't give you much hope for a recovery. You had a terrible head injury. Every day I prayed for you. I think that is the only thing that saved you."

"Thank you, Mother." Beth wiped away her tears. "I've got to say this, then I'll never mention it again. I was in that coma for a reason. To right a wrong that happened a long time ago. I know you don't know what to make of my saying such things. I won't cause you any stress by acting less than normal, but let me believe what I do. It can hurt no one. Not even me."

Joan nodded her head. She would grant her daughter's wish. She would not question her strange words or actions. She was only grateful to have her family back together again. She pulled the car back onto the road and continued on toward home. She had no doubts that Beth believed she had been to Brier Cliff before. But time would take care of that. She would get better, and as Beth said, her fantasies hurt no one.

Joan pulled the car into the driveway cut out from the rock in the side of the mountain and stopped the car so they could look up at the house. The house was just as Beth remembered with the two tall columns and porch winding around all sides. The outside was still in need of paint. Everything was the same. Beth had no doubts she had been here before.

In the house, Beth looked over everything and exclaimed to her mother what a good job she had done. The pictures of Elizabeth and Willow still adorned the foyer. Beth felt tears rise to her eyes as she looked up at them. Nothing had changed except for a different portrait hanging there. A portrait of Dillon MacCarthy. She stood for a long time and looked up into his handsome face. How well she remembered his strong arms around her and his lips on hers. But when had the picture been painted? she asked herself. She looked at the date on the corner of the painting. The year 1866 met her eyes.

Beth turned to her mother. "Where did this portrait come from?" She had not asked about the portraits of Elizabeth and Willow, only the one of Dillon.

Joanna laughed. "I see you think him as handsome as I do." She wheeled Beth into the sitting room before she answered. "Cora had mentioned the portraits of the Preston sisters. I found them in the attic, along with the picture of Brier Cliff in the 1860s. But the one of the young man I found much later in a closet in the spare bedroom. It was packed in a crate, as though it were to be shipped someplace. Cora hasn't been here since I hung it, so I haven't thought to ask her who it might be." She pushed Beth's wheelchair in front of the settee and sat down to talk with her. "It is probably a distant cousin or such. I am sure Cora will know."

"Or a husband of one of the sisters," Beth added with a smile on her face. Why else would Dillon's portrait be at Brier Cliff? The thought lightened her heart.

Joan nodded her head in agreement. "That is a possibility. I need to find out. Even if he is not related to the Preston family, I will still let his portrait hang. He is such a handsome man. He is dressed in a Civil War uniform. I think the picture goes with the decor. Don't you agree?"

"Yes," Beth agreed, "let his portrait hang. It only adds to the decor as you say."

Her mother fussed over and pampered her until Beth found it unbearable. She retired to her bed early. Alone in her room, she lay upon her bed and wondered if Elizabeth had survived the shooting. And if not, why was Dillon's portrait hanging downstairs? There were too many questions that she needed answered.

The next day, Beth wanted to go into the yard. Joan would allow it only if she was accompanied. Beth held to her mother's arm and walked out into the lovely manicured lawn. She was surprised to see the trees had been cut down, and what once had been Cora's cottage was visible from the big house. The house was far different than she remembered. It was in prefect order, freshly painted and well kept. She asked her mother about it.

"Cora lived there until she sold the property. The cottage has always been part of Brier Cliff. Cora's grandparents built it as a guesthouse. She said the main house was too big for one person, and the little house was all she needed. She lived there for twenty years," Joan answered. She pointed toward two older buildings standing a good distance from the cottage. "Your father plans to restore those buildings. One was a stable, the other a barn. He wants to get some horses. Won't that be great? You can ride anytime you wish." She led Beth to a lawn chair and helped her sit down. "You're going to love this place, dear. There is a college in town where you can take classes and stay at home. And the ocean is practically at our front door."

"I love it already," Beth answered. Then she remembered the graveyard. She knew she could find answers there. "Mother, is there an old cemetery on the property? I'd love to see it."

"I've never been there, but Cora says there is."

"Can we walk there?" Beth was excited.

Her mother shook her head. "It's a good distance into the woods. You're not well enough to walk there today. Maybe later when you're feeling stronger."

Her mother was right. Beth resigned herself to wait for the answers she sought. She looked around at the property and marveled at its beauty. No wonder her mother and father loved it so.

Joan helped her daughter back into the house after a short time outside. She was so weak from the accident she could not sit for any length of time. Back in the house, her mother took her into the kitchen. A servant stood at the stove with her back to Beth. But she would know Nell anywhere. "Nell."

The servant turned at her name. "Yes, miss."

Beth took the servant's hand. "It is so good to see you. You look well."

Nell looked to Joan. Joan motioned for the servant to ignore the strange behavior. Nell did so. "Thank you, miss. I'm glad you're well enough to come home. Your mother missed you."

"Thank you," Beth answered quietly. She knew Nell was only humoring her. She had no memory of what had happened while she was in a coma.

Later that evening, after dinner, the phone rang. Joan answered it. She turned to Beth and smiled. "Yes, she got home. She's doing well, but she still is not strong." There was a long pause. "All right, I'll tell her. Thank you for calling."

She turned to her daughter. "That was Cora. She wanted to know how you were doing. She wants to come visit once you're on your feet. She said to tell you she is looking forward to talking with you but that she will wait until you're stronger."

Beth was disappointed. She longed to talk with Cora and find out what had happened to Elizabeth and Dillon. Her mother noticed her disappointment. "There's time for visiting later, dear. Right now you need to concentrate on getting better."

There was little she could say. She realized she was not that strong yet. Even now she was exhausted, and she had done nothing all day but walk out into the yard. She excused herself and slowly made her way up to her bedroom. She undressed and put on her nightclothes. The knock at the door surprised her. "Yes," she called.

Joan stuck her head around the door. "I just wanted to see if you were all right." She walked into the room and sat down beside her daughter on the bed.

"Mother." Beth was exasperated with the constant attention. "I am fine. Please relax and let me enjoy being home."

"I am sorry." Joan was visibly hurt and looked away so that her daughter would not see the tears that came to her eyes. "Have patience with me, dear. I almost lost you, and I feel responsible."

Beth was instantly sorry. She leaned toward her mother and took her into her arms. "I am the one to be sorry. I am just tired. And you were not to blame for that accident." It felt good to be in her mother's arms. They had always shared a special friendship, and Beth had missed that. She was grateful that her mother's fate had not turned out to be the same as Elizabeth's mother's.

Joan's eyes again misted with tears. "Thank you, dear. Will you permit me to tuck you in like I did when you were a child?"

Beth smiled as she lay down and allowed her mother to draw the blanket over her. Joan then knelt and kissed her cheek. "You don't know how glad your father and I are to have you home. There was a time we thought you were not going to come home."

"I'm going to be fine. I love you, Mother," Beth answered.

"And I love you." Joan left the room and closed the door behind her.

In the next week, Beth began to move around a little more by herself and seemed to be gaining some strength in her legs. This morning she had come downstairs to find that her mother and her father had gone out riding. She pulled a book from the bookshelf and seated herself in the chair facing the fire and propped her feet up on the ottoman to read.

She enjoyed the warm fire her father had built in the fireplace and opened the book and began to read when Nell entered the room carrying a cup of hot tea. She set it down beside her and turned to leave. Beth stopped her.

"Nell, sit and talk with me for a moment." Beth looked up at the servant, taking in her changed appearance. She looked the same, but now she had an air of authority about her that she didn't have before. She carried herself like someone who knew what she wanted out of life. Beth liked the change in her.

Nell turned back to the girl. "Miss, your mother and father do not pay me to sit and talk. I have chores to do."

"Please. For only a moment. Then I'll let you get back to your chores," Beth asked with a trace of emotion in her voice.

Nell was instantly sorry for her remarks. She knew the girl was recovering from a serious accident and needed reassurance. There were many things that were confusing to her. Nell took a chair across from her and waited for Beth to begin.

"Thank you." Beth smiled. "You don't know how much your presence here means. Everything is so different than the first time I was here."

Nell didn't know what that meant, but she knew she was to go along with whatever the young mistress said. Her mother had explained that she was under the impression that she had visited Brier Cliff before. It had to do with her head injury. Beth continued when Nell did not respond. "Tell me about yourself. Do you have any family?"

Nell folded her hands in her lap. "Yes, miss. I have a husband and two daughters."

Beth smiled. She was so glad that Nell had someone in her life. Before, she had dedicated her life to Brier Cliff. "Tell me about them."

"My husband is a carpenter. He helped in the restoration of Brier Cliff. We have been married for twenty-five years. My two daughters are grown and moved away. I have three grandchildren. I rarely get to see them except on holidays. Christmas is a big holiday at our home. The girls and their husbands and children come to visit, and we have a big dinner." Nell was embarrassed that she had rambled so. She stopped and waited for Beth to respond.

"That is wonderful. I am so happy for you. But what of Cora?" Beth had to ask. She wanted to know if things were as before.

Nell was surprised at the question. She had worked for Cora in the past, but she did not have a personal relationship with her. "I see her only occasionally. We speak, but that is about all."

Beth realized everything was different between Cora and Nell. No longer did Nell consider Cora her aunt. It was better that she not ask anymore about her.

Nell rose to her feet. "If that is all, I'll get back to work." Nell knew she was cutting the young woman short, but she did not believe in making friends with her employees.

Beth merely nodded her head. Nell quickly left the room. She sat back in her chair and thought how things were so different. Nell was different. She was not the friend she had been in the past.

Beth knew that she had to stop before everyone thought her insane. She needed to wait until she spoke with Cora. And the way things were going with her recovery, she knew that would be a long wait. She relaxed back in her chair and continued with her book. But her mind was not on what she reading, and she found that she had to reread pages over. Finally she gave up and closed the book. She closed her eyes and, though she thought herself not tired, fell to sleep. She woke when she heard the front door open and her mother and her father entered the house. She looked toward the doorway as they entered the room.

Joan leaned down and kissed her cheek. "You look so much better today."

"Thank you, Mother." She smiled up at her parents, thinking again what a handsome couple they made. "Did you enjoy your ride?" She didn't have to ask. The evidence was on her mother's flushed cheeks.

"Yes, we did." Her mother and her father seated themselves on the settee and took each other's hand. "We had a wonderful time. Your father's leg is healing nicely, and he had no pain today while on the horse. Isn't that wonderful? We can't wait until you can join us. You are going to love it.

Our property is so lovely, and the horses are so well behaved. You'll have no trouble at all with handling them."

Beth returned her mother's smile. "I'm looking forward to riding, but the way I feel now, I doubt it will be anytime soon."

"Are you still in pain?" Concern showed on her mother's face.

"Not a lot. I am just weak. But I feel stronger every day." She tried to reassure her mother.

"Have you had lunch?" her mother asked as she rose to her feet.

"No," Beth answered. "I was waiting for you."

"Good." She held out her hand to her husband. "We'll just go upstairs and change, and we'll all have lunch together."

As the two were leaving the room, Charles leaned over and kissed his daughter's cheek. "You look great, kitten." He used his pet name for her.

She couldn't help but smile. Her father had called her kitten since she had been a little girl. "Thanks, Daddy." She reverted back to the name she had called him many years ago. He seemed pleased as he turned to follow his wife from the room.

Beth removed her feet from the ottoman and picked up her cane, which was sitting by her chair, to make her way into the kitchen. Nell stood at the stove preparing lunch. She did not turn to acknowledge her presence. Beth thought to herself, the old Nell would have turned with a welcoming smile on her face. But those times were gone. She pulled out a chair and seated herself. "Nell, could I have a cup of coffee? I can't seem to manage this cane and the cup at the same time, or I would get it myself." She apologized for interrupting her from her chores.

Nell turned around and pulled a cup from the top shelf of the cabinet and poured the coffee into it. She set the cup in front of the young girl without a word and went back to her chores. With her back to Beth, she said. "I forgot to tell you that Mrs. Albright called today when you were taking a nap."

"Mrs. Albright?" Beth asked as she spooned sugar into her cup.

"Yes. That is Cora's married name," she said as she turned to remove a hot pot from the stove.

Beth was instantly alert. "Cora? What did she say?"

"She wanted to know how you were doing and if you were up to a visitor," Nell answered.

"And what did you tell her?" Beth was annoyed that she had not been called to the phone. But of course, Nell would not wake her from a nap.

"I told her that your mother wanted you not to receive visitors at this time. That you were not up to it yet." She turned back to the stove and continued with what she was doing.

Now Beth was angry. She had waited a long time to talk with Cora, and she was completely up to talking to a friend. She started to reprimand the servant, but she realized she was only following her mother's orders. And she would not say anything to her mother. She worried constantly about her, and she would not make her feel any worse than she did already.

Beth leaned back in her chair and sipped at her coffee. She wondered when her mother would think her up to receiving callers? She was slightly exasperated with her mother's constant attention. She was old enough to know when she felt like receiving visitors.

Her parents joined her in the kitchen for lunch. They had an enjoyable time, with her mother monopolizing most of the conversation with talk of what she planned to do to Brier Cliff. Beth loved to hear her chatter on about the house. Beth loved it too and wanted it restored to its former glory, as her mother liked to say.

Later that day, Beth went into town for a doctor's appointment. She hated being chauffeured around in a wheelchair but knew she could not walk any great distance. The doctor was pleased with her progress and encouraged her to continue at home with her exercises. He prescribed a lesser medication for the pain and said he would have her off it in less than two months at the rate she was going.

When they pulled up to Brier Cliff, Beth was surprised to see her father standing by the veranda holding the reins to a horse. It was a beautiful black mare, which probably stood only twenty hands high.

Joan came around the car and helped Beth out. "For you, sweetheart," her mother said with a huge smile on her face. "For when you're better."

Beth was very pleased as she came up to the horse and began to pet its mane. She was very friendly and nuzzled Beth for more attention. Beth laughed and turned to her father. "Thank you, both."

"We have been wanting to get you your own horse but didn't know the right time. We thought if you got the horse before you were able to ride, you could get to know it and make friends. But I can see she is already making friends to you."

"Thank you again." The horse continued to ply for Beth's attention. "I love her."

Beth retired early that evening. She was very tired from her trip into town. She was so grateful for having such wonderful parents even though her mother was slightly overprotective. She smiled as she climbed into bed and turned out the lamp by her bed. Within minutes, she was asleep.

Chapter 15

Time closes one door
and opens another.

TIME AFTER TIME

There had been many changes to Brier Cliff in the five months since Beth had been home from the hospital. The house had a new coat of paint, and the mansion once again stood majestic and proud on the cliff facing the ocean. The stables were rebuilt, and Charles had purchased three horses for the family to ride. Each morning after breakfast, Joan and Charles rode out over their property. They enjoyed this time together. Charles was once again back on his feet, but at times, he needed the assistance of a cane. Beth had yet to ride the horses. She did not trust her legs to sit astride one. The barn was under construction but had slowed because of the colder weather.

Beth had made a lot of progress in the last five months. She could walk now without her cane. But she still tired easily. The doctor had cut out her pain medication entirely, and she was doing well without it. She spent most of her days with her parents. They tried to include her in all their activities. But sometimes she felt like a third wheel. She should be grateful, but she was lonely in a way she never knew before. She had her books and her family, but there was something missing in her life. She could put a name to it, but she did not, for fear that her heart would break.

Beth had registered for classes at the college in town, but she had only signed up for two a week. She thought she was not ready for a full schedule, and her mother and father agreed. Those two classes gave her the opportunity to meet young people her own age, and she enjoyed being away from the house. She had spent all of the five months here, except for her visits to the doctor. She was ready to get away for a few hours a couple times a week.

Beth thought often of contacting Cora. She did not because she didn't know what she would say. How could she explain what had happened to her while in a coma? Cora would think her insane. She had not called since the last time, many months before.

Beth had walked out into the yard to think. She needed to bring some prospective back into her life. She needed to put this behind her, but she could not until she knew the truth. The air was cold so she had put on a sweater. The trees around the property were changing into a multitude of color, and she could remember nothing as beautiful. The seasons continued to change, and the birds still sang, and the ocean still beat upon the shore. But Beth's life was at a standstill.

She wrapped her arms around herself to stop a chill that ran through her. The day was so still. Everything seemed at peace. She headed across the lawn to a lounge chair and sat down. She looked up at the house and sensed that it was awakening from a long sleep. Everything was changing around her, but she could not go forward, and certainly not backward. Her mother had said that the house gave off a sense of peace to anyone that entered her doors. But Beth did not find the peace she longed for.

Today she was alone. Her mother and father had gone into town to buy new drapes for their bedroom. Beth had declined their invitation to go along. She said she wanted to relax and read. Now, alone, she wished she had gone. Maybe that would have lightened her mood and taken her mind off her troubles. It was a beautiful day. The sky was a dark blue, and the sun shone bright. But even that could not bring Beth out of her depression. She flipped open the book she carried with her and reclined back into the lounge chair. She had just started to read when the sound of a car coming up the driveway caught her attention. The car pulling to a stop in front of the house made her sit up. She was surprised to see Cora step out of the car and start toward her. Her heart picked up its pace, and a smile came to her face.

"Good morning." Cora smiled as she seated herself in a chair that Beth offered her. "I see you are enjoying a good book. When you're through with that one, you can borrow another from me. I have a whole library that is not being used."

Beth could not help but to stare. Cora looked like a woman of sixty instead of eighty. She was dressed in brown corduroy pants with white blouse and matching jacket. She looked marvelous. She finally answered, "Thank you. I love to select some books from your library. I have been reading this book for the second time, but it's good, and I still enjoy it."

She had waited for this for a very long time. But now she was at a loss for words.

Beth stood. "Let us go into the house where it is warmer. Father built a fire in the sitting room, and I know Nell will have a pot of coffee."

Cora rose and followed Beth through the yard to the house.

The fire burning in the fireplace gave off a welcome warmth, and a feeling of comfort penetrated the sitting room. Cora took a chair, and Beth excused herself to go to the kitchen and pour them a cup of coffee. She set down the cup of coffee on a stand at Cora's side and took a chair opposite her. "Nell makes wonderful coffee. I hope you enjoy it."

Cora blew across the rim of the cup and took a sip. She smiled and nodded her head in approval. "I know all about Nell's coffee. She worked for me at one time, remember?"

"Yes, of course," was all the Beth could think to say. She had wanted this meeting, but now she was nervous and knew what she had to say would sound foolish.

Cora looked around her. "Your mother has done a fine job on this old place."

Beth did not reply. She knew Cora had come for a reason. She decided to wait patiently for her to begin.

Cora finally turned her eyes on the young girl. "I will get right to the point. In the hospital you spoke of my mother. You called her Willow. No one knew my mother was Willow Preston. My grandfather went to a lot of trouble to hide that fact. How is it that you knew? Not even my close friends know that."

Beth chose her words carefully. She wanted her words to be the right words. And most important, she wanted Cora to believe her. After a moment's hesitation, she said, "During my coma, I was at Brier Cliff. I know how that sounds, but it is true. I was here, not only in this time, but in the time of your mother and her sister, Elizabeth." Beth nodded toward the portrait of Dillon. "I know that that painting is of Dillon MacCarthy, the man your aunt, Elizabeth, loved. I know because I have met him and your grandmother and your grandfather." Beth paused, waiting for some sort of denial that this was possible. When none came, she continued. "I knew you at the hospital because I have met you before, not as you are now, but as you were once in a different lifetime." She stopped there and looked deep into Cora's eyes. She must believe. She had to know how things could have been.

Cora only shook her head. "I should get up right now and leave. I don't for two reasons. One is the fact that you know the name of the man in the portrait. I didn't tell your mother that. I had forgotten about his portrait. I had packed it away to send to my niece. She had wanted it for her home. Your mother must have found it and hung it up since my last visit. And second, you knew my mother was Willow. So"—she leaned back in her chair—"tell your story, girl, and it better be a good one if you want me to believe it."

Beth hesitated for a moment. "What I have to tell you about your mother may hurt. But I want you to know the truth."

Cora only shook her head. "Nothing you could tell me about her will be of any surprise."

Beth began to tell her story. The more she talked, the more interested Cora became. At times she sat on the edge of her seat to listen more intently to what she had to say. Several times she would interrupt with a gasp or a shake of her head. When Beth came to the part of Charles's accident, she burst into laughter. Beth stopped and waited until she gained control of herself. Cora cleared her throat and stifled down a laugh. "That old coot," she said affectionately. "He always told me it was a war injury. I later found out the truth." Beth continued to relate the events that happened to her during her time in a coma. She talked for more than an hour before she came to the part of Willow shooting Elizabeth. Cora's face turned white. But she didn't interrupt, so Beth continued until the end. Afterward Cora stared at her for a long time before she found her voice to speak.

"As hard as it is for a levelheaded woman such as myself to say, I believe you. You know too many facts for it to be a lie. I found out most of what you told me from Elizabeth's journal, which I took out of the house when I sold it. It is now in a safe-deposit box in my bank. I wanted no one to read what was in that journal," Cora said. She relaxed back in her chair. "I think I need another cup of coffee before I begin my story."

She sat and waited for Beth to return with two more cups of coffee.

Cora sipped on her drink before she began. "You got the story right. Every detail," she began. "Elizabeth's journal does begin on her nineteenth birthday and the events that took place on that day. She did meet Dillon at a ball to celebrate South Carolina's succession from the Union. They fell in love right from the first day they met. And Willow was jealous. He was the only man she couldn't control with her beauty. My mother did become pregnant by the young artist James Randolph, but they never married. My grandfather did receive an injury to his leg, much the same as the injury your father received. He always told me it was an old war injury. I found out in Elizabeth's journal the truth. And Willow did shoot Elizabeth in the stables as she was about to leave with Dillon. Every detail. Just as it is written down in the journal." Cora still found it hard to believe that this young girl could have lived Elizabeth's life, but the facts were there, and she couldn't deny them. "But what you want to know is what happened after the shooting. You say you woke from the coma after Elizabeth was shot and know nothing more?"

Beth shook her head. "Yes. That is all I know."

"Elizabeth entered the stable and saw Willow holding the gun on Dillon. She ran to her sister and fell against her, trying to knock the gun from Willow's hand. The gun discharged, and Elizabeth was shot. But the wound was in the shoulder. She didn't die. Dillon carried her into the house, and Joanna tended to her wound. The Northern troops were so close everyone was afraid they had heard the shot. They locked the doors and waited for the Yankees to find them and set fire to the house.

No one could leave because of Elizabeth. She was bleeding too badly to move. So they sat there, in the dark, afraid for their very lives. Willow was in shock. She didn't mean to harm her sister. For all she had done, she did love Elizabeth. Charles had taken the gun from her hand and had dragged her back into the house. He had deposited her in a chair, and there she sat, dazed and confused, more sick than any of them knew.

The Yankees marched right by Brier Cliff, so close the family could smell their tobacco smoke and hear the men talking among themselves. The fog and rain helped to hide them from the soldiers. They remained in their places until all noise of the troops faded into the night.

Dillon stayed until Elizabeth was able to tell him she would be all right. He then rode back to his troops and finished out the war. Brier Cliff was one of the lucky ones. Most houses were burned to the ground in the face of the marching troops. It stands today, just as it did then. By that time, the war was all but over for the South. In April of that same year, the South surrendered, and peace was declared. But it took a long time for the South to recover from this war. The Prestons were no exception. It took many years for Charles to get back on his feet, but there was a lot of demand for lumber since most of the South had been burned to the ground. He and his family prospered.

Charles sent Willow away to an institution where she remained for several years.

Elizabeth and Dillon took me right after they were married. Grandfather had the birth records changed to list Elizabeth and Dillon as my parents. No one knew the truth.

Willow was able to leave the institution and return home. Grandfather had kept her illness a secret from everyone. She could return with no ridicule from friends and neighbors. She married a young man from Manassas, Virginia, and lived out her life as happy as she would allow herself to be. She never had any children, which was probably for the best. But she had what she wanted. She lived the life of an aristocrat. She had her friends and gave her benefits for charities, and she donated her time to some worthy cause. And she gave of her own money to help needy orphans. She tried to be a good citizen. Elizabeth and Willow never spoke of what had happened. They lived out their lives without telling another living person. They loved one another. Elizabeth was proud of what her sister accomplished. I would have never known if I had not read it in the journal.

And she was good to Elizabeth and her children. We wanted for nothing when she was around. At Christmas she spoiled us outrageously. She was a good aunt, but she was never my mother.

Willow accomplished a lot in her life. She tried to make up for all the hurt she had caused. I think she did that. Mother told me that Aunt Willow had the largest funeral this town had ever seen. It was even attended by the governor of the state. She was well liked by everyone.

Dillon became a lawyer, and he and Elizabeth lived here at Brier Cliff with her parents. They raised four other children besides myself. Two boys and three girls. A large and happy family. They loved one another. Even as a child, I knew that. He had a way of looking at her. It was as though he thought the sun rose and set in his wife's eyes. And she felt the same about him. Even as they grew older, they still held hands in front of everyone. He liked to take her hand and lead her out into the garden. She loved flowers, and Brier Cliff was a showplace in those days. The gardens could not be matched by any in the state. In the evenings, they would sit on the veranda in their porch swing, and his arm was always around her shoulder. After her parents were gone and all the children were grown and left home, they remained at Brier Cliff until the end. Both my parents loved this place. I would have never sold it until I found the right person. I believe I chose the right family to live here.

My grandparents lived a long and prosperous life. My grandmother died two years before my grandfather. My mother used to say that that was for the best. Grandmother could not have survived without him. She was a devoted wife to him all her life. He was a good man. I know he loved my grandmother. He provided well for his family. What else could a person say about another? He was one of the most influential men in this state. They left this house to Elizabeth and her family.

Dillon died in 1910 and, till his last breath, loved Elizabeth with all his heart. She died the next year, eager to join her beloved husband in the hereafter.

Their love has left a legacy of happiness among all the children, grandchildren, and great-grandchildren. Elizabeth and Dillon will never be dead as long as this family survives. They left a part of themselves in each of us.

Willow was widowed ten years after her marriage. Her husband left her very well-to-do. She died in 1906. She left everything to me. I never knew why until I read the journal. You see, my parents never told me I didn't belong to them. But no one could have had a better mother and father than I did. I never missed out on any of the love because I was adopted. I would have wanted it no other way." Cora reached into her jacket pocket and pulled out a folded piece of paper.

"This is a copy of the last entry in Elizabeth's journal. I copied it only today. You would ask, why? That I can't tell you. It's something I felt I had to do. Now I understand why. I am sure you will want to read it." She handed the paper to Beth.

She unfolded the paper and stared down at the neat scribe.

June 26 1866

> Today, at long last, I am to wed. I have dressed in my grandmother's and mother's wedding dress. I am very pleased with it and am sure Dillon will think it as lovely as I do. I am alone in my room. Mother and my attendants have left me to wait for the music that will signal my march down the stairs. Poppa waits in his room, very nervous and as emotional as I am. It is a beautiful day, a perfect day for a wedding. But part of my heart aches for my dear sister who will not be here to see me wed. She is in an institution. She has been there almost a year. We had hopes that she would be

well enough to attend, but her doctors say she is not ready for any contact with her family. We are not able to even visit. It is a sad thing, but I'm in hope that one day soon she will be well. I have no ill feelings against her. Instead, I love her all the more. I know this was an accident. I am confident that she would never have harmed anyone. Enough of that. Little Cora is staying with Mother and Father until Dillon and I return from Maryland. She is all of six months old, and we love her as if she were our own. She will be part of our family once we return. I look forward to being a mother to her and giving her the love she deserves, the love her mother would want me to give to her. This is a day for happiness, and I am extremely happy. I am wedding the man I love more than my own life. He is to wear his uniform, and I know he will be most handsome. The war is long over, but Poppa says it is fitting that he wear his uniform. He said the old South will never be dead to many of her citizens. I hope and pray every day for the people of the South. We are a long way from being over that terrible war, but the Southern people are a strong lot, and we are well on our way to being a new and better people. Dillon and I will be a part of that new generation of Southerners. Our children will grow up in a new and better country. We have made plans to travel to Maryland to visit his family. But we will be returning in three months. We are to live here at Brier Cliff. My parents are very happy with that. Poppa had the guesthouse remodeled, and we will live there until the children start to come. Then we will move back here to the main house. The guesthouse is plenty big enough for our immediate family. I know Poppa and Mother wish us in the main house as soon as possible. Brier Cliff is more than big enough for two families, my father has said. I hear the music, and Poppa is knocking on the door. I call out to him to wait one moment. This will be my last entry in this dear journal. I have only a few things left to say. I am so grateful for my life and the way things turned out. We survived a terrible war. Our family stayed together, and we were made stronger because of the struggles we went through those years. I know that something more powerful than any man had a hand in the events that took place those years at Brier Cliff. I thank God every day for the miracle that protected myself, my family, and Dillon. Farewell, dear journal. A new life awaits me on the other side of my bedroom door.

Beth felt tears rise to her eyes. "What a wonderful story of two wonderful people, Elizabeth and Dillon." It was a long moment before she could speak. She fought to keep back her tears, but it was of no use. She let them come. After a moment, she regained her composure and smiled at her old friend.

"Tell me about your life," she said as she wiped the tears from her eyes. "I have wondered these months how things changed for you. Are you married?"

"Yes." She smiled, remembering her husband. "To a very good man that gave me three boys. We lived a good life for over forty years. He died five years ago. We lived here at Brier Cliff. After the death of my husband, and my children were grown and gone, I moved into the guest cottage. But this house has only known love. And I know that your family will carry on the tradition."

"How can I ever thank you for sharing this with me? You don't know how happy it makes me to know that Elizabeth and Dillon's love did not come to a tragic end."

Cora smiled. "I think I detected some feeling for my father in your voice when you spoke of him. Am I right?"

Beth lowered her head. "How could I not? You see his portrait hanging in this room. Is he not the most handsome of men? And besides that, he cared so much for Elizabeth. Even Willow's haunting beauty could not sway that love. You must remember I was Elizabeth throughout this whole thing. I am not ashamed to say that I loved him too. But he was not of my time. For me to feel as I do is foolish. But how do you stop your heart from loving?"

"I can understand your feelings for him. He was a wonderful man. I have met few like him in my life. You were lucky to know him as you did." She stood and came to Beth. She held out her hand. "I think I owe you my thanks, for without you, who knows what our future would have been."

Beth walked her to the door and bid her good-bye. Cora promised to return in a few days. She had enjoyed their conversation and wanted to get to know Beth better. Beth's heart was light as she looked up at the portraits on the wall. It was true that Brier Cliff had only known love and happiness.

Beth left the house again and walked through the woods to the cemetery. The cemetery wasn't as it had been. It was mowed and well taken care of. The Prestons' headstone dominated the grounds. There on the stone was Elizabeth's name and that of her husband's. A joy overtook Beth's heart. They were together even in death.

At the far end of the cemetery, she found two identical stones. One had the name of Thomas Winters and beneath it the word "Confederacy" and beneath that was written, "seventeen years of age." Beth smiled. Charles had not forgotten. The second stone read, "Sam Davies," and beneath it was written, "Union." Beth knew that Charles had been responsible for this and that the stones had not been placed here until many years after the war. It was done in a gesture of respect for the men who died in the war.

    Beth made her way slowly through the woods to the clearing. Her heart was light as she thought of all the changes that had taken place since her last visit to Brier Cliff. She stopped as she heard the sound of horses' hooves coming in her direction. She wondered if one of her parents were the rider, but it was a Confederate soldier, leaning low in the saddle, urging the horse into a faster run. He had a full beard and long shaggy hair, but there was no mistaking who the rider was. Dillon MacCarthy! He was galloping across the clearing, heading toward the young girl that stood beneath a tree waiting for him. Beth's heart leap into her throat, and she felt tears running down her cheeks. Elizabeth stood there, waiting for the man she loved. He pulled the horse up short and jumped down. She ran into his waiting arms. They embraced for a long moment before he pulled away and brought his lips down on hers. This time it was Elizabeth that pulled away, only to draw him back into her arms to hold him against her breast. She held him like that for a long time. Their tears mixed as one as they held each other there in the bright sunlight. Dillon had come home.

    He lifted her into his arms and carried her to the horse to set her upon it. He threw his legs up behind her and turned the horse toward home. Together they rode away and disappeared from Beth's view.

    Beth could only stand there with tears running freely down her face. She knew that they were saying good-bye to her. That she would not see them again. She wiped at her tears and continued on through the woods back to Brier cliff.

    She returned home and could not contain the happiness she felt. Only one thing was missing in her life at that moment. Someone she could love as much as she loved Dillon MacCarthy.

    Beth went to bed early that night with a light heart. Even her parents remarked on the change in her mood from when they had left for their shopping trip. She had explained that Cora had visited and that they had had a wonderful talk. They had become friends, and Beth was to visit her in a few days. They had accepted her explanation, glad that something had brought their daughter back to her old self.

    Beth turned out the light and pulled the blanket to her chin. With a smile on her face, she closed her eyes and fell asleep. She began to dream.

    She was sitting at a round table with her parents in an expensive restaurant. An orchestra of musicians was on a platform behind her playing music of current popular tunes. Couples, dressed in long gowns and suits, were dancing in the center of the room.

Beth was wearing a long navy blue gown. It had thin straps and fit tight down to her ankles. It had a split on the side that ran up to her thigh. Her blonde hair was pulled tightly to her head and braided in a French braid. Tiny wisps of hair curled at her ears and fell onto her forehead. In her ears, she wore diamond earrings that her mother had loaned her for this night.

Joan was dressed equally elegantly in a gown of dark red. It had three-quarter-length sleeves and fell from the waist into a full skirt. Beth thought she looked like a queen with her hair done up and set on top of her head in tiny curls. Her father sat in the middle of the two in a dark suit and tie. He was a very handsome man who could have attracted any woman in the room, but he had eyes for only his wife. Today was her birthday, and he had taken the family out to celebrate. They were enjoying a fine candlelit dinner, and afterward Charles had planned for a large cake to be carried out with thirty-nine candles. Beth knew her mother would object to the thirty-nine candles. She didn't want anyone to know her age. But Charles thought it great fun to tease her about her age.

When the cake arrived with the blazing candles, Joan blushed a bright red. Charles and Beth had to laugh. They burst into song, singing, "Happy birthday." Everyone in the room joined in, and Joan could not have been more embarrassed.

They each took a piece of cake and ordered coffee. Charles told the waiters to pass the remaining cake around the room. It was such a large cake there was no doubt that it would suffice.

Beth was eating her cake and thoroughly enjoying herself when she felt a tap on her shoulder. She turned around and gasped. The man standing over her was tall and dark, dressed in an army uniform. He was the image of Dillon MacCarthy.

"May I ask you for this dance?" He smiled, revealing even white teeth.

The orchestra was playing a slow song at that moment. Beth could only nod her head in agreement. The young man took her hand and led her out onto the dance floor.

His hand around her waist was firm as he twirled her around the room. She could only look up into his handsome face. She knew she was being foolish, but she could not get over how much he looked like the man she loved. But he didn't seem to notice. He led her around the room until they came to the French doors opening onto a patio. He stopped and, without a word, led her through the doors and out into the night air. At the banister, he stopped and turned to her. His voice was soft and low. "I thought this day would never come when we could be alone."

She looked up at him in wonder. Did he know her? Was this Dillon MacCarthy?

He lowered his head to hers and captured her lips with his own. "You're so lovely, Beth," he whispered against her ear.

Beth's heart was beating almost out of her chest. This couldn't be Dillon. This man wasn't wearing a Confederate uniform, but an army uniform. He was the picture of Dillon, but he could not be."

She let him kiss her again. This time she returned the kiss. She wrapped her arms around his neck and held him to her. His arms came around her waist to hold her tightly against him. Long moments passed before he pulled away from her embrace and smiled down into her flushed face. "May I see you again?"

"Yes." Her answer escaped her in a soft breath.

The music could be heard from the patio, so he took her into his arms and danced with her there in the moonlight. They twirled around the patio, each looking into the other's face. When the music stopped, they stopped, but he continued to hold her around the waist.

"I'd better get you back to your parents. They'll become worried when they don't see us out on the dance floor." He took her hand and led her through the crowd to her table. It was at that moment that Beth saw the bracelet. It was the same as the one Dillon wore. She could not imagine who this man was. But she was happy that he had chosen her out of all the women in the restaurant to dance with.

Her father smiled and offered the young man his hand. "Good to see you again, son. Stop by the house before you leave. Beth can take you for a ride on our new horses."

"Thank you, sir. I will." He turned to Beth. "May I have the pleasure of another dance later?"

She nodded her head and sat watching him disappear into the crowd.

Beth woke with a jerk. She sat up in bed and turned on the lamp sitting on her nightstand. She was still shaking from her dream. What could it mean? Was it only a product of her desire to find a man such as Dillon? Or could it mean something more? She calmed herself as much as possible and turned out the lamp and lay back down. Hours passed before she found sleep.

Three days from Cora's visit, the invitation came. Beth was so excited that she had received it that she took extra care with her appearance. She dressed in a black pantsuit and white silk blouse. On her feet, she wore two-inch heels. She pulled her hair away from her face and curled it with a curling iron. It fell to her shoulders in soft waves. She applied makeup and just a touch of lipstick. She stood in front of the mirror for a long time before she was satisfied that she looked all right.

She took her mother's car into town and parked beside a two-story house that reflected the owner. The grounds were well taken care of. A white picket fence bordered the lawn and ran around the house. The house looked like a gingerbread house with all the fancy wood trim around the windows and door. She rang the doorbell and waited for Cora to answer. Moments passed before the door was opened by a young man. He was tall with dark hair and startling green eyes.

Beth gasped. "Dillon!" She grabbed the doorjamb to keep from falling to her knees. It was the man from her dream! He was the image of Dillon!

He held open the door for her to enter. His smile was branded into her heart. It was Dillon's smile. "No. Adam," he said. She entered the house and found a chair to sit in, afraid her wobbly legs would not hold her. "Dillon was my great-grandfather's name." He looked down at her with those beautiful blue-green eyes, and her heart stopped for a second.

She could only stare up at him. He was dressed in an army uniform and looked very handsome. She felt her heart pick up its pace. She gasped aloud when she saw the gold bracelet adorning his wrist. It was the same one Dillon gave Elizabeth so many years ago.

He noticed her stare and held out his arm to show her the bracelet more closely. "A present from my great-aunt Cora. In fact, she gave it to me only today. I am sorry I didn't introduce myself. I am Adam MacCarthy. I only arrived a few hours ago. I am on leave, and my great-aunt Cora has agreed to let me stay with her the month I am in the States."

He seated himself across from her in a chair. "Is something wrong? You keep staring at me."

"No," she managed. "No. It is just you look so like the picture my parents have at Brier Cliff of Dillon MacCarthy."

He laughed. "Your family owns Brier Cliff now? Well, that explains why you are looking at me so. Everyone tells me I look like my great-grandfather. It must be true."

Beth's heart raced at the sight of his beautiful smile. She nodded her head. "You do."

He looked deep into her eyes. He saw something there that he had never seen before. Her eyes were a reflection of the gentleness of her soul. It startled him that he would think such things of a girl he had only just met. "My aunt will be out in a moment. She said for me to entertain you until then." He rose from the chair and walked to close the door behind them.